"Maeve, don't do this to yourself," Will said gently.

"I feel for you and what happened with your child, but your life has to go on."

She forced herself to look him in the eye. "I shouldn't have made love to you knowing it would come to this. It was selfish. I'm sorry," she apologized.

"Sorry?" He gave a humorless laugh, then shifted away from her on the bed. "You convinced me I shouldn't go ahead and marry. Made passionate love with me. And now you're just going to walk away?"

"I'm sorry, Will," she repeated, miserable.

Later, she would weep. Right now, she had to leave. What a fool she was! He was right to despise her. She'd screwed up both their lives.

She jammed her feet in her sandals. "Goodbye, Will."

He turned his back on her without a word.

Tears blurring her eyes, Maeve walked out of the room, down the stairs. And out of his life.

Dear Reader,

Writing The Second Promise was especially enjoyable, as it's set in my own backyard, so to speak. The Mornington Peninsula, in southeastern Australia, is a beautiful spot, with its bayside and ocean beaches, rolling pastureland and numerous vineyards.

Every story begins with a single idea. The spark for The Second Promise was the large clifftop estates at the southern tip of the peninsula. From the road, the only thing visible might be an opening in a huge hedge or a high brick wall with just a glimpse of a long curving driveway. Yet from the water the houses shine in brilliant sunlight, dotted like gems high above the sparkling blue sea. The intriguing juxtaposition of the mysterious with the open-yet-unattainable provided a foundation for this story about honorable secrets and forbidden love.

Will Beaumont lives alone in one of those big houses on the cliff. Maeve Arden considers it part of her job to find out why. She creates a garden for Will—whom she loves but cannot have—which she hopes will put the magic of childhood back into his life. Inadvertently Maeve also puts something of her own secret longings into the garden. Through enriching Will's life, Maeve finds that love's healing power allows her to overcome past sorrows, opening a way to a future together.

I do hope you enjoy my story. I love to hear from readers. Please write me c/o Harlequin Enterprises, Ltd., 225 Duncan Mill Road, Don Mills, Ontario, Canada, M3B 3K9; or e-mail me at www.superauthors.com.

Joan Kilby

The Second Promise
Joan Kilby

TORONTO • NEW YORK • LONDON
AMSTERDAM • PARIS • SYDNEY • HAMBURG
STOCKHOLM • ATHENS • TOKYO • MILAN • MADRID
PRAGUE • WARSAW • BUDAPEST • AUCKLAND

ISBN 0-373-70965-X

THE SECOND PROMISE

Copyright © 2001 by Joan Kilby.

The Second Promise

PROLOGUE

Christmas morning, Melbourne.

WILL TURNED his six-month-old niece, Caelyn, in his arms so she could watch her elder brothers and sisters open presents. Little Caelyn's warm, sweet-smelling body nestled snugly in the crook of his arm and her tiny hand curled around his finger.

"Another year and you'll be opening your own presents," Will assured her as he tore the paper off a soft toy. "Look, a lion! Grrr." He nuzzled the orange mane into Caelyn's neck until she giggled, her dark-blue eyes flashing with glee.

Will's sister Julie crouched before his chair with a camera. "Smile, Caelyn. Smile at your uncle Will." She snapped the photo and sat back on her heels. "When are you going to settle down and have a family, Will? You don't want to be like Dad and wait till you're an old man to have children."

No, he definitely did not. Will's father had been fifty-five when Will was born. By the time Will was old enough to play footy or cricket, William Sr. was walking with a cane. And by the time Will was ten, his father was dead of a heart attack.

He thought about his big house on the bay just begging to be filled with children's laughter, and the hollow spaces in his heart seemed to expand. He'd turned thirty-six last month; he had to get cracking. "Soon," he told Julie. "I'll be starting a family soon."

"You'll need a wife," his brother-in-law, Mike, reminded him jokingly, before a water pistol aimed by his eldest boy got him in the neck. "Hey, not in the house!" Mike spun and tickled the laughing child under the arms until he dropped the water pistol.

Enviously, Will watched Mike cavort with his children as they spilled out of the family room and into the backyard, shrieking with laughter in the summer sun.

"Will won't have any trouble finding a wife." Julie had put down the camera and was handing him a glass of eggnog.

"Cheers." Will sipped the frosty drink. Since he'd broken up with Maree four years ago there'd been no one serious in his life. The sporty, carefree girls who hung out at the Surf Lifesaving Club were too young to really talk to, and most women his age were either married already or increasingly set in their ways, even as they searched for some elusive romantic ideal.

He had tried to find love, and for a while with Maree, he'd thought he had. The years since they'd parted had eroded his belief in happily-ever-after, but not his desire for a family. The tricky part of marriage was finding that special woman who wanted children as much as he. He knew if he just took a rational approach, he could solve the problem.

After all, he had the rest of his life under control.

CHAPTER ONE

MAEVE ARDEN CONSIDERED a big part of her job as a garden designer was noticing things about her prospective clients. With Will Beaumont the first thing she noticed was his eyes. They were cobalt blue, logical and assessing, but with a hint of humor in their depths.

"Hi," she greeted Will, who'd just opened his front door to her. "I'm Maeve."

"Ah, Art Hodgins's daughter. He talks about you a lot."

"Art talks a lot, period," she said cheerfully. "But I wouldn't have him any other way."

Her father spoke frequently of Will's sterling qualities as a boss but had somehow neglected to mention his good looks. Will's brown hair was damp, his feet bare beneath freshly pressed chinos, and he wore a Hawaiian shirt. Not exactly Maeve's image of the head of a company, but she liked the incongruity. It made him, and therefore her job, more interesting. "Nice shirt."

With a half smile, Will Beaumont fingered the hem of dark swirling blues and fluorescent pinks and greens. "I wear it to annoy my accountant."

Maeve, who dressed for more practical purposes in work boots, khaki cargo pants and a white muslin shirt buttoned over a black crop top, grinned. She removed her hat to fan her face. Wisps of long dark hair blew up with each pass of the broad brim. It was only seven-thirty on a January morning and already the day was a scorcher.

Will slipped his feet into the leather thongs sitting beside the welcome mat. "Come. I'll show you the garden."

"I've already seen that it'll be a big job." The front yard was choked with weeds and overgrown shrubbery, and dried stalks drooped from stone urns flanking the steps. The large two-story art deco house done in cream and pale gold was beautiful; the garden, a mess.

Will led the way around the three-car garage, past a bungalow, to the back of the house. Maeve flipped open her clipboard and paused to do a rough sketch of the existing garden. The property was bounded by high walls and hedges, and sloped to a breath-taking view of Port Phillip Bay, with Melbourne in the distance.

"I understand you're friends with other clients of mine, Alex and Ginger White," she said, drawing in the Monterey Bay fig tree that dominated the south side of the terraced lawn.

"They raved about you," Will said, watching over her shoulder. "Claimed you're some kind of magician. I was very impressed with what you did with their place."

"Thank you." If Alex and Ginger thought she was a magician, it was because she'd done her homework. She'd made note of their clothes and furnishings, their car, even their choice of pets. She'd asked a million questions about their lifestyle, what they expected from their garden and how they planned to use it. Then she'd used her artistic and botanical skills to create a green space uniquely suited to them.

"This place has fantastic potential," she said, flipping to a new page. "What exactly did you have in mind for your garden?"

He frowned over her question. "Low maintenance is the main thing," he said briskly. "Maybe a few flowers…"

She sighed at his response. "Do you entertain business associates, friends…?"

"Yes, of course. I have a built-in barbecue up by the patio. And then there's the pool." He led her down stone steps to the second terrace, where blue water shimmered beneath the dazzling sun. Bordered by roses and hibiscus, the pool stretched about forty feet in length, with a marble sheen finish and blue mosaic tiling around the edge. Maeve noticed damp patches on the concrete surrounding the pool and drying footprints on the path leading up to the patio. She glanced at Will's hair, drying on top to reveal gold streaks among the brown. He spent plenty of time in the water. Or on it.

"Very nice," she said of the pool; then, fingering

a badly blighted leaf, she added, "Pity about the roses."

"Will they have to go?"

Hearing disappointment, she asked, "What is it you particularly like about them?"

He thought for a moment, hands deep in his pockets. "The scent, I suppose."

"I know some wonderfully scented roses. Or I could plant gardenias. They have a beautiful fragrance." She pulled a tape measure from the pocket of her cargo pants. "Hold this, please," she said, giving the end to Will. She walked the length of the pool, wrote down the measurement on her clipboard and walked back, reeling the tape in until she was standing in front of him. "White flowers are lovely by moonlight. Do you swim at night?"

"Sure, when it's warm enough." His frank gaze washed over her, intimate and humorous. "Do you?"

"When the opportunity arises." Maeve tugged, and the tape snapped back into its case. *Those eyes.*

She tipped back her hat to gaze up at the house, imagining it from the bay, with the cream stucco repeating the pale-gold sand at the base of the cliff and the sky reflecting blue in the plate-glass windows. Projecting, she saw it surrounded by lush healthy vegetation.

"It's a wonderful house," she said. "Awfully big for one person, though." She glanced at him, eyebrows raised. "Or are you married?"

The humor faded from his expression. A tendon in his jaw twitched. "Is that relevant?"

"If I'm going to design your garden I'll need to know something about you. I want to make the outdoor living space uniquely yours."

"It's not meant to be a work of art. Just needs a little pruning and weeding here and there."

"Are you married?" Maeve asked again, reminding him of the question. And reminding herself that patience was a virtue.

"No." He was massively indifferent.

"Fiancé?"

He frowned. "No."

"Girlfriend?"

"Now, I know *that's* not relevant." He sounded exasperated, and slightly defensive, almost angry.

She waited silently. Sometimes people needed a couple of sessions to open up. Sometimes they talked so much she couldn't get past the verbiage to their real selves. What she wanted was a glimpse of the real Will Beaumont, something she could translate into a garden that would provide him inner peace. After the turmoil in her life, she was a great believer in inner peace.

"Oh, all right," he said at last. "Lately I've been thinking it's time I settled down." He shrugged off the admission with a disarming grin. "What can I say? My biological clock is ticking."

Maeve pictured a white pavilion and elegantly dressed guests mingling, champagne glasses in hand, among the flowers. "The second terrace would be a wonderful place to have the wedding ceremony,'' she said, enthusiastic. ''You and your bride could stand here overlooking the bay, with your guests over there—''

''Are you a wedding planner or a gardener?''

Maeve's cheeks grew warm. ''Sorry.''

But she was getting somewhere at last. Women. Love. Marriage. Touchy subjects of some significance to Will.

Relevant? Definitely.

She set off along the wall that separated the first terrace from the second, feeling the heat emanating from the stones. Crickets shrilled in the dry undergrowth, and the scent of tea-tree from the cliffs below hung on the salt-laden air. Methodically, she cataloged the plants and shrubs that needed pulling or pruning or treating for disease, and those that could remain. Will followed a discreet three feet away.

''Pity the place was allowed to go so wild,'' she commented as they came to an overgrown stand of rhododendrons. ''Once weeds gain a foothold they're hard to get out.''

Will snapped off a leaf and twirled the stem between his fingers. ''I've been preoccupied with my business lately, and the garden kind of got away from me.''

Maeve took the leaf from his hand, inspected the underside and shook her head at the evidence of spider mite infestation.

''Is it serious?'' he asked.

A faint groove curved around his lips. Under favorable conditions, she thought, a dimple might grow in that spot. "Nothing's so serious it can't be fixed."

As she circled the bungalow, she examined a young gum tree that had sprung up next to the small brick building. Cracks spread through the concrete base where the tree's roots burrowed underneath. "I'd recommend taking this tree out. Do you use the bungalow?"

"It's my workshop." Will opened the door and flicked on the light.

Maeve stepped into the room. The wide wooden benches lining the walls were scattered with voltmeters, coiled wire, batteries and plastic casings, plus odds and ends she couldn't identify. "You don't get enough of electronics at your factory?"

"I like to tinker."

Turning to go, Maeve saw propped against the back wall behind the door a bright-yellow surfboard. A wet suit hung from a hook next to it. She had a sudden image of sun-sparkled water and Will riding the crest of a wave in a perfectly balanced crouch, his lean-muscled body sleek against a brilliant blue sky. "Do you do much surfing?"

Will ran a loving hand along the top curve of the surfboard. "When I was younger I almost turned pro."

"Really? What made you choose engineering, instead?"

"I quit school when I was sixteen. Spent my

nights working in a convenience store and my days at the beach. I'd sit out there for hours every day, waiting for the perfect wave, and all the while my mind would be ticking over, thinking about things.''

"Hopes? Dreams?" she asked. "Relationships?"

He flashed her a bemused glance. "Practical things. Physical things. How things work, like the thermostat in a cooling system or the electronics of a car. I had ideas for inventions, things I could build myself." He made a sweeping gesture that took in his workshop and the projects under way. "With my limited knowledge I could only get so far...so I went back to high school and then on to university."

She had to admire someone with that much drive and ambition. "It's wonderful to be able to work at something you love."

"Yeah... It's good, but the business side of it...I don't know. More headaches than it's worth sometimes." He broke off with a shake of his head. "You're not interested in all this."

"Yes, I am," she said seriously. "I'm interested in everything about you." She blushed, realizing how he might take that remark. "I mean—"

"Please don't spoil it by explaining." He smiled widely.

Bingo. One dimple, on the right side of his mouth. Great grin, warm and teasing. Some woman was going to be very lucky....

Maeve moved across to the Monterey Bay fig tree. Its broad limbs and glossy dark leaves gave welcome shade to that half of the yard. Stepping over the high, ridged roots, she ran a hand caressingly over a thick smooth limb. "This would be a perfect place for a swing," she suggested idly, pulling her pencil from behind her ear to make a note on her clipboard.

"Or a tree fort." His gaze was lost in the soaring tangle of greenery. She couldn't see his expression, but she heard the wistful note in his voice.

Every once in a while clients came along who subconsciously communicated an inner need or a desire for something more from their garden than simply a place to relax and entertain. Such clients, and the gardens Maeve created as an expression of their inner selves, demanded her greatest intuitive and interpretative skills. Yet they were also the most rewarding.

Looking at Will Beaumont, successful owner of his own electronics manufacturing company, she wouldn't have thought him the type to need her special gifts. But the tingling in her nerve endings as her gaze went from the neglected grounds to his pensive blue eyes suggested Will might be just such a client.

"Do you plan on having kids?" she asked, suppressing the inevitable ache she felt when she talked about children. Ordinarily, she didn't initiate such conversations, but she had a job to do.

His eyes lit. "Absolutely. I love kids."

Maeve walked on quickly. From her perspective, his enthusiasm seemed painfully innocent.

"Do you have children?" he asked, falling into step.

She shook her head, stumbling on a tuft of grass. *Not anymore. Never again.* She said nothing. Any answer she gave would only lead to questions she'd spent the past five years avoiding.

They'd come full circle, and once again stood where the grass ended at the asphalt driveway. "If you're going to have kids, you'll want to fence off the backyard," Maeve suggested briskly.

"True," Will agreed, watching her. "Do you want some water? You look a little pale."

"I'm fine," she said. "Really." She flipped through her clipboard to a plastic sheet encasing business cards, extracted one and handed it to him. "This fellow does specialty wrought-iron fencing for me. Since a wedding is in your future plans, we could do something appropriate for the occasion—a kissing gate. I know they're a little old-fashioned, but they're very romantic."

"A kissing gate? I've never heard of that." His dimple reappeared. "You'll have to show me how to use it."

She plucked the card from his fingers and slid it back into its slot. "That will be a job for the future Mrs. Beaumont."

"The position is vacant," he teased. "All comers considered."

For Maeve, flirting was more bittersweet than fun when there could be no future in it. She smiled and changed the subject. "Shall I draw up a plan and prepare a price estimate to rejuvenate your garden?"

His humorous gaze turned assessing. Then, abruptly, he started toward the patio. "Come inside. I'll give you my card with a number where you can contact me during the day."

Shade cloth and bougainvillea cooled the slate-floored patio. Cushioned chairs were set around a redgum table. Nice spot, Maeve thought. Add a few large pot plants, maybe a staghorn fern hanging from the wall, and it would be even more inviting.

She followed him through a terra-cotta-tiled family room adjoining the kitchen, to a study off the dining room. His briefcase sat open on a chair, and business documents were spread out on the desk, along with his wallet and car keys.

Maeve's gaze automatically gravitated to the papers he'd been working on. She just had time to notice a financial consultant's report on Aussie Electronics before Will shuffled the documents together, placed them inside the briefcase and shut the lid.

"Top secret, huh?" she said, wondering at the sudden frown that flattened the arch in his eyebrows.

"Just business." He snapped the locks shut and spun the dials. Then he handed her a card from his wallet. "You can reach me on this number during the day and on my cell phone anytime."

Maeve slipped the card into one of the pockets of her cargo pants. In turn, she gave him one of her own.

"'Maeve Arden,'" he read. "Your last name is different from Art's. Are you married?"

"I was. I divorced five years ago." Her split-up with Graham had been less rancorous than sad. Grief over Kristy had overwhelmed other disappointments and left Maeve with a lingering sense of unfinished business.

"Dad will be pleased to know I'm working for you," she said. "If you decide to use my services, that is." Already she wanted this job; Will's garden was ripe with possibilities and rife with unfulfilled dreams. She didn't know exactly how she knew that; she simply accepted that she did. She'd learned not to analyze the source of her intuition, for fear of stifling the flow.

"If I weren't so busy at work I'd have gotten several quotes, but personal recommendations go a long way with me. If I like what you propose, I'll probably go with that."

She met his eyes. "You won't regret it."

"If you're your father's daughter, I'm sure I won't. Art is the best foreman I've ever had." He led the way back through the house to the front steps. "I look forward to seeing your design. When can you have something ready?"

At this time of year she was working flat-out, but for someone her father admired as much as Will Beaumont, she would put aside some of her non-essential tasks. "I'll do up a preliminary plan in the next few days. Before I finalize it I'd like to come back for a more thorough look over the grounds and to ask you a few more questions.''

"Fine. Say Thursday, around six?''

She wrote down the time and day, then tucked her clipboard under her arm. She'd noted many details today, but the most important information she'd gleaned was imprinted not on the pad's lined pages but on her brain. Not facts and figures, but the suppressed longing in a man's voice when he spoke of a child's tree fort.

Maeve climbed into her truck and poked her head out the window. "I'll see you Thursday.''

Will leaned on the roof above her window. "Afterward we could grab a bite to eat in Sorrento,'' he suggested casually. "There's this great seafood restaurant down by the water—''

Tempted despite herself, she searched her mind for an excuse. He'd be fun to go out with, but encouraging him wouldn't be fair. She heard a faint ringing from inside the house. "Is that your phone?''

He glanced over his shoulder and straightened away from the ute. "I suppose it is.''

Maeve put the truck in gear. "Catch you later.''

In the rearview mirror, she saw him shake his head, his smile bemused, clearly in no rush to answer his phone. She laughed to herself. This job could be interesting. And challenging.

The biggest challenge of all would be restraining her attraction to Will Beaumont.

CHAPTER TWO

MAEVE PARKED BENEATH the peppermint gum in the side yard of her cottage in the village of Mount Eliza, a half hour up the coast from Will's place in Sorrento. The front door stood open in the vain hope of attracting a passing breeze, and her father's worn work boots rested to one side of the mat.

Good. Art was home. She wanted to have a word with him about his moving back to a place of his own. He'd recovered from the mild heart attack he'd suffered last winter, and although she loved him and enjoyed his company, they both needed to get on with their own lives.

Maeve kicked off her boots and pushed through the screen door to enter the relative cool of the hallway. Wandin Cottage wasn't as grand as some of the houses she worked at, but what did she or her father need with grandeur? He'd been a working man all his life and she preferred the outdoors to fancy decor.

She slung her hat on a hook, picked up the pile of letters on the hall table and walked down the narrow hallway to the kitchen, which lay at the back of the house.

Art stood at the stove, burly in a white T-shirt and brown work pants, with her frilly pink apron tied around his neck and waist. His hair had turned completely white after the heart attack, but his eyebrows were still black and bushy.

Maeve came up from behind and gave him a hug. "Hamburgers again. You know you don't have to cook for me."

"You can't do a full day's work, then come home and eat rabbit food," he growled, flattening a sizzling patty with the back of his spatula. Then his habitual frown lightened into what for him passed as a smile. "Never thought I'd say it, but I like cooking for my daughter. It's good having company over a meal."

Maeve forced herself to return his smile, though her heart sank. "There's something we need to talk about."

"Sure, Maevie, love, but before I forget, Tony called. He wants to know if you ordered the paving blocks for the Cummings place."

"Thanks. I'll phone him back later." Maeve got herself a bottle of mineral water from the fridge and leaned against the counter, sorting the junk mail from the bills, dropping the flyers straight into the recycling box. "I did a landscaping quote for your boss, Will Beaumont, this morning."

Art flipped the burger and smashed down the other side. "You don't say!"

"He's got a beautiful place on the cliff at Sorrento. The garden'll be a lot of work, but it has great potential.''

''After I was let go from my old job, not a soul wanted to hire a man in his fifties who'd had a heart attack. Will Beaumont did.'' Art pointed his spatula at her. ''You make sure you do a good job for him, you hear?''

'''Course I will, Art. He thinks pretty highly of you, too.'' She grimaced at the size of her nursery bill and moved it to the bottom of the pile.

''Beaumont doesn't waste time with a lot of manipulative bullshit about productivity and teamwork,'' Art went on, stirring the onions frying alongside the hamburgers. ''He respects a person's ability to do a job and lets him get on with it.''

Maeve barely heard him. Tucked between the quarry bill and the phone bill was a small green envelope addressed in the strongly slanting handwriting she'd never thought she'd see again. *Graham.*

''And if something screws up he doesn't hold it against you, just expects you to fix the problem,'' Art rambled. ''He doesn't waste words, either. I can't bear a man who rabbits on about nothing.''

That outrageous statement shook Maeve out of painful memories of her brief marriage and made her smile.

Art pointed his spatula at her. ''He'd been a good 'un for you, Maevie.''

''Don't think so,'' she said, taking a sip of her water. ''He's in the market for a wife.''

Art turned off the heat under the frying pan. "All the more reason."

"Dad, forget it. Please." Her life might be an emotional desert, but at least she'd more or less recovered her equilibrium. For a whole year after Kristy's death she'd barely functioned. No one but her friend Rose knew all she'd been through. She was not ready for another plunge into matrimony and motherhood. Probably she never would be.

"Okay, okay," Art said. "These burgers are ready. Want to cut up some rolls?"

Glad of an excuse to set Graham's unopened letter aside, Maeve sliced hamburger rolls and slid them under the griller to toast. "There's something lurking under the surface with Will," she said. "Something I can't quite put my finger on."

"Will Beaumont is the most straightforward bloke a man could hope to meet," Art declared. He waggled his fingers at her. "I suppose you got one of your weird 'feelings' about him."

Maeve turned away from the fridge, her arms loaded with bottles of condiments. "I just got a glimpse. Not enough to go on. He's missing something. Something to do with love."

Art snorted. "Will Beaumont missing out in love? I wouldn't think so. You should see the way the girls on the production line follow him with their eyes when he walks by."

"I'll admit he's got sex appeal, but that doesn't necessarily have anything to do with love," Maeve said dryly. "However, I could be wrong. He's a hard one to read."

Art slid the hamburgers onto a plate and brought them to the table. "He's been under a lot of pressure lately, always in a meeting with the accountant. There are rumors going around that the company's in trouble financially."

"Really? He's got a great big house and a Mercedes parked out front." The memory of Will shoving papers into his briefcase—papers he didn't want her to see—flashed through her mind.

Art sat at the head of the table and fixed his hamburger with "the lot"—bacon, onions, a slice of beetroot, cheese, mayo, tomato and lettuce; then he topped the whole quivering mass with a fried egg. "What was it you wanted to talk to me about?" he asked, before opening his mouth wide and biting deep.

Maeve, who'd contented herself with lettuce and tomato, put her hamburger back on her plate and took a deep breath instead of a bite. "Do you ever miss having your own place?"

Art chewed and swallowed. "My word, no. That housing unit was as lonely as a monk's cell, after your mother passed on." He was about to take another bite, then lowered his burger and fixed her with his shrewd gaze. "Perhaps it's you who miss having your place to yourself."

Suddenly, she couldn't tell him. Couldn't inflict another loss on her father. "Of course not," she said, laughing to prove the foolishness of such an idea. "It's great having you here."

He smiled tentatively. "Who else would you get to cook for you, eh?"

After dinner Art took himself off to the front veranda for his one smoke of the day. Maeve propped the green envelope on the windowsill in front of the sink, and ran hot water to build up a soapy froth. What did Graham want after all these years? The return address was care of the yacht harbor in Sydney, so she assumed he still had his sailboat.

After she'd stacked the last clean plate in the dish rack, she swept the floor and tidied the pantry. Then she sat at the table and attended to her bills, her checkbook at hand. At last, there was nothing for it but to read Graham's letter. With trembling fingers she tore open the envelope:

> Dear Maeve, I've been thinking of you a lot
> lately. I'm sailing for Fiji at the end of March.
> Before I go, I want to see you again. I'll be in
> Mornington sometime in the next few weeks.
> Will call when I get in. Graham. P.S. Remember how we used to make love at sea under the
> stars?

Maeve's hands dropped to her lap and the letter slipped through her motionless fingers to the floor. For a moment she did remember. Was there a part of her that still loved Graham? They'd had some good times before Kristy died. Some bad times, too, but that was part of marriage. If he was backtracking all this way just to see her, he must still care.

Did she?

WILL ARRIVED HOME from work late on Thursday evening to find Maeve's ute in his driveway and Maeve sitting on the tailgate. Every red blood cell in his body went on alert. She'd cast off her shirt, and the scant black crop top left an expanse of taut brown skin above her cargo pants. Her dark hair was pulled into a long ponytail, which hung over her shoulder. In one hand she held a half-empty bottle of water and in the other a wide-brimmed hat, with which she fanned herself.

"I hope you haven't been waiting long," he said, emerging from the Merc. "The production line broke down just as I was leaving, and I stayed until it was fixed."

She hopped from the tailgate and brushed off the back of her pants. "It's okay. I mowed the lawn while I waited."

"Such enterprise." Will opened his front door. "Come in. We'll get a cold drink and you can grill me."

Maeve kicked off her boots and stepped past him into the entry hall. He watched her gaze lift to the overhead skylight, then sweep up the curved staircase to the landing. There, round windows like portholes let in more light. Finally she peeked sideways to the lounge room, which glowed warmly in shades of cream, yellow and terra-cotta.

"I love your house," she said, turning to him with a surprised smile. "I didn't take it all in the last time I was here. It's perfect."

"Thanks." The house was light and bright, reflecting the sun and the sea, with hardly a straight line or a sharp angle in the place. After he and Maree had split, he'd needed a place where he could feel positive about the future. A home he could grow into.

But as he led the way down the hall to the kitchen, Maeve amended her verdict. "Almost perfect. So far I haven't seen a single plant."

He glanced over his shoulder to see her eyes sparkling. "And you won't. I always forget to water them, so now I don't bother trying to grow any." He opened a bar fridge in the family room, displaying a dozen types of specialty beer, plus several bottles of white wine and different types of water. "What'll you have?"

"Something nonalcoholic with ice, thanks."

Will made her a tonic and lime juice, then chose a Red Dog lager for himself, and they sat at the patio table. Maeve flipped her clipboard open and proceeded to question him on everything from his favorite color to his astrological sign. Her dark-brown eyes studied him with such intense concentration, she might have been trying to read the convolutions of his brain.

And when she bent her head to note his answers with green-stained fingers, Will studied her. Although she wore no makeup, her tanned skin was smooth and her vivid coloring a collection of contrasts: dark hair, white teeth, deep-red lips. Her mouth was wide and full, curling at the corners in a cupid's bow. Her large eyes full of laughter a few minutes ago, were now serious.

"Do you have any siblings?" She brushed back a strand of hair that had fallen across her cheek, drawing his attention to the translucent moonstones that studded her lobes.

After a moment of silence she glanced up expectantly, and he realized he'd forgotten the question.

"Siblings," she repeated.

"Two sisters and a brother."

Her gaze remained fixed on his. "What number child are you?"

"I'm the eldest."

"Star sign?"

"Capricorn."

She frowned down at her clipboard, muttering, "Capricorn and Libra—bad mix."

"Who's a Libran?"

She didn't answer, and he smiled to see a blush creep into her cheeks. "Do you believe in astrology?" he asked.

"Not really." Her gaze sharpened. "I mean, yes."

Will drank from his beer. "'Our fate lies not in the stars, but in ourselves.' Or words to that effect. I feel I know you already, through your father."

"Oh?" She put down her pen and eyed him warily.

"For instance, I know you like pancakes topped with fresh fruit for breakfast on Sunday morning. And that you use rainwater to wash your hair." His fingers flexed as he found himself wondering if her hair was as smooth and soft as it appeared.

"What else did he say about me?"

Will racked his brain, and couldn't think of anything she might object to. "Nothing personal. No deep dark secrets."

Maeve appeared relieved, and his fascination with her grew. But this session was about him, and she hadn't forgotten that. "So," she said, going back to her clipboard, "who was next—your brother or a sister?"

"My sister Julie. But why? What does my childhood have to do with this garden?"

"You never know," she replied, writing down his answer.

He leaned forward, trying unsuccessfully to read her handwriting upside down. "Are you licensed to practice psychiatry in this state?"

Her mouth twitched, but she ignored his question and went on. "Did you grow up in the city or the country?"

"I grew up here on the peninsula on a small mixed farm. When I was ten, we moved into the town of Mornington." Will shifted in his chair, crossed one leg over his knee. "What about your family? Art mentioned he has a son overseas."

"My brother, Bill, lives in New Mexico. He's an astronomer."

"Is he searching the galaxy for extraterrestrial life forms?" Will joked.

"Yes," Maeve answered seriously. "Now, when you were on the farm you must have played outside a lot. Do you remember the feelings you associate with being outdoors at an early age?"

He was about to make a flippant remark, when he stopped and thought twice. Perhaps the smell of the freshly mown grass called forth memories, or maybe it was Maeve's gentle prodding, but suddenly the past came back in a flash of vivid imagery. That time in his life before his father died. Before he'd had to grow up too quickly.

"Freedom," he said at last. "I could go anywhere, do anything I liked, from dawn to dusk. My brother and sisters and I roamed the beaches and the paddocks for miles around. We weren't restricted by time or place or fear of strangers. Freedom and security—they were what I felt. Two rare and precious commodities. But they're gone from today's world. You can't get them back."

"I can try," she said.

He eyed her skeptically. "If you can create the illusion of childhood in a garden, I'll believe you really are a magician."

"The magic comes from within," she said quietly. "You have it, too. Everyone does. You just need to find it."

She paused to sip her drink, the melting ice cubes tinkling faintly as she lifted her glass. To Will, the curve of her throat seemed at that moment both unbearably vulnerable and unimaginably strong. Magic within? He didn't think so. Not him.

She lowered her glass and repositioned her pen above the paper. "Did you have a special place you liked to go to as a child? A place that was yours and yours alone?"

"Why are you asking all these questions?" All of a sudden he felt vulnerable himself.

"I told you. I want to know you." Her huge dark eyes were hypnotic; her smooth low voice was mesmerizing.

"There was a place," he admitted slowly, "at the bottom of the garden where jasmine grew over the fence. The vines were wildly overgrown—they must have been at least six feet thick. Next to the fence I hollowed out a cubby for myself. On hot days it was cool and filled with green light. Perfumed by the jasmine." He chuckled. "I would pretend I was an Arabian sheik living in my tent at an oasis. My golden retriever was my camel." He threw her another skeptical glance. "Not the sort of landscaping you had in mind, I'm sure."

"You'd be surprised." She closed her clipboard. "I'll just go take a few more measurements. I want to check out those lilacs by the brick wall."

"Mind if I tag along?" Will said, rising. Then, through the open sliding doors came the sound of the door chimes.

"Saved by the bell—again." Her mouth hinted at a smile, then she strode off across the lawn.

Will went to open the front door and found Ida,

his oldest friend and practically his best mate, on the doorstep. With her auburn hair and creamy complexion, Ida would have been a knockout if not for the burn scars that marred the right side of her face, puckering the skin from the outer corner of her eye all the way down to her chin.

"Hi, Will. You're not busy, are you?" she asked, stepping past him into the entry hall.

"No." Even after all these years, Will never saw the scars without experiencing a stab of guilt.

Today Ida looked slighter than usual in a slim gray skirt and white fitted blouse.

"Good, because I need to talk."

"Of course. Come through to the patio."

They stopped in the kitchen to get Will another beer and to pour Ida a glass of chardonnay.

"Can I have some mineral water with that?" she asked, rummaging in Will's pantry for pretzels. "I've been feeling a little queasy all week. Must have a tummy bug."

Will handed her the wine spritzer. "What's up?"

"Wait till we're sitting." Carrying her glass and the bag of pretzels, Ida led the way out the sliding glass doors to the patio table. When they were seated, she took a sip of her drink, put her glass down and looked Will straight in the eye. "I've decided to have a child."

Will choked on his beer. "What?"

"I said, I'm going to have a child. On my own."

"You can't be serious."

Ida waved a pretzel at him. "I didn't mention it

until now because I was afraid you'd try to talk me out of the idea before I'd even made up my mind. But I've thought long and hard and I'm very sure this is what I want. Now it's just a question of finding someone to donate sperm."

"But on your own! Don't you want to get married someday?"

"Who'd marry me?"

"Come on, Ida," Will chided. "You're smart, successful, beautiful—"

"Stop it, Will. I might have been beautiful once," she conceded, touching her forefinger to the fine ridges of scar tissue on her cheek. "Since this happened…forget it."

Will fell silent, gnawed by guilt. Her scars, caused by burns from a deep-fat fryer in the fast-food joint where they'd both worked as university students, were his fault. She'd been standing over the fryer when he'd come along, on his way to the back room with his lunch. He'd stepped in a spot of grease, slipped, and his drink had flown into the fryer. He'd gone down, escaping the spray of boiling fat. Ida had caught it in the face. Thanks to her generous, forgiving nature, she'd never held the accident against him.

"Okay, so you'll never make it in the movies, but you do all right, don't you? I mean, your law practice is thriving, you own your house outright, you drive a brand-new BMW—" He broke off, wondering whether he was trying to convince himself or her.

"In terms of material success, yes, I'm doing fine. But it's not enough anymore. What I want is a family."

"I can understand that. I'd like a family, too. I've been thinking it's time I settled down."

"There you go. I'm thirty-seven, Will. It's time to face facts. Maybe somewhere on this ever-shrinking Earth is a man who would love me for who I am, but I can't wait forever to meet him."

Will traced a path through the condensation on his glass. If only he could have fallen in love with her. But he'd known Ida since they were children, long before the fryer incident and the scarring. He loved her like a brother; the right chemistry just wasn't there. "You'll meet someone. Thirty-seven isn't old."

Ida snorted. "My biological clock has turned into a time bomb. If it weren't physiologically unlikely, I'd swear I was getting hot flashes just thinking about my next birthday."

"What about that guy from San Diego—Rick, wasn't it? The one who was here setting up the Melbourne outlet for Borders bookstore. He seemed nice."

"He's gone back to the States," Ida said with the dismissive gesture Will had come to associate with her covering up some hurt. "He wasn't serious."

"You always downplay any feelings a guy might have for you." Will had thought the relationship was serious, at least on Ida's part. He'd liked Rick, but if Rick had hurt her, Will wanted to shake him till his brain rattled. Ida hated anyone feeling sorry for her, though, even him, so he just nodded and sipped his beer.

A rustle in the bushes next to the brick wall caught his attention. Maeve emerged on the lawn. Despite the shimmering heat, she looked cool as a spring flower in her loose white shirt. Unaware of his scrutiny, she was making notes on her clipboard, head bent, wisps of shining dark hair falling over her high cheekbones. Then the warm breeze ruffled the page, and she glanced up. Seeing him watching her, she smiled.

Will froze, glass to his lips, as the oddest sensation stole over him, a kind of warmth in his midsection. A smile curved his lips as their gazes held, and the warmth expanded throughout his body, transporting him to a state of unexpected well-being.

"Who's that?" Ida asked.

"Huh? Oh, that's Maeve. She's a landscape gardener, and the daughter of my foreman at the factory. She's got some sensational ideas for the garden."

"She's lovely. If you're looking to settle down, you don't need to look farther than your own backyard."

"I asked her out and she refused," Will said with a frown. "No reason. Just refused."

"Maybe she was having a bad day."

"Maybe."

Maeve disappeared behind the Monterey Bay fig,

and Will turned back to Ida. "I understand your wanting a child, but do you really have to do it on your own?"

Ida's chin lifted. "What's wrong with that?"

Will shoved both hands through his hair. "For starters, a child needs a mother *and* a father. I realize it doesn't always work out that way and I'd never judge anyone whose marriage breaks up, but, damn it, you have to try."

Ida leaned forward, her hazel eyes shimmering. "I have tried, Will. What do you think I've been doing for the past fifteen years—playing hard to get?"

"But think of the child. It's not fair to deliberately deprive a kid of having a father." No one understood better than he what growing up without a father was like.

Ida's mouth pulled tight. "*Life* isn't fair. Is it fair for me to remain childless when I want so badly to have a baby?"

"No, but..."

She got up and strode across the deck to lean against the post, arms tightly crossed. "I was hoping for your moral support. If that's not possible, at least spare me your condemnation."

Will rose and put his arms around her, and felt her lean into him. "I'm sorry," he said. "But I wouldn't be your friend if I didn't try to talk you out of this crazy idea."

"No, I'm sorry," she said, wiping her wet cheeks with the heel of her hand. "My emotions are all over the place lately. I know what I want is selfish, but I'm feeling desperate. I hate that. It's so pathetic.''

"Hey, hey, hey," Will said soothingly, and stroked her back. "You're not selfish or pathetic. It's just that you deserve more. Your baby deserves more. I thought you were waiting for Mr. Right to come along.''

She managed a ragged laugh. "Mr. Right must have taken a wrong turn. Or maybe he saw me first. I've given up, Will. I've tried so hard for so long. Plastic surgery can only do so much. My appearance is as good as it's ever going to get. The only dates I've had since my accident have been with friends or co-workers who feel sorry for me.''

"And Rick," he reminded her. "But I don't believe he or anyone else went out with you because they felt sorry for you.''

With an impatient sigh, she pushed away from Will and paced back to her seat. "I thought Rick was different, yet when his time was up here in Melbourne, he just left.''

"Have you heard from him at all?''

"He phoned once, but I could tell it was just a duty call. I'm not prepared to wait around any longer on the off chance I might meet someone else. If I'm going to have a child, I want it to be soon.''

Will was silent a moment, struggling to accept what she was saying. He came back to his seat, prepared to be a help, not a hindrance. "Okay, you're serious. Let's take it from there. What about the father? Who will it be? Are you planning to tell him?''

"I don't have an arrangement with anyone yet." She gazed down at her hands with an oddly shy smile. "Although I do have a candidate in mind."

Will relaxed a little and leaned back against his chair. At least, she wasn't planning on a series of one-night stands with anonymous lovers.

"And, of course, I'll tell him," Ida went on. "It wouldn't be fair not to. He could have as much or as little contact as he wished. My only stipulation would be that if he opted to take on the fatherhood thing, he be prepared to stick with it. For the child's sake."

"I hope whoever you're thinking of is good enough for you. He'd have to be a pretty special guy."

Ida glanced up at him. "Oh, he's special, all right."

Will gazed at her determined, tear-stained face.

She gazed right back at him.

Light dawned. "You mean me?"

"Would you? I hate the idea of using a sperm bank and having a complete stranger father my baby."

"I—I'm incredibly flattered. I just don't know what to say. I don't know what to think."

"You don't have to make up your mind right away. I know it's a lot to spring on someone. But would you at least contemplate it? Please?"

His gut reaction was to decline, but for Ida he would consider the proposal. "Sure. I'll think about it."

"Thank you." She checked her watch and sighed. "I'd better go. I've got so much work to catch up on."

Will walked her out to her car. Ida opened her door and paused to search his face worriedly. "Will, whatever you decide it's okay. I don't want anything to hurt our friendship."

"Nothing will hurt our friendship." He still felt a little stunned as he leaned down to kiss her lightly on the lips. He wanted to be a father, but this wasn't the way he'd expected it to happen. What was the point of having children if you weren't part of a family?

CHAPTER THREE

MAEVE CLOSED her clipboard and wandered back to the patio. Her plan wasn't as complete as she would have liked. But then, she didn't feel she knew everything she needed to about Will. Sometimes she just had to start with the barest of an idea, and elaborate as she got to know her characters, the way a writer might.

She spread the sheets of graph paper with her roughed-in design on the table and waited for Will to return from seeing his friend—girlfriend?—out. He came through the sliding doors looking as though he'd been hit hard over the head and was still seeing stars. "Everything all right?" she asked.

"Huh?" He gave his head a little shake. "Yes. Fine. Are you finished taking measurements?"

Maeve indicated the graph paper. "See what you think."

Will turned the paper sideways to read her tiny writing. "It's all Greek to me."

"Latin, actually," Maeve said. "Sorry if it's confusing, but using the species names of plants is second nature."

"Where did you study?"

"Melbourne University. I have a PhD in botany."

Will's eyebrows disappeared upward into a lock of sun-streaked chestnut hair. "I would have thought you'd be teaching or doing research, with a degree like that."

Maeve shrugged. "I experiment in situ in my own modest way, but I prefer growing plants to studying them, especially when I have the go-ahead to do my own thing. Which is really your thing, of course. You can get back to me on the estimate, if you like. My phone number's on the letterhead, or you can e-mail me."

"When would you be able to start?" he asked.

She thought for a moment. "I'm booked solid for the next two weeks, but I'll try to rearrange some of my less-urgent jobs. I could get back here on Monday to take out that tree by the bungalow."

"I appreciate your rearranging work for me."

She knew he wouldn't understand if she told him his garden was already growing inside her mind. "You...you've been so good to my father."

"Nothing he didn't earn." For some reason Will's mouth flattened and a frown line appeared between his eyes. He went into the house and returned a moment later carrying a checkbook. "You'll be needing money for materials, I presume?"

Maeve handed him the second piece of paper from her clipboard. "Half of that will be enough to get me going. Labor costs are charged at an hourly rate."

Will glanced over the itemized list and scribbled off a check. "Might as well pay for all the materials now to avoid delays in the future."

"If you say so." Clients weren't usually so quick to offer money—especially those supposedly in financial straits. Mentally, she gave herself a shake; sometimes she analyzed things too much. She wrote him out a receipt, then folded his check and tucked it into her breast pocket. "I take it this means I've got the job."

"Looks that way." He stacked the papers and set them aside. "Are you busy Saturday night?"

"No, but—"

"There's a jazz concert at the Briar's winery this weekend," he said over her objection. "We could take a picnic supper, sit under those big old gums and watch the cockatoos flap home to roost while the sun sets over the hills…"

Maeve smiled and held up a hand to stop his flow of words. "That sounds wonderful, but I can't."

"Can't, or won't?" he asked bluntly.

She hesitated, glanced away, then faced him squarely. "Won't."

"May I ask why?"

"I…don't get involved with clients." She couldn't meet his eyes.

He shook his head. "I don't buy it."

"Okay. How about, I don't think seeing you is a good idea given that you're my father's employer."

"Bullshit," he said politely.

"Okay…" Time to get serious, even though—no, especially because—part of her badly wanted to see him again. Her chin rose. "I don't find you attractive."

Will didn't even flinch. He studied her face as though trying to decide why she was lying to him. Finally, he said quietly, "Tell me the real reason."

She drew in a deep breath, shaken that his calm rational eyes saw through her so easily. When she spoke, the truth made her voice tremble. "I'm just not ready for a relationship right now. Sometimes I don't know if I ever will be again."

His frown softened into concern. "You must have been hurt badly."

She glanced away. "You could say that."

"Your ex-husband?"

"He…was part of it. Look, I really don't want to talk about it. It's personal and deeply painful, and not something I share with many people. Trust me, it wouldn't work between us."

"Maybe if I ask you again in a week or two—"

"No! I mean, I'm sorry, but there's absolutely no hope that I'll change my mind. You'd just be wasting your time."

She gazed at him, troubled to see that his expression was one of quiet determination.

"I won't pressure you," he said. "But when you change your mind, I'll be waiting."

"Don't," she said, putting her hat on. "Don't wait for me."

WILL ROSE AT FIVE the next morning, groggy with the heat. He'd spent a sleepless night, his mind in turmoil over the upcoming meeting with Paul, his company accountant and friend since university. Electronic engineering, not economics, was Will's field, but he didn't have to be John Kenneth Galbraith to realize that his company was in trouble.

Today he had to make a decision on the financial consultant's recommendation to close the Mornington factory and relocate offshore. Production costs were high; wages were higher. Cheap imports threatened his place in the market, and shareholders were pushing for an increased profit margin. After an initial, almost phenomenal, success, his tamperproof, infrared security alarm was being priced out of the world market. The only way to keep his business afloat, the money boys said, was to transfer production to Indonesia.

Such a move would throw his employees out of work. He hated that idea; it went against everything he stood for, everything he'd worked for. On the other hand, if Aussie Electronics went down, they would all lose their jobs anyway.

He ate a fried-egg sandwich while he stood at the edge of the patio in nothing but his shorts. When the hell would this weather break? Not a cloud marred the pure-blue sky, although the towers of Melbourne in the distance were hazy with smog. Usually a cool change blew through after a four- or five-day cycle of rising heat, but this was the seventh day in a row of temperatures over one hundred degrees.

The image of Maeve's trusting smile appeared before him. *You've been so good to my father.*

Maeve herself, with her graceful movements and her perceptive dark eyes, had been on his mind in spite of his efforts to forget her. He couldn't shake the feeling that she could see into his heart, and was at least intrigued with what she saw. So why this refusal to go out with him?

Then, there was Ida. Her astonishing request completed this triumvirate of mind-boggling, gut-wrenching problems. He wanted to help her out. He couldn't see any logical reason he shouldn't help her out. But something in him balked at being nothing more than a sperm donor.

He arrived at his factory an hour later. Aussie Electronics occupied a long, low-slung building in an industrial park on the outskirts of Mornington, twenty miles north on the peninsula. Will parked the Merc in front of the building, noting that Paul's car was already in one of the visitors' slots.

"'Morning, Renée," Will said as he walked through reception. Renée was a petite blonde in her forties who'd trained as a secretary, then stayed home with her children while they were young. Will had rescued her from a dead-end job and he'd been more than repaid by her organizational skills and efficiency.

Renée's hands stilled on the keyboard of her computer. "Paul's waiting for you in the meeting room."

Will felt her troubled gaze follow him as he

walked through the door that led to the inner offices, and he clenched his fists. Surely, with good references and a record of five years' steady employment she wouldn't have to go back to flipping burgers.

Paul was seated at the long oval table, papers spread around him. His short dark hair glistened with gel and he wore city garb—a black suit and a conservative gray tie. He was more than an accountant to Will's company; Will relied on him for many of the business management tasks he himself had little time for.

"Paul, you old bastard," Will said, grasping his hand in a firm shake before pulling out a chair across from the accountant. "Don't you know it's summer?"

Paul gave him a mildly reproving once-over. "I hope you're not going to wear that bloody Hawaiian shirt when we meet with the Indonesian delegation in Jakarta next month."

Will glanced down at his colorful attire, and grinned. "Don't you know the casual look has reached this country's boardrooms?"

Paul gave a bark of laughter. "And you're such a slave to fashion."

Will's smile flickered. "Time to get serious, Paul. Kmart and Target both canceled their orders for my security alarm. They've decided to stock the Japanese model. It's manufactured in Singapore and sells for ten percent less."

"Bloody hell."

"Exactly." Will dropped his briefcase on the table and sat heavily. The Japanese alarm, new on the market, was almost identical to his own invention, with just enough superficial differences to get around the patent laws. "I've not only lost my number-one position in sales, but I'm being pushed right out of the market."

"You've got other products," Paul said. "Timers, switches, medical instrumentation..."

"Sure, and they're doing okay, but they're not big earners. Not big enough to make up for losing the tamperproof alarm, at any rate. And since I floated those shares on the open market I've got third parties demanding increasing profit." He indicated a sheaf of papers in front of Paul. "So you've looked at these documents sent over by the Indonesian Department of Trade?"

Paul nodded. "They're offering all sorts of tax incentives. Economically, it's very viable."

"True," Will said. "Although Indonesia's had a lot of internal political trouble lately. The people aren't too keen on foreign investors."

Paul spread his hands. "No sweat. The government officials I've communicated with assure me the situation is under control."

"I saw on the news the other night that students are protesting in the capital."

Paul shrugged. "Students are always protesting. It's what they do. The government will love you for creating jobs."

"Too bad I have to destroy them here," Will said sharply.

"Listen, mate, good guys finish last. You've got to close the factory and make your move while you're still solvent. Six months from now your Mornington employees won't even remember your name."

"They'll be cursing it." Will pushed back his chair and rose to gaze out the floor-to-ceiling windows. Beyond the paddocks where horses grazed, rows of grapevines curved up the slope of the hill. Over the years Will had gotten to know each of his employees. Most of them were skilled, hardworking and loyal. He didn't want to let them down.

Or lose control of what he'd worked so hard to build.

But he knew Paul was right. Close the factory was the only logical thing to do. Will's chest squeezed tight, as though he were being crushed. "After all the satisfaction of growing the company, it hurts to send it down the drain."

"Not down the drain, just overseas. It's not the same thing at all," Paul assured him. "If you want, I'll make the announcement and you can distance yourself from the dirty deed."

"No," Will said, straightening. "I'm responsible to my employees. I'll tell them."

Paul passed across some stapled pages. "I've drawn up a list of employees and their redundancy payouts. Everything's ready to go. I just need your signature."

Glancing down the page, Will frowned. "These

amounts are awfully low. Most of my employees have families.''

''They're the minimum entitlements required by law.''

''Double them.''

''You can't afford—''

''Just do it!'' Will swore softly but fervently, rubbing a hand across his face. ''Sorry, mate, I know you're only trying to do what's best for the company.''

Paul leaned forward and gripped Will's shoulder. ''Everything'll be okay. You'll see.''

Will nodded, and forced himself to concentrate on what had to be done. ''To fulfill current contracts, production has to continue for another three months.''

''I'll notify the appropriate people in Jakarta and put the paperwork in motion,'' Paul said. ''I've got agents there looking for suitable factory space. Do you have anyone in mind to go over and help with the start-up?''

''Art Hodgins would be my first choice.'' *Three months.* He was giving his employees the ax and then expecting them to continue to work for him for three whole months.

''If I were you, I'd delay making the announcement until closer to the shutdown date,'' Paul said, as though he'd read Will's thoughts. ''You're only required to give two weeks' notice. Any more than that and you're asking for trouble.''

''People need time to find new jobs. It won't be easy for some,'' he said, thinking of Art Hodgins—

and Pat and Mick and Vlad and a dozen others over the age of fifty. Although, in the case of Art, Will could delay the problem by getting him involved in the set-up overseas.

"You're shooting yourself in the foot," Paul said. "But maybe for you they'll carry on. I've never seen a company with so few industrial relations problems." He glanced at his watch as he tucked the rest of his papers in his briefcase. "I've got another appointment in Mornington—but what do you say we meet for an early lunch at the Grand Hotel?"

Just the thought of sitting in a pub, pretending to have a good time right after he'd lowered the boom on his employees, had Will shaking his head. There was only one place he wanted to be after this—alone on his surfboard between the sky and the sea. But that would have to wait until the end of the working day. "Thanks, mate, not today. Let's get together soon, though." He pushed himself to his feet.

And then, all too quickly, Will was facing the expectant faces of the hundred or so men and women who worked for him. There was some nervous laughter as he cleared his throat, and a few people exchanged apprehensive glances. When he began to speak, the room fell quiet. From the shocked looks on every face as his message sank in, he realized that whatever rumors had gone around, no one had expected the factory to actually close.

Shock swiftly gave way to muttered whispering. Then, McLeod, a hard-bitten man who'd been with the company only a few months but who seemed always to be complaining, demanded belligerently to know why.

Art Hodgins quelled the rising storm of protest, shouting that Will Beaumont wouldn't be closing his doors unless he was up against the wall. When the noise died down, Art turned to Will with quiet dignity. "I'm sure we're all sorry you're losing what you've worked so hard to build."

Will nodded briefly, fighting a rising sense of shame. Paul stepped forward to outline the steps being taken to save the company, namely, relocating to Indonesia. Rumblings of anger and betrayal echoing in his mind, Will escaped back to his office to deal with the morbid and mortifying task of burying his dead company.

MAEVE KICKED OFF her boots and pushed through the front door of her cottage. She'd just been to the wholesale nursery to order plants for Will's garden and had gotten an excellent mid-season sale price on two dozen gardenia bushes, plus found a gorgeous specimen of a deeply scented mauve rose called Moonlight Mist. She couldn't wait to see how they looked in Will's garden.

"Hi, Dad," she called. "I'm home."

No answer. Art's boots were in their usual place on the mat outside the front door. The mail had been collected and piled on the hall table. She walked down the long hallway, passing the shut bedroom doors, listening to the silence. "Dad?"

The house seemed unnaturally quiet. The kitchen

was empty, with no signs of cooking. Or indeed, of any life at all.

Apprehension jabbed under her ribs. Quickly, she strode back down the hall to his bedroom. Wherever he was, Art was fine, she told herself. He'd walked down to the milk bar for a paper or a pouch of the tobacco he rolled his single cigarette of the day from. But if that was the case, why hadn't she passed him on the street?

"Dad?" She knocked at his closed door. "Are you in there?"

Pressing her ear to the door she heard a grunt of assent. Sighing with relief, she opened the door. "Are you okay?"

He was lying on his bed, hands folded on his chest, staring at the ceiling. Fear clutched at her again. He hadn't gone to bed during the day since his heart attack. When he turned his head to look at her, his face was gray and the lines on his forehead and around his mouth appeared more deeply etched.

She came farther into the room. "What's wrong?"

"Nothin'. Was just about to fix dinner." He pushed himself to a sitting position and swung his legs over the edge of the bed, then seemed to lose the energy to get up.

Maeve sat beside him and put an arm around his shoulders, alarmed to smell whiskey on his breath. Art liked a shot of Johnny Walker now and then, but he was too frugal to go in for drinking in a big way. "What's wrong?" she repeated. "Are you ill? Tell me."

Art sighed and dragged a hand over his stubbly face. "My job is finished. Aussie Electronics is closing the Mornington plant and moving to Indonesia."

"What! When?" Her father had survived one redundancy, but at his age he'd been lucky to get hired at Aussie Electronics. For him, getting another job would be virtually impossible.

"Three months." Art reached for the empty glass on the bedside table and swilled back the last drops of whiskey. Then he stared at the floor.

"But I don't understand. Why?" Her father's morose apathy scared her. The past five years had been hard on him—first Mum going, then Kristy, then his heart attack. Now this. Her father was no longer the big, bluff man she'd believed invincible when she was a child.

"Supposedly we can't compete with cheaper imports. They claim wages here are too high. A hundred jobs gone, just like that—" he snapped his fingers "—and me only three years away from retirement."

"But you said Will Beaumont prided himself on his company being Australian owned and operated. Why would he move it overseas?"

Scowling, Art rose and paced the bedroom. "Money, what else? He'll make better profits if wages are lower. How do these bastards think the average Joe is going to buy their fancy imported products if they keep shipping jobs out of the country?" he demanded. "Answer me that!"

Behind the fury, she could see that Art was frightened. Not that he would admit such a thing to anyone. Especially to his daughter. "Can't you do something?" she asked. "Organize the employees to take over the company?"

As quickly as his outrage had flared, it died. Art lowered himself into a chair with the slowness of the aged. "Buy out a multimillion-dollar electronics business that requires ongoing research and development of new products? Not a hope. Will is a proud man. He'd never agree to handing over control, much less being an employee in his own company. Nor could we carry on without him."

"Oh, Dad." She knelt beside his chair and put her arms around his shoulders. She'd meant to console him, but she ended up shaking him. If her father sank into inaction, he was lost. "Don't give up. You can fight it somehow."

Art seemed to make a conscious effort to straighten his shoulders. "I'll be right, Sprout, you'll see. Nothin' for you to worry about."

She squeezed his hand and managed a reassuring smile, knowing she would worry, even though she could do nothing about her father's predicament.

On the other hand, she *could* control what she did with her life. She was damned if she would work for the man who'd dumped her father back on the unemployment heap. And to think she'd been feeling sorry she'd turned down Will's invitation to the jazz concert.

"I need to do something," she said, rising. "Don't worry about dinner. I'll pick up some fish and chips for us on my way back. I shouldn't be more than an hour."

She was halfway to Sorrento before it occurred to her that she could have called Will Beaumont on the phone to cancel the job. But she'd still have to mail his check back, and, damn it, she wanted to give him a piece of her mind. If she called, he could simply hang up on her.

Her hands gripped the wheel as her foot pressed harder on the accelerator and she took a curve at ten miles an hour over the speed limit. The thought of her father pottering around the house like an old man when all he wanted was to be working and earning his own way fueled her indignation. Art had a right to a job. A right to his full pension after decades in the workforce. She thumped her fist on the steering wheel. A right to dignity.

She came over the rise that led into Sorrento. Before her, the ferry dock jutted into the bay and the limestone heritage buildings mounted the hill, interspersed with trendy boutiques and surf shops.

Will Beaumont seemed like a decent man, she told herself as she drove through town. She should give him the benefit of the doubt, not blast him. But when she pulled up his long driveway and saw him untying his surfboard from the roof rack of his silver-gray Mercedes, she was outraged. While her father had been drowning his sorrows, the man responsible had been out surfing.

Bastard.

"Maeve. G'day," Will said, his voice lifting in surprise as she got out of the ute. He was still in his wet suit, the top half peeled to his waist, exposing a chest and shoulders lean and hard with muscle. His smile faded as the look on her face registered. "I see you heard the news."

"I heard, all right. Why are you shutting down the factory and moving it overseas?" She pulled the check he'd given her from her breast pocket, prepared to rip it into pieces. She'd been going to create a wonderland in his backyard. A special place for him and his future family. Not bloody likely.

His warm blue eyes turned cold as he spied the check in her hand. "The move is necessary to save the business."

"Doesn't it bother you that you'll be putting my father and a hundred other workers out of jobs?"

His fingers curled around the edge of his surfboard, knuckles white. "I'm sorry about your father. And the others, too, of course."

She glared at him, not bothering to hide her anger. Some things were too rotten to gloss over with the mask of politeness. "My father is fifty-seven. Where is he going to get another job at that age? Or do you think he should go overseas and work for fifty cents an hour?"

"It's not what I wanted to happen. I'll do my best

to help my people find other employment." His quiet voice held an edge.

"'Your people'?" she spat. "You don't own them. Save your hypocritical explanations and useless platitudes for the factory. Just don't count on anyone believing a word."

He propped the surfboard against the car and faced her squarely. "You're a businesswoman. Surely, you can understand that if you're not turning a profit you won't stay in business for long."

"Not turning a profit? How can that be? Your top-selling product is a super-duper alarm system that not even my father can afford to buy."

"A rip-off model has come on the market, undercutting me," he countered sharply. "I don't want to move production offshore, but it's that or shut the business down altogether."

"How can you afford this house if your company is doing so poorly?" she demanded. "I don't see you suffering."

"I bought this house five years ago, when times were good and real estate prices were low. Not that it's any of your business."

"You drive a Mercedes," she said, grasping for ammunition. She had him on the defensive, so why did she feel she was being backed into a corner?

"I wanted a car with safety features…a family car," he said, his voice hardening with every word. "Are you finished?"

Damn it, she wanted so badly to hate him. The surfboard caught her eye. *Aha, Nero fiddling while*

Rome burned. "Shouldn't you have been thinking up ways to save Aussie Electronics, instead of going surfing like some irresponsible teenager?"

He didn't flinch from her accusing gaze. "Surfing clears my mind. It puts me in a head space where I can see alternatives to problems."

Intrigued despite herself, she cataloged the information. "Really?" she had to ask. "What is it about surfing that does that for you?"

"I've got a theory," he said slowly, taken aback at her abrupt change of tack, "that the ocean's horizontal planes promote lateral thinking."

Was he joking? He looked serious. Yet as she stared at him, he grinned sheepishly, as though he knew that even if his theory made sense to him, it sounded crazy to others.

"But waves are vertical," she objected.

He slapped the roof of the Mercedes. "This is the surface of the ocean." Then he slanted his hand at a sixty-degree angle to the roof. "This is the wave." With his other hand he intersected the wave and the ocean. "This is the surfboard with me on it. At the juncture of the two tangible planes is a third, imaginary, dimension, where anything can happen."

It didn't make rational sense, but, God help her, she could see it. Her mind translated his abstract notion into a vision of cascading drifts of blue and white flowers with, here and there, the unexpected blossom of red or purple—

No, it was too late for that. The check fluttered between her fingers in the light breeze.

He glanced at it, seeming to catch her thoughts. "I hope you'll still do my garden."

Her fingers tightened, crushing the flimsy bit of paper. With Art out of work, they would need the money. She gazed into Will's blue eyes and saw intelligence and compassion, qualities as attractive to her as his physical appearance. He was a good man caught in difficult circumstances.

Then she thought of Art, a broken man.

And she just…couldn't…do it.

"Go to hell." She stuffed the check in his hand, ran back to her utility truck and tore down the driveway and out of his life, before she could change her mind.

CHAPTER FOUR

BLOODY HELL. She had no right to blame him. No one wanted Aussie Electronics to stay in Australia more than Will Beaumont.

Will watched her ute's rear lights flash red as she braked briefly at the end of the driveway, before squealing across the bitumen and roaring down the road.

Still cursing, he hauled his surfboard to the back of the house and flung it against the wall, salt crusted and sprinkled with sand. After peeling off his wet suit, he dropped it beside the board, little caring he was committing the unpardonable sin of leaving board and suit unrinsed.

Nor did he bother rinsing himself off after discarding his damp bathing suit; he just pulled on a pair of gray shorts and a dark-purple short-sleeved shirt, grabbed Maeve's quotation off the hall table and strode back out to the Merc.

He wanted his garden fixed up, damn it. She'd signed a contract. She couldn't just quit because she thought he was some evil capitalist who destroyed people's lives for fun and profit.

Glancing at the address on the letterhead, he

brought the car's powerful engine to life and sped out of the driveway, steering with one hand and doing up buttons with the other.

He caught up with her in the town of Rosebud, where traffic slowed for stoplights and beachgoers streamed across the road from the waterfront park to the takeaways and ice cream parlors on the other side. Waiting at the red light, he had a moment to wonder whether stress might be forcing him into uncharacteristically irrational behavior. He was chasing his gardener up the peninsula, for goodness' sake.

Whether, however, his actions were foolish or merely futile, a big part of him, he realized, wanted to confront not Maeve but her father. He hadn't had a chance to talk to Art alone after he'd broken the news to the employees, and he hated to think Art saw him as the bad guy.

So if he wasn't the bad guy, who was? Some banker who wouldn't be happy until he made three-thousand-percent profit? The government for relaxing import tariffs? Or did fault lie with people who bought cheap imported goods? Supporting local industry had become a luxury not everyone could afford.

He pulled up behind Maeve, but she didn't notice him. Or refused to notice. He considered beeping the horn but decided against it. He didn't want to appear aggressive; he just wanted to talk to her. As the light changed to green, she spotted him in her rearview mirror.

Maybe she would pull off into the small parking lot that ran parallel to the road. Then again, he mused as she sped off, maybe not.

He followed her all the way home. She didn't look in the mirror again until she turned off the highway into the village of Mount Eliza. He smiled. She was woman enough to want to know if he was still following. Maybe to want him to keep following. Yeah, right. Just like she wanted to go out with him.

Through the leafy streets, down a winding, dead-end road he trailed her, before pulling up at last in front of a sage-green weatherboard cottage with painted wooden filigree lining the veranda roof. Wandin Cottage, proclaimed a sign above the door. The garden was a mass of flowers, shaded by huge golden-limbed gums with sun-dappled leaves.

Maeve parked and went inside, shutting the door firmly behind her without a glance his way.

A minute later Will was tapping the brass door knocker. Five minutes passed. Now she was just being rude.

Art opened the door. His hair was smoothly combed and his white T-shirt was tucked neatly into work pants.

Will suddenly felt like a sixteen-year-old facing his father. Despite their employee-employer relationship, Will had sensed that Art had always taken a paternal interest in him; even, Will sometimes thought, a fatherly pride.

Today Art was a troubled man, angry with his favorite son.

Will pushed a hand through his hair and did up his top button. "G'day, Art. How're you going?"

Art nodded, his seamed face wary, but appeared prepared to be friendly. "What can I do for you?"

"I came to see Maeve. You may not have known, but she gave me a quote on some landscaping the other day, and I wanted to talk to her about it."

"Maeve said she'd canceled on you." Art looked more troubled than ever. "I want to apologize for her, Will. I told her that my job and hers were two separate things and that she should honor her contract. But she wouldn't have it."

Hell, Will said silently. Art wasn't angry at him; he was upset because his daughter hadn't done the right thing. Or maybe he was angry, too, but felt conflicted out of loyalty and a belief in fair play. Will never should have come here, invading their space, imposing on Art's good nature. However, he would look frivolous if he left now. "May I talk to her?"

"Don't know that it'll do any good, but go ahead and try." Art stepped back and allowed Will inside. "She's in the backyard. Come through."

The dim hallway was cool, papered with pale floral print and hung with botanical drawings of flowering herbs. In the kitchen, newspapers were spread out on the table. The employment section. *Ouch.* With a glance at Art, Will pushed through the screen door.

Maeve was reaching high on a bush to snip a long stalk bearing a lush white flower almost as big as her head. Peonies. His grandmother had grown them.

"Hi," he said.

She ignored him and laid the blossom in the basket at her feet.

What flowers grew in Maeve's garden? They were too many and various for him to identify even half of them. From brightly colored to delicately pale, they grew at every level from ground to tree. They twined along the fence, overflowed from tubs, hung in pots from the veranda. Beside a swinging garden bench of carved wood was a raised herb garden planted in a hexagram. On the other side of the yard, next to the garage, was a miniature nursery with rows of potted seedlings and baby shrubs. Behind a low hedge in what still must be her property was a greenhouse.

"This is really nice," he said, truly impressed. The whole place was cool, fragrant and inviting. Except for her.

Aggressively, she thrust the hand holding her clippers forward; her other hand was planted on her hip. "What do you want?"

"A fair trial, for starters."

"You chased me all the way up the peninsula just to persuade me that deep down you're really a great guy? That none of it's your fault. You're ruled by global markets, free trade, forces beyond your control? Listen, mate, I've heard it all before and I'm sick of it. If you believe in something, you make a stand."

"It's not that simple," he began. "You see—"

"Save it," she said with indifference, then turned back to the peony bush and lopped off a dead head. "Anyway, what do you care what I think?"

Good question. And one he wasn't prepared to answer right now.

"I just want you to do my garden." He brandished her signed, typewritten quote. "We made a deal."

That instant he remembered that he'd made a deal, too—with her father. A contract signed before Christmas, which had more than ten months to run. She met his gaze with a level, sardonic stare.

"So sue me." She bent to pick up her basket.

"I'll pay you double." He saw her hesitate, and triumph surged through him. Until he remembered it was because of him that she and her father would be hungry for money.

Holding her basket in front of her with both hands on the curving handle, she eyed him with disdain. "You can't keep your company in the red. How could you afford to pay me double?"

"That's not your concern." From the corner of his eye he glimpsed Art's face at the kitchen window. Then Maeve's father ducked away.

"You can't buy my respect," Maeve said. "And I wouldn't take your blood money if I was starving." She reached into her pocket for a small notepad, scribbled something on it and handed it to him. "Just to be nice, I'll give you the number of a colleague of mine—Peter Davies. He'll do a good job."

Will crumpled the scrap of paper. He wanted *her*.

He wanted the magic she'd promised. And although he hated to admit it, she was right. He wanted, at least in her eyes, to not be the bad guy.

He was losing perspective, he told himself. Having lost control of his company, he was desperate to control other aspects of his life. He forced himself to smooth out the paper, fold it properly and tuck it in his pocket.

The garden wasn't that important. Maeve's opinion of him wasn't life threatening.

"I need to talk to your father before I go. I'll catch you later."

He was about to return to the house, when he spotted a solar panel lying on its side up against the wall of the garden shed. "What's this?"

She shrugged, clearly through talking to him but bound by innate courtesy to answer. "Just part of an experiment I'm running. Dad was trying to figure out a way to increase the energy output of the solar panel so I could heat a large volume of running water. So far he hasn't had any luck."

Will crouched to examine the electronic control box connecting the solar panel with a twelve-volt battery. "You wouldn't get a lot of heating capacity out of a panel this size," he agreed. "Why not use a larger one?"

"I can't afford it."

"What's your experiment about?"

"Look, don't worry about it. It's just something I was trying out to help my friend Rose. She raises hydroponic herbs for a living."

"Tell me. Maybe I can help."

"I doubt it." He waited. "Oh, all right. You know that in hydroponics, plants grow in a soilless medium and water containing nutrients flows over the roots."

He nodded.

"Well, my experiment aims to determine the optimum temperature of the hydroponic solution so as to boost production. I want to test growth rates of a variety of herbs at three different temperatures."

"That sounds interesting. How are you regulating the water temperature?"

"That's the other problem," she said, sounding frustrated. "I've got a water heater but not the technology to produce three different temperatures simultaneously, which I have to do to ensure that—"

"Other factors influencing plant growth are equal. I get it." He turned the control box over in his hands. This was just the type of problem he loved to sink his teeth into. "If I could take this to my workshop, I could have a go at fixing it."

"No, thank you." She plucked it out of his hands. "Goodbye."

"You sure?"

"I'm sure."

He cast a last reluctant glance at the solar panel, and went back to the house. After knocking once, he pushed open the screen door.

Art looked up from his newspaper, unabashed at openly searching for another job. "Get what you wanted from her?"

"Er, no."

"Expect the worst and you'll never be disappointed," Art intoned with grim satisfaction.

"I disagree, although I can see why you might hold that opinion. But there's a silver lining in every cloud. I planned to talk to you at work tomorrow about an offer I hope you'll take up, but if it's convenient, we could talk now."

"All right. Will it affect Maeve?"

"I suppose it would, indirectly."

"Then I'll call her in. Care for a beer?"

"Thanks."

Art reached into the fridge for a pair of thick green bottles, the type that usually contained imported German beer.

"I brew my own," Art said, setting the bottle and a clean glass in front of Will.

"Ah." Will reached for it, anticipating the cold tart flavor with relish. "Where did you get all the bottles?"

Art tipped his head and winked. "That, me old son, was a labor of love."

The phone rang, and Art crossed the kitchen to answer it. "Hello? Yep, hang on a tick." He carried the receiver to the back door, stretching the phone cord as far as it could reach. "Maevie! Phone."

Maeve came in, dropped her basket on the counter and took the receiver from her father, averting her gaze from Will as she leaned against the counter. "Hello?"

As Maeve listened, her face turned pale. Lowering her voice, she walked as far away as the phone cord would allow, to stand in the doorway between kitchen and lounge room, her back to them.

"Pour carefully," Art said, pretending not to notice. "You don't want the sediment in the bottom of the bottle."

"I used to make beer when I was at university." Will expertly tilted his glass and poured, then held it up to the light, all the while aware of Maeve. "Nice color. Wheat beer, is it?"

Art looked pleased. "Bit of an aficionado, are you?"

"Passionate." His gaze flicked to Maeve. Her shoulders were hunched and stiff. "What footy team do you barrack for?"

"Collingwood Magpies," Art proclaimed. "Like my father and grandfather before me."

"I'm a Carlton Blues fan myself." Will sipped his beer. "Hey, this is good."

Art nodded, but his smile was forced. He, too, was aware of Maeve's tension. "Her ex-husband," he explained in a low voice.

"We should give her some privacy." Will started to rise.

Abruptly, she hung up.

Art swiveled in his chair. "Maevie, love, you okay?"

Dry-eyed and drawn, she nodded. She glanced at the full beer in Will's hand. "I'll be out in the garden."

"Will has something important to discuss with

me,'' Art said, as she started to leave. "You're to stay and hear it, too.''

"More bad news?'' Her voice was bitter.

"Maevie, be polite,'' Art said quietly.

"You might as well listen,'' Will said. "I'm sure Art will want to talk it over with you, in any case.''

Maeve got herself a bottle of mineral water from the fridge and sat next to her father. She pushed up her sleeves and leaned on the table, faint scratches visible on her tanned forearms. "Well, what is it?''

Will cleared his throat and spoke directly to Art. "When the new factory starts up in Jakarta, we'll need someone to run things at first and show the workers how to operate the machines. I'd like you to go across and be that person. It'd be a short-term contract, six months or so, but would delay the need for that—'' He gestured to the employment section of the newspaper.

Mouth open, Art sat back hard in his chair. "Me? Work in Indonesia?'' He glanced at Maeve and snorted. "Can you picture it, Maevie?''

"Not in a million years.'' Turning to Will, she spoke angrily. "Art has a heart condition. The heat would kill him. Why, he's never even been out of the state.''

"I'm trying to help, not hurt him,'' Will said. Okay, so she was upset by her phone conversation, but that was no reason to take it out on him.

"You're offering him this job to make yourself look like the caring employer so I'll come back and work on your garden!''

"What kind of businessman would pay someone to work overseas just so that man's daughter will prune a few bushes?" Will scoffed.

"Prune a few bushes!"

"Settle down, you two." Art held up his broad gnarled hands. "Maeve, stop trying to protect me. Will, I appreciate your offer, but Maeve's right—I'm too old and set in my ways to be gallivanting off to Indonesia."

"Your accommodations would be taken care of—air-conditioned, of course," he added with a pointed glance at Maeve. "You'd be supplied with a car, possibly even a driver."

Art shook his head, his black eyebrows pulled together in a frown. "No, Will, it just won't do for me," he said firmly, but without heat. "Jim Knowles—now, he'd be a good 'un for the job. He even speaks a bit of the lingo."

"Knowles is a fine worker, but he doesn't have the experience the job requires."

Art remained obdurate. "Sorry. No can do."

Will could see he wouldn't get any further today—with either of them. "Don't say no straight away. Give yourself some time to think about it, okay?"

Maeve answered, "Don't hold your breath."

"I only do that when I'm in over my head," Will said, giving her a cool smile. He drained his beer and rose. "Thanks for the drink, Art."

"How can you get set up for overseas production

in just three months?'' Art asked, walking him to the door. Maeve followed slowly.

"The factory we're considering buying used to produce electronic toys for a British toy company. It's already got most of the equipment we need.'' And there's a plentiful supply of cheap local labor, he could have added, quoting Paul, but he didn't. "Think it over and we'll talk again soon.''

He said goodbye, and was strapping himself into the Merc, when Maeve came forward to lean in the open window. Her fingers curled over the lower ledge, grass stained and strong.

"Make sure Peter sees that tree by the bungalow,'' she said. "You'll have problems down the track if it's not removed.''

"We could both rest easier if you did the job yourself.'' No response. He put the key in the ignition. "Take care of Art.''

Frowning, she nodded. "Of course.''

He started the car, then realized this could be the last time he'd see her. He left his foot lightly on the brake; a second passed but he didn't shift into drive. "You looked pale when you were talking to your ex-husband... Is he a problem?''

"No. Not at all.'' She tugged on the end of her long braid.

He sighed heavily. "I know you don't believe it, but I do care about Art, and, by extension, about his family.''

"Sure you do.'' She stepped away from the car. Abruptly, he took his foot from the brake.

As he pulled away from the curb, he glanced in his rearview mirror. She was still standing there, staring after him. And then he turned the corner, and she disappeared from view.

Okay, so Maeve wasn't for him. He hated that she'd never given him a chance, but he had to accept it.

And get on with life.

AN IDEA TOOK ROOT slowly in his mind over the next few days. In a low mood, he tried at first to banish it as unworkable. When that didn't succeed, he tried to chase it away with accusations of "ridiculous" and "ill-advised." By the time he came around to accepting his idea as the solution to his and Ida's problems, he wondered why he hadn't thought of it earlier. Here was a woman whose friendship he'd valued for twenty-five years. He wanted children himself, and he'd do anything for her.

Five days after his confrontation with Maeve, Will left work and took the Mornington Road turn-off. He parked along the curb outside a block of upmarket new units near the water. Ida's shiny black BMW sat in her driveway.

"Hi, Will," she said after opening the door to his knock. Her smile welcomed, but her eyes held uncertainty, as if she were afraid he'd come to tell her no. She stepped back to allow him inside, then led the way into the kitchen. There, she poured him a beer and handed it to him with a nervous smile.

"What's up?"

He took a drink, wetting his dry throat.

"I've given your request a lot of thought and I'd be happy to father a baby for you."

Ida broke into a relieved smile. "Thank you, Will. Thank you so much." Then suddenly, her smile faded and she regarded him with a worried frown. "Hang on. Why would you agree now, after all you said about a child needing to belong to a two-parent family?"

"Because I have a suggestion that will overcome that obstacle and prove beneficial to us both." His plan had nothing to do with any lingering guilt over being the cause of her problems. He didn't even know why that thought flashed into his mind. He went on quickly, before the notion could grow. "You and I will get married."

Ida laughed. "Are you out of your mind? We're just friends."

"That's exactly why it will work. We'll never fall out of love and hurt each other." The way he and Maree had when they couldn't, or wouldn't, meet each other's expectations. She'd wanted to move to Sydney to further her career, whereas he'd wanted to start a family.

Will dropped into a chair at the chrome-and-glass breakfast table, placed his beer on the table and leaned forward eagerly. "We're both practical, down-to-earth people who aren't waiting for some mythical love-of-our-lives to come along."

Ida slowly sat, too, and twisted the silver ring on

her right hand. "It sounds sad when you put it like that."

"But it's not," he insisted. "It just means we skip the starry-eyed stage, and the subsequent disillusionment."

Ida raised an eyebrow. "So we can what—go straight to boredom?"

He rolled his eyes. "And I thought *I* was cynical."

"You are," she agreed, laughing. "That's partly why we get along so well. But you make it sound so passionless and predictable. Where's the mystique?"

"That's the beauty of it. We've known each other so long, there won't be any surprises."

"You're sweeping me off my feet with logic." She paused. "I'm past having romantic aspirations, but *you* could still fall in love. I don't mean with me. Not for a moment do I imagine we would fall in love after all these years as friends. But are you absolutely sure you want a marriage of convenience?"

Maeve's magnificent smile flashed into his mind. He got to his feet and paced the tiny granite-and-oak kitchen, pushing away feelings of lost opportunity. Maeve was the first woman he'd been seriously attracted to in a long while, but she wasn't interested. She'd been definite on the subject.

"It's not as though I haven't wanted to fall in love," he said. "Every woman I've dated since Maree, I've thought, 'This could be the one.' Each time

I've been disappointed. Maybe I expect too much. Maybe I'm looking in the wrong places. I don't know."

"Maybe you're too rational," Ida suggested. "Love is something you feel in your heart, not deduce from common interests and goals."

"The thing is, I want children and I don't want to be an old man when they're born. Romantic love aside, I care about you more than almost anyone. I'm sorry it can't be more. I would do my absolute best to be a good partner to you."

Tears shone in Ida's eyes. "I believe you, Will. I'm going to take you up on this crazy offer before you have a chance to think again. Before I have a chance to think about what I'm doing to you—binding you to me."

Will reached out and pulled her to her feet. "You'll be doing me the biggest favor of my life."

He wrapped his arms around her in a warm, brotherly hug. Ida would be good for him. Maybe their marriage wouldn't be the flight of passion he'd once hoped for, but it would be solid and lasting.

"We could have an open marriage," she offered, gazing anxiously at him. "My opportunities are limited, but you'll find yourself attracted to other women."

It was likely, he had to admit, though the idea of an open marriage didn't sit right with him. Marriage to him meant one man, one woman; faithfulness and trust.

"Or," she added when he didn't reply, "there's such a thing as recreational sex between friends."

"I knew you just wanted me for my body," Will teased. Turning serious, he added, "Whichever option we choose, *both* of us should be comfortable with it." She nodded, and he touched a gentle finger to her damp cheek, wiping away the moisture. Would they have a boy first? Or a girl? It didn't matter, he decided, exhilarated at the idea of having any child at all. He felt as though he'd just caught the perfect wave and was taking the ride of his life.

"When shall we get married?" Ida said, excitement showing in her bright eyes. "I'll have to get a dress, send out invitations—" She broke off, adding worriedly, "You do want a real wedding?"

Will didn't really care, but he could see it mattered to Ida. He owed her. Even though she would deny it. "Whatever you want. I thought we could have the ceremony in my garden."

"Oh, yes. I'd love that."

"Good. Then how about toward the end of summer— Damn."

"What is it?"

He slumped against the bench top, shoving a hand through his hair. "Maeve quit on me. She's angry because I had to sack her father along with all the other employees."

"Oh, Will. I forgot for a moment you were going through that. Was it awful?"

"Pretty bad. Don't worry about the garden— I've got the name of another landscaper."

"But from what you said, Maeve had a great design worked out. Starting over would take time we don't have. Would it help if I talked to her?"

"No, leave it," he said quickly, hoping to erase the thought before Ida had it fixed in her mind. Getting engaged so soon after asking Maeve out would do nothing to enhance his image in Maeve's eyes. Not that it mattered now, but still...

"Are you sure?" Ida persisted. "I really feel I could talk her around. After all, she doesn't have any quarrel with me."

"Don't bother. Please. I'll get another gardener." He glanced at the wall clock, thinking of the Indonesian documents he still had to read. "I'd better get going."

At the front door he paused to clear his throat, foolishly embarrassed. "Er, when did you want to get pregnant?"

Ida laughed nervously and turned pink. "Since we're getting married, why don't we wait till after the ceremony."

"Sure." He hid his relief. Making love to Ida would feel weird, almost incestuous, and apparently she felt the same way. They had plenty to work out between them, but they'd manage.

Because they were friends.

CHAPTER FIVE

WATERING CAN IN HAND, Maeve moved along the narrow aisles of black plastic pots containing mid-size annuals. She gave each plant a drink and pulled the odd weed from pots of purple-and-white petunias, yellow pansies and pink-and-white Sweet William. They would look good in the big urns at the front of Will's house. Except…she wasn't going to work on Will's garden.

Footsteps tapped along the driveway. Around the side of the house appeared the woman with the scarred face Maeve had seen at Will's. Professional looking and perfectly groomed in a tan linen suit dress. Tan pumps. Neat gold studs in her ears.

"Hi," the woman said. "I knocked on the front door, and your father said to come around the back. I'm Ida, Will Beaumont's fiancée."

Fiancée? Maeve straightened, dusting the dirt off her hands, wondering if she'd somehow slipped sideways into a parallel universe. "I didn't know Will was engaged."

"It was pretty sudden," Ida admitted, spots of color blooming in her cheeks. "But we've known each other for years."

Maeve fought down a surge of jealousy. She debated mentioning that just last week Will had asked her out to dinner. Then immediately discarded the idea. Why cause trouble?

"Congratulations," she managed to say. "What can I do for you?"

Ida came closer. "Will told me you'd decided not to work on his garden and why. He said he was going to contact another landscaper, but I wanted to talk to you first. Ask you to reconsider." She paused. "He doesn't know I'm here. In fact, he told me not to come. But I understand how much he wants you to do his garden."

Maeve set her watering can aside. She'd been feeling bad about reneging on her contract. Art had made sure of that. And now Ida. Stalling, Maeve asked, "Would you like a cold drink?"

"That would be great. Can you believe this heat?" Ida lifted her wavy hair away from her face.

"It's a job just keeping my plants watered." Maeve went to the bar fridge in the garage and handed Ida a bottle of flavored mineral water. "Have a seat," she added, gesturing to the swing.

Ida sat, then pushed off in a gentle rocking motion. "I'm sorry about your father. If it helps, Will is really cut up about what's happening to his company and his employees."

Maeve stared at the ground, silent. Sure, Will felt bad. But he'd still have a job and a paycheck when the dust settled.

"He's really a great guy," Ida went on. "Smart,

generous, kind. Loyal. For our university graduation ball he turned down an invitation from a girl he liked and took me, instead, because I was so scarred nobody else would ask me for a date.''

Maeve searched inside herself for anger at the man who'd invited her out and then not a week later asked another woman to marry him. A guy as attractive as Will could have opted for beauty in his choice of bride. Instead, he'd chosen character and personality, which presumably meant he possessed those qualities himself.

''So you two have been a couple before?'' she asked, puzzled by the chronology of events.

Ida looked startled, then wary. ''No,'' she said slowly. ''As I said, our engagement is very recent. Kind of surprised us both.''

''How long have you known each other?'' Maeve asked.

''Since we were children.'' Ida smiled at some memory. ''We shared a table in grade five, and Will annoyed me because he was always borrowing my colored marking pens and using them up. Then one day some older boys were picking on me. Will stood up to them and got a black eye for his trouble. The next day I brought him his own set of colored pens. We've been friends ever since.''

''What a wonderful story,'' Maeve said. ''So it was a case of 'best friends who don't realize they love each other.'''

Ida turned her head slightly so Maeve could see only the scarred side. ''Er, something like that.''

Maeve found Ida's expression hard to read, not just because of the scarring but because she was obviously practiced in hiding her feelings. "What happened to your face? If you don't mind my asking."

Ida faced her squarely. "I'd rather people ask than studiously ignore. I was burned by a splash from a deep-fat fryer. It would have been much worse if Will hadn't been there. He applied first aid, called an ambulance. I owe him a lot."

Maeve owed him nothing, but she liked Ida. "What do you look for in a garden?"

A lopsided grin chased away the shadows and brought out a charm Maeve suspected Ida didn't see when she looked in the mirror.

"My ideal garden would be green concrete, plastic trees and a garden gnome. In other words, so low maintenance not even I could kill it." She raised her shoulders in a self-deprecating shrug. "I'm pretty hopeless when it comes to gardening."

"Sounds like you and Will make a good pair," Maeve joked. "What I had in mind for Will's place is fairly low maintenance. For some clients I come back quarterly to maintain the garden and tackle big jobs like pruning and ground preparation."

"Does that mean you've changed your mind and will do the garden?" Ida asked.

Maeve smiled. "We'll see."

"I don't know if Will mentioned it, but we plan on starting a family soon," Ida said, almost shyly.

"I got the impression he was interested in having

children," Maeve said stiffly. "Large portions of the garden would be child oriented."

"You must love kids," Ida said.

How on earth did she come to that conclusion? Maeve needed a moment to find her voice. "Other people's kids are okay."

"Oh, but having your own must be much better." Ida hugged herself, eyes closed, like a child dreaming of Christmas. "I can't wait to have a baby."

Once upon a time, Maeve had felt like that. Eyes stinging, she rose and went over to a thick hedge-like stand of tall silver-green stalks. Releasing the catch on her secateurs, she asked, "Would you like some lavender?"

Opening her eyes, Ida leaned over and brushed the heads of several of the dusky-purple flowers, filling the air with the distinctive bittersweet scent. "It's beautiful, but what would I do with it?"

"Put it in a vase in your entryway," Maeve said, snipping fragrant stalks. "Lavender's also nice in the bathroom. And good in sachets, or drunk as a tea if you have a headache."

"I don't have a vase big enough to hold all this," Ida said, accepting the bundle. "But I'll take it, anyway, and worry about that later. Thanks."

"It's nothing." Maeve moved into the bed of dahlias. "Would you like some of these? They need thinning, too. I'm having to cut back everything at the moment."

"They'd be wasted on me. I'm hardly ever home and I don't have the room to do flowers justice."

"You're going to have lots of room soon."

Ida nodded. Yet for someone so blessed, she didn't seem totally happy. Maybe Maeve was just imagining something was missing when Ida spoke of her coming marriage, but she sensed both Ida and Will were keeping secrets, and she'd have given anything to know what they were.

One thing was certain; while Maeve was gardener, there would be no green cement or plastic trees in Will's garden.

Will and Ida's garden, that is.

ON SATURDAY MORNING Will was yanked from dreamland by the roar of a chainsaw starting up. The high-pitched whine that followed brought him upright in bed to check the bedside clock. For crying out loud, it was only 8:05.

Ordinarily, he awoke at dawn. Weekends, he'd be in the surf by seven and on his way home for breakfast by ten. But last night he'd gone to the Surf Lifesaving Club for a beer, sort of an impromptu, single-handed buck's night. He'd had the idea he would test his reaction to relinquishing his bachelorhood. And women.

In the moment of heightened lucidity brought on by a couple of beers, he'd realized he felt no pain over giving up his freedom. What hurt was giving up Maeve before he'd had a chance to try to win her. The sense of lost opportunities had sparked a kind of grief, and he'd drunk more than his usual limit.

This morning, he was paying the price with a dry

mouth and pounding head as the ear-splitting roar of another machine of destruction joined the whine of the chainsaw. The racket sounded close enough to be in his own backyard. Bleary-eyed, Will dragged himself out of bed to close the window.

What the hell…!

The chainsaw-wielding demon was on the roof of his bungalow! His back to Will, he sliced through the limbs of the gum tree before dropping them into a mulching machine, which vibrated and screamed as it chewed the wood into sawdust.

Will hadn't authorized this. He hadn't even had a chance to call the landscaper Maeve had recommended. She must have called herself, but the guy had a nerve starting work without Will's say-so.

Will rubbed his eyes and looked again. The fellow was wearing khaki cargo pants, work boots and a black crop top over a strong tanned back and gently muscular arms that gleamed with perspiration. He was a she. And although her long dark hair was nowhere in evidence, he could tell by the figure and stance that she was Maeve Arden.

He hardly knew what he felt as he drew back from the window. Elation—that she'd come to restore his garden. Annoyance—that she'd chosen to start first thing in the morning with the chainsaw. Irritation—that she hadn't informed him she'd decided to honor her contract.

Anticipation—at the thought of seeing her again.

Will popped a couple of headache tablets, showered and shaved, then stepped outside in shorts and a loose cotton shirt, ready to tell her off. Because her back was to him and the noise was so great, he had to walk around to the other side of the bungalow to get her attention. "Hello. *Hello.*"

She didn't hear. Of course, she didn't hear. She wore protective earmuffs as well as plastic safety glasses. Her mouth tight with concentration, she guided the heavy chainsaw through the trunk of the gum tree. With an expert flick of her strong wrists, she twisted the chainsaw so that the branchless top of the tree dropped neatly into the gaping maw of the mulcher. She paused to scratch her nose with the back of a gloved hand. And saw him.

Frowning, she shut off the chainsaw. Will waited until the mulcher had pulverized its latest victim and the noise had dropped, before he shouted, "I thought you couldn't bring yourself to work for me."

She removed her hat to wipe the perspiration from her forehead, and her long braid, tucked under the brim, snaked over her shoulder. "I changed my mind."

She changed her mind. "How very…female of you."

On second thought, this conversation could wait until he'd had breakfast. He started to leave.

"A cold drink would be nice," she called after him.

The sound of the chainsaw accompanied his retreat to the house. There he slammed an ice tray onto the bench top to loosen the cubes, and dumped the ice into a glass pitcher. He filled the pitcher with cranberry juice, then toasted and buttered a stack of raisin bread and carried everything to the patio table. He ate half the raisin toast, drank two glasses of juice, and finally began to feel a little better.

More than capable of tackling Mary, Mary, quite contrary.

But when she stepped onto the patio, her tanned skin glistening beneath the crop top, he forgot what his problem was. She tilted a glass of juice to her lips and drank it down in one gulp, exposing her slender throat.

She reached for the toast. Before she could pick up a piece, he pushed the plate toward her. "Care for some toast?"

Her lips curled upward in a closemouthed smile of seemingly incredible sweetness that nevertheless made him think of a mischievous imp. "Thank you, I would."

"So," he said, folding his arms over his chest, "are you here because I offered you double the pay?"

"I'm here because I signed a contract. I honor my promises. And for some strange reason, my father thinks the world of you. He might fret himself into another heart attack if I let you down." She bit into her toast and chewed forcefully. "And because Ida came to see me."

"Oh." He couldn't think of anything he wanted to say on the subject of Ida. But it didn't matter, because Maeve had already moved on.

"I expect only the money I quoted on my estimate…"

He nodded. He was getting off cheap. In more ways than one.

"Plus, you'll find my father another job—not in Indonesia."

He was shocked into silence. Which she obviously took as acquiescence, for she grabbed another piece of toast and got up to leave. "Thanks for breakfast."

The last time she'd been here, he hadn't been able to get her to stop asking questions; now she wouldn't spare him an extra word. "Is this going to be a habit?" he asked, following her off the patio. "Working on Saturday mornings, I mean. I'd like to know so I can put my earplugs in the night before."

"Sorry about the noise," she said cheerfully. "I'm making up for lost time. I'll have to work a few weekends if I want to get your place finished before the end of summer. Don't worry. Once the lopping and pruning are done, it won't be so noisy."

"I thought you had an assistant for the heavy work."

"Tony helps out on his family vineyard on weekends." She tucked a wisp of dark hair behind her ear. The movement released a scent of clean sweat and warm skin.

Suddenly, Will didn't want to leave her. "I'll get changed into something less comfortable and give you a hand."

"That's not necessary," she said, coiling her braid on the crown of her head and jamming her hat on top.

"Maybe it is. You see—" His brain stalled while trying to come up with a plausible reason to help her do the job he was paying her for. "Ida and I are getting married in a couple of months and I want the garden looking nice for the ceremony," he said at last.

Maeve stared at him. "So what were you about, asking me out to dinner and jazz concerts?"

"That was before Ida and I decided to marry." He would have explained further, but what could he add that wouldn't in some way diminish Ida?

"Okay you can help. I want to get it done, too. I may be going out of town at the end of the summer." She whirled around and strode off across the lawn.

Will went back into the house and put on long pants and boots. In the laundry room, he clapped on a hat, picked up his secateurs and gloves and joined Maeve out by the rhododendrons. She was armed with a saw and a pair of lethal-looking, long-handled clippers.

She glanced at his garden shears and offered him the saw. "I'll do the fine pruning. You can remove the dead branches. See, like this one—no green leaves, twigs snap instead of bend."

"I may not know a sepal from a stamen, but I know a dead branch when I see it." He took the saw and set to work.

Twenty minutes later, he'd removed half the deadwood in the stand, and sweat was dripping between his shoulder blades. Pausing to wipe the moisture from his forehead, he said, "Are you going on holiday at the end of summer?" A thought struck, making him add, "With your ex-husband?"

She gazed at him through the rhododendrons, her face half obscured by the long glossy leaves. "He wants me to sail to Fiji with him."

A jolt of jealousy and loss went through Will. She looked like a—what were those wood nymph things—dryads? Yes, a dryad, with her smooth olive complexion, mahogany eyes and ebony hair. If he leaned a smidgen closer, he could kiss her. Not that he would, of course.

"What does he do for a living?" Will asked, needing to stay with rational, ordinary topics.

"Graham's a doctor," she said slowly. "When our dau— When our marriage broke up, he quit his medical practice, and now he spends most of his time sailing around the South Pacific, going from island to island."

"How does he survive financially?"

"He works locum for a few months, then takes off on his boat till the money runs out. You don't need much to live on with that kind of lifestyle."

"And now he wants you back," Will said, guessing. "Are you going to sail with him?"

Her dark eyes held his. "I'm beginning to think I should."

He was wrong, surely, about the attraction he

thought he'd glimpsed just now in her eyes. And the double meaning underlying her words. But he couldn't mistake his reaction to her—the pulsing blood and the shortness of breath. It was only physical, he told himself. Doubtless, if he got to know Maeve he would discover all sorts of faults and weaknesses. Yeah, like he really believed that. "I'll just take these branches over to the mulcher."

By the time he'd done that, she had the electric hedge trimmer out and was starting to clip a smooth surface across the box hedge. "Get me the ladder from the back of the ute, please," she said, any trace of intimacy gone. "Then rake up the trimmings as they come down."

She was enjoying this. "Yes, sir, Boss."

One corner of her mouth lifted. "You said you wanted to help."

"I had in mind something a little less menial."

"Huh! You haven't seen menial till you've spread manure."

He grinned and went to fetch the ladder.

WILL COULDN'T REMEMBER ever enjoying yard work before. He'd definitely never lain in bed two nights afterward recalling the fun time he'd had ripping out diseased plants and throwing them in the back of a utility truck. Of course, some of that enjoyment could have come from spending time with Maeve.

Correction. *All* the pleasure derived from being with Maeve. Even though she'd barely unbent the whole time.

So where did that leave him and Ida?

He couldn't go through with the wedding. It wasn't fair to Ida. It wasn't fair to him.

Who knows, maybe Ida, too, had had second thoughts about marrying. He could still donate sperm, if that was what she wanted. He'd even go to prenatal classes with her. He would help her in every way he could, short of making her Mrs. Will Beaumont.

On Monday after work, instead of heading down the peninsula to Sorrento, he crossed the highway and started the crawl down Mornington's main street. Ida's law office was located at the end of the street, just before the park. Great when he was meeting her for an impromptu lunch on the beach, but hellacious when he was snared in bumper-to-bumper summer tourist traffic and trying to catch her before she shot past in the other direction.

He was in luck, though. When he walked through the door into the air-conditioned office, Ida's secretary, Sally, glanced up and smiled. "You're just in time."

Ida emerged from her office, her purse in one hand and a soft-sided leather case bulging with briefs in the other.

"Will!" Her face lit, then she did something she'd never done before at the sight of him: she blushed.

Okay, that settled it. This arrangement was a mistake. It was affecting a lifetime friendship. Thank goodness, they weren't too far down the road toward matrimony and could still turn back.

"Hi," he said, giving her shoulder a friendly squeeze. "Got time for a drink? I need to talk to you."

She glanced at her briefcase and grimaced, however, the excited smile she turned on him told another story. "I've got heaps of work, but, yes, you can buy me a drink. There's something I want to talk to you about, too."

"What is it?" He wondered if he should offer to carry her briefcase. It looked heavy, but he'd never done anything like that before, mainly because he hadn't thought she'd let him.

"Wait till we get to the restaurant. 'Bye, Sally," she called to her secretary. "See you tomorrow." Ida struggled to hold both briefcase and purse in one hand as she opened the door.

"Here, let me take that." Will made a grab for the briefcase, but she yanked it out of his reach.

"I'm fine," she said. "It's only in the third trimester that I shouldn't lift heavy objects."

"Huh?"

But she'd hurried ahead, through the lane to the all-day car park where she had a reserved spot for her BMW. There, she dropped her case in the boot and twirled to him, smiling and unencumbered. "Shall we go to the Seahorse? I'm starving."

"Sure."

They strolled down the street toward the water-front bistro that served Mediterranean food. "You're in a good mood,'' he commented a few minutes later, as they seated themselves at an outdoor table shaded by a market umbrella.

Ida smiled hugely. "I've got good news."

"Did Rick call?" He couldn't think what else would engender such elation, although he felt a little guilty at the forceful wave of relief that flowed over him at the thought of Rick back on the scene; it would let Will off the hook.

"No, silly." Ida batted away the notion with her hand and spoke to a passing waiter. "A large lemonade, please."

"Lemonade?" Will's eyebrows rose.

Ida just smiled smugly and picked up a menu.

"I'll have a Tuborg," Will said to the waiter. "And an order of calamari for two, to start." As the waiter walked away, he turned to Ida, "So, what's your news?"

"You first. You had something to tell me."

He took in her smiling face. This wasn't going to be easy. Not just because of Ida's potential reaction might be, but because, suddenly, not having a family to look forward to filled him with an enormous sense of loss. "Ladies first."

"No, you go ahead."

"I insist."

"Oh, all right. I'm going to have a baby."

Will swallowed. She was still set on the idea. "Yeah, we already talked about that."

Ida laughed. "No, I mean, I'm *going* to have a baby."

He gazed at her blankly.

"I went to the doctor at lunchtime today. I'm pregnant!"

"Pregnant! How did that happen? We haven't even kissed!"

"Quit looking like a stunned mullet," Ida said, laughing. "It wasn't an immaculate conception, you idiot."

"Then whose is it?"

Her smile faltered. "Rick's, of course. There hasn't been anyone else for a long time."

"Hell, Ida, have you told him?"

The waiter brought their drinks and the plate of calamari, took their dinner orders and left.

Ida nibbled on a crispy ring of fried squid. "I called him," she said, equivocating.

"Did you let him know he was going to be a father?"

Her hazel eyes widened. "Yes."

"Really?" Will said skeptically. He couldn't believe Rick would deny his own child. Or leave Ida in the lurch. "What did he say, exactly?"

"He's been very busy, he's sorry he hasn't called, he hopes I'll visit him someday—"

"What did he say about the baby?"

Twirling her straw in her glass, Ida stared across the bay. When she spoke at last she was quietly resigned. "He's not ready for children."

Will swore under his breath. "Give me his phone number. I'll talk to him."

Ida's gaze snapped back. "Don't you dare!"

Taken aback at her vehemence, Will sputtered, "Why not?"

"I...I will not be further humiliated." She reached across the table and grasped his hand. "Oh, Will, thank goodness I have you. I never realized just how much I value your friendship. And now that I know I'm pregnant, now that a real live baby is growing inside me, I realize how right you are about a child needing a mother and a father. There's no way I'd want to raise one alone." Tears welled. "I'm so happy and grateful we're going to get married. Please tell me it's okay that the first baby won't be yours."

What could he say? It hadn't even occurred to her that he might have changed his mind about marrying her. And what kind of jerk proposed, then backed out almost immediately? He put aside his doubts. Ida needed him. And she was right; they were no longer talking hypothetically. There was a baby on the way who also needed him.

"Of course, it's okay," he said, squeezing her hand in return. "I'm going to love that baby."

He truly believed he spoke the truth. A relationship with Maeve, even if he pursued her, even if she were interested, would undoubtedly be as short-lived as all his others. He was ready for something lasting. Ida and her baby—*their* baby—would give him what he wanted out of life.

The relief on Ida's face was palpable. "I knew you wouldn't let me down. Oh, Will, we'll have fun, you'll see. A brand-new adventure." She pulled a tissue from her purse and dabbed at her eyes. "At least, now I know why I've been so emotional lately..." She paused to blow her nose. "Hormones."

"How far along are you?"

"Six weeks. When I missed my last period I didn't think anything of it. Rick and I were using protection, and my periods are irregular, anyway."

"So what made you suspect you were pregnant?"

"When I threw up at work for the third day in a row, Sally bought a pregnancy test and insisted I take it. The test turned out positive, and today the doctor confirmed it. I'm going to be a mother." She shook her head in wonderment. "I'm so thrilled. I wake up grinning and go to sleep with a smile on my face."

Will smiled, too, just to see her so happy.

Their food came, and Ida fell upon her dinner ravenously. "I'm getting an ultrasound next week," she said between bites. "Two o'clock on Wednesday. Will you be able to make it?"

He pulled out his electronic pocket organizer and punched in the date. "I've got a meeting with a local supplier, but I can probably reschedule. I'll just make a note of the time—" he tapped it in "—and confirm within the next few days. Maybe we should get married right away at the registry office, instead of waiting for the garden to get fixed up."

"Can't we wait?" Ida said, sounding disappointed. "I won't start showing for a few months, and I'd love to have the reception on the lawn over-looking the bay.''

"All you want is a big party," he teased. "What about the ceremony? I thought the vows were the most important part."

Ida's smile faded a little. "Let's not forget why we're doing this, Will. I'm overjoyed to be starting a family with you, but I'm not confusing our relationship with the real thing."

Her clear-eyed honesty took his breath away. Here was a window of opportunity. He could respond by telling her of his misgivings. Then he remembered the baby.

"I like the idea of a party, though," Ida added. "How about an engagement party?"

Will couldn't think of a good reason why not, so Ida, as she worked her way through her moussaka, made enthusiastic plans to invite their friends and family to celebrate their engagement. Will listened, nodded and responded appropriately. The new status quo was firmly in place.

At last, Ida sat back, replete, and checked her watch. "I'd better go—I've got so much to do." She pulled out her wallet and tossed some money on the table for her meal.

Will did the same, and together they walked back to the parking lot. The sun was low across the bay and cast a golden glow over the old buildings. "What are you working on that's keeping you so busy?"

"The usual. Conveyancing, divorces... There

seems to be a spurt of both at the moment.'' They came to her car, and she turned to him, eyes luminous in the dusk. ''Don't forget the ultrasound. Just think, we'll be able to see his tiny heart beating and count his fingers and toes.''

''How do you know it's a he?'' he teased. ''Maybe it's a she.''

Ida placed a hand lightly on her abdomen. ''I don't care what it is as long as he or she is healthy.''

''Make sure you get enough rest. And eat well.''

Ida laughed softly. ''No worries there. Oh, hey, didn't you want to talk to me about something?''

Will hesitated, then got out his pocket organizer again. ''Shall we set a date for the wedding? How about the third Saturday in March? The twenty-fifth. It should still be warm enough for an outdoor wedding and will give Maeve time to get the garden in shape.'' He felt guilty just speaking her name. ''I'll call my family tonight.''

Ida gave him a sheepish smile. ''I already called mine. Mum's thrilled.''

Will felt vaguely uncomfortable at the thought of facing Ida's parents. ''Did you tell her it's a platonic marriage?''

''I did. I wouldn't want everyone to know, but I think it's only fair to be honest to our families. Mum's just happy I'm not going to be a single mother, and doesn't care about the rest.'' She stood on tiptoe to kiss him on the cheek. ''Talk to you soon.''

Instead of driving directly home, Will went by his

mother's house, a modest bungalow in an older part of Mornington. He usually visited Phyllis once a week and performed some chore such as mowing the lawn or cleaning the gutters. But mostly he came to talk. She had a way of putting life in perspective.

He parked behind her Toyota and slowly got out of the car. On the short trip over here he'd imagined her being pleased, if somewhat surprised, to hear of his engagement to Ida. And thrilled at the prospect of another grandchild. Now, as he walked up the footpath to the sound of the TV blaring through the screened window, he was less sure of her reaction.

He knocked once and went in. "Hi. It's me, Will."

"Come through, darl'," his mother called. "*Sale of the Century* is just finishing."

Her eyes still focused on the TV screen, Phyllis leaned up from her recliner and pushed back her frizzy blond hair so he could peck her on the cheek. Will sprawled on the sofa, knowing it was no use trying to talk while her favorite program was on.

Finally she clicked the TV off with the remote control and set aside the book of crossword puzzles she'd held on her lap. Pushing her glasses higher on her nose, she smiled at Will. "How's it going, darl'? Like a cuppa?"

"No, thanks. I just came from dinner with Ida." He paused, wondering how to continue. Ordinarily, he communicated easily with his mother, but tonight he couldn't find the words. Luckily, Phyllis was never in short supply.

"I ran into her a couple of weeks ago in the supermarket," Phyllis chatted on. "Looked a little tired, poor girl. I still can't quite believe she's a lawyer with her own practice. Pity she never married."

The perfect opening. "Funny you should say that," he replied. "She is getting married."

"Really?" Phyllis stared. "She never said a word to me."

"It's...sudden." He swallowed past a lump in his throat. "Maybe I will have that cup of tea, after all."

"Sure thing, darl'." She pushed herself out of the recliner, tugged her sweat shirt down and padded to the kitchen in her sheepskin moccasins. "Who's the lucky man?" she said, putting on the electric kettle. "That bloke from America?"

Will followed her into the kitchen. "No...." He peered through the curtains at the backyard. "Your grass is looking a bit long. I'll come by with my mower soon."

"Come on Sunday. I'll put on a leg of lamb. Julie and her mob might be out, as well." Phyllis emptied the remains of a package of assorted cream biscuits onto a plate, as Will got out the cups.

A few minutes later they were seated at the kitchen table with their cups of tea.

"So give me all the goss on Ida," Phyllis said. She pushed the plate of biscuits toward Will and pulled a cigarette from the pack lying on the windowsill. "Do you know this fellow she's marrying?"

"Er, yes. In fact, I know him very well."

"Come on, then." Phyllis lit up, her blue eyes avid behind the spiral of smoke.

"He is me. I mean, I. *I* am marrying Ida." He took a swig of scalding black tea and burned his tongue.

She stared at him blankly. "You and Ida are getting married? Why? Don't get me wrong. I love Ida like a daughter already. I just didn't think you loved her like a woman."

"I don't."

"So why are you doing this?"

"We both want a family and we've both given up on the notion of romantic love. That sounds negative, but it's not. We've been good friends for a long time. We'll make a go of it."

Phyllis inhaled deeply of her cigarette, then blew out a long stream of smoke. "God knows, I want to see you settled. And a woman can never have too many grandchildren. But what happens if, down the track, you fall in love with someone else."

Maeve. He brushed thoughts of her aside. What he felt for her was earthy and real, but he couldn't call it love. Yet he shifted uncomfortably. "Some things are more important than romantic love."

Deep inside, the hole he'd ignored for years suddenly revealed itself as a chasm. Who cared? he asked himself angrily. Ida and the baby would fill the gap. That was the whole point.

"What happened with Maree?" Phyllis asked. "I never did understand why you two split."

There had been several reasons, but only one that mattered. "I wanted kids and she wasn't ready. She was only twenty-five and had big career plans."

"Does Ida know you don't love her?"

He nodded. "She doesn't love me, either. We're going into this with our eyes open."

Phyllis peered at him. "Mmm. Even so, think carefully before you take this step. You're very guarded about your emotions." Thoughtfully, she knocked the ash off the tip of her cigarette into the ashtray. "It's a pity your father died when you were so young. As the eldest, I think you took it hardest."

Will had no answer to that.

Phyllis leaned over the table, fixing him with her sternest gaze. "Whatever happens, I want you to promise me two things."

Will reached for his favorite biscuit. "Sure."

"Don't say it so casual, as if I were asking you to go to the milk bar for a loaf of bread," she said sharply. "This is important. To you and to Ida."

"Okay. What is it?"

"Promise me you won't hurt Ida. Lifelong friendship is something to treasure. If you two screw this up, you could end up with nothing."

"That's easy to promise. I'd never do anything to hurt Ida. What's the second thing?"

She stubbed out her cigarette. "Be true to yourself."

"Mother, trust me. I've thought this through. I honestly believe marrying Ida will be the best thing for me. And her."

Phyllis scrutinized him silently. "Fine, then," she said at last. "Congratulations."

Will brushed together some crumbs and pushed them under the plate. "There's one other thing— Ida's pregnant."

"Jeez, Will." Phyllis reached for another cigarette. "Is it your baby?"

"It is now." Will placed his hand on hers to stop her from lighting up. "Do I still have your blessing?"

Seconds passed before acceptance came. Then she smiled, eyes moist. "For what it's worth, yes."

"It's worth a lot." He rose from his chair and pulled his mother into a hug. "Thanks."

Her cheeks were wet when she drew back. "Be happy."

"I will. Now, can *you* promise *me* something? Give up smoking. Do it for the baby, if not for yourself."

"I'll think about it."

Will drove home with the warm breeze blowing through the open windows of the Mercedes. He was already happy. In spite of Maeve. In spite of the mess his business was in. Soon he and Ida would be a family. With a baby he would call his own. He topped the rise and glided into Sorrento, the bay spread out before him, pink and gold and blue in the setting sun. Life was good.

CHAPTER SIX

THE FOLLOWING SATURDAY Will rose early, pulled on a pair of swim trunks and padded downstairs to boot up his computer. When his Web browser's home page filled the screen, he brought up the Web site for surfing information along the Victorian coast. His house overlooked the calm waters of Port Phillip Bay, but just a few miles across the narrow peninsula, Sorrento ocean beach was a favorite surfing spot. Photos of the breaking waves, updated every morning, showed Sorrento was looking good with waves four to six feet high.

When he got to the beach, a small cadre of surfers was riding the swells, waiting for the next big one. Will pulled off his shirt and felt the breeze on his bare chest. He tugged on his wet suit and reverently unwrapped his yellow Malibu. It had been a Christmas present to himself, custom shaped to his specifications.

He tucked the board under his arm and jogged into the surf. The water was cool, as always in Bass Strait because it was chilled by currents from the Antarctic. The breaking waves washed over him as he paddled out, sending chilly rivulets down the neck of his wet suit. But by the time he'd positioned himself beyond the breakers, he was warm with exertion. He nodded to the guy sitting on his board twenty feet away. Mouse. Bleached hair, tattoos down both arms, a ring through his eyebrow and a stud through his lower lip. Beyond Mouse were a couple of kids, probably not more than twelve or thirteen, locals who'd started out on body boards and had graduated to surfboards last summer. They reminded Will of himself at that age.

He waited out a couple of sets of waves, studying the break, and the height and the direction of the curl. The third wave of the next set he rode to shore, curving back on the curl when he got too close to one of the youngsters.

Will paddled out again, pleased with his new board, but sat out a few more waves, watching, waiting. He felt troubled, even here on the water. Maeve was occupying too many of his thoughts—thoughts that should be reserved for Ida and the baby. When Maeve was around, he found himself looking for her impish smile or anticipating one of her penetrating glances.

A spray of cold water whipping off the top of a wave caught him on the cheek, bringing him back to the present. His eyes narrowed as he judged the distance and speed of the approaching swell, estimating the height and the moment it would start to break. He swiveled his board in the water and, glancing over his shoulder, started paddling. Surfing, like business—and love—was all a matter of timing.

He rose to his feet, squinting into the bright sun, dazzled by the gleam of sunlight on water. The flat brilliant surface reminded him of a beam of photons on a solar panel—

Something clicked in his brain—images coalesced into ideas in a nanosecond of blazing insight. Elated, he slid down the slope of the crashing wave on a rush of speed and adrenaline. The answer to increasing the efficiency of the solar panel lay in creating a multiplier effect that would increase the rate of movement of electrons through the silicon layer. And he knew just how to accomplish that.

Creativity, as much as necessity, was the mother of invention. And what he'd just thought of was the mother of all inventions.

Maeve couldn't help but be impressed.

IDA STARED at the telephone as if it were a hanging judge and she the guilty party. There was no reason to be so scared, she told herself. It was only a phone call. "Hi, Rick," she would say. "How's the weather? By the way, I'm having a baby and you're the father."

She'd told Will she'd already called Rick, but that had been a lie. The part about Rick not being ready for children was true, though. He'd mentioned it in casual conversation early in their acquaintanceship. So she hadn't needed to call him to know what he'd say to her being pregnant. He would probably offer child support—he was a decent guy, after all—but he wouldn't ask her to marry him.

Okay, so she'd told him a time or two that she regarded their relationship as a fling, but he should have been able to see past that. If he'd really loved her he wouldn't have been put off so easily.

Ida picked up the receiver and quickly dialed Rick's number in San Diego before she could lose her nerve. Will was right: Rick deserved to know he was going to be a father.

"Hello?" Rick's voice sounded in her ear. Then, after a silence, he said, "Anybody there?"

Dry-mouthed, Ida couldn't answer. She dropped the receiver gently back in the cradle. What was the point in setting herself up for rejection?

"YOU'RE SURE Maeve won't mind my taking the panel to work on?" Will asked Art through the driver's window of his Merc. Knowing perfectly well she would.

"I'm positive. This thing has driven her mad," Art replied. He gave a last tug on the cord lashing the solar panel into the boot and stepped away from the car. "She shouldn't be too much longer. Have a beer and wait. You can ask her yourself."

And ruin his strategic timing? "Thanks, I've got to go."

He put the car in reverse and stuck his head out the window, as Art guided him back through the narrow gateway in the sage-green picket fence.

Half an hour later, Will approached his own house, his gaze drawn to the big stone urns flanking the front steps. They'd been stripped of dead stalks and replanted with masses of brightly colored flowers. Maeve had been here.

When he pulled to a stop in front of the garage and spotted her dark-green utility truck, the breath stuck in his lungs.

Maeve was still here.

Because he wanted to, he didn't go looking for her. Instead, he untied the cord around the solar panel, lifted it carefully out of the trunk and carried it into his workshop. Sunlight fell on the white-and-silver panel as he laid it on the bench, and glancing up, he realized that as well as removing the gum tree, she'd cut back the ivy growing over the windows.

"Will?" he heard her call.

She stood framed by the open door, wearing khaki cargo pants and her black crop top. Tiny silver hoops threaded with a single turquoise bead looped through her ears, and green-handled pruning shears peeked from one of the many pockets on her pants.

"Hi," he said, walking over. The smudge of dirt on her cheek only added to her aura of strength and earthiness. The woman was an Amazon.

"I need you to make a decision about the papaya tree," she said, pushing back long wisps of dark hair from her forehead with the back of her gloved hand.

"I didn't even know I had a papaya tree," he replied, rocking back on his heels, hands in his pockets.

"It's in the northeast corner, behind the lilacs. Come, I'll show you."

Will followed her across the lawn and around the clump of lilac bushes. Hidden next to the brick wall that separated his property from his neighbor's stood a small tree with a spindly trunk and a cluster of palmate leaves at the top.

"I don't know why anyone would plant a papaya tree in such a shady spot," Maeve said, forced to stand close to him in the confined space. "It doesn't look as though it's ever borne fruit, but if I move it, you might get lucky."

"Fine, put it anywhere you like." Her scent filled his nostrils. After the easy camaraderie of their last session, he felt awkward. He was aware of Maeve as a woman and unable to do anything about it.

"The sunny area between the Monterey Bay fig and the pool would be perfect," she said. "I should warn you, though. The move could prove too much. The tree might die."

"Is this the right time of year for moving trees?" He avoided looking at her, for to turn his head would mean gazing into her eyes, which were just inches away.

"No, but I have plans for this corner." She, too, held herself perfectly still. Crickets thrummed in the undergrowth.

"Such as?"

She shook her head. "You'll have to wait and see."

"Well, if the papaya won't bear fruit in this location, what have we got to lose?"

"That's what I think, but I don't like to jeopardize

a mature plant unless the owner is aware of the risk.''

Will racked his brain, but he couldn't think of another thing to say about the papaya tree.

Abruptly, Maeve started to walk back. He followed. When they were out in the open again, he noticed she put a good three feet between them.

"How's Ida?" she asked.

"Fine. In fact, she's—" He broke off before he could say, *she's pregnant.* His sisters never told anyone they were expecting until they'd successfully passed the first trimester. They might simply be superstitious. Then again, there might be good reason for caution. Maeve was waiting for him to finish his thought, so he told her lamely, "She's just fine."

She gave him one of her lingering, penetrating looks. "She mentioned you and she went to university together, and that you were her date for the graduation ball. Took you two a long time to decide you were in love."

He shrugged. "What is love?"

"Don't you know?"

"Sure. I just meant…" He trailed off, not sure what he'd meant. "Bloody hot again today," he muttered, turning his gaze to the cloudless sky.

"You never told me much about your father," she said.

"My father! What makes you ask about him?"

"The lilacs made me think of him." An enigmatic smile curled her lips for a moment. Then she sobered. "I think you said he died when you were a child."

"He had a heart attack when he was sixty-five." He didn't want to talk about his father. He had too many conflicting feelings where William Sr. was concerned. Reluctantly, he added, "I was ten years old."

"He must have been quite a bit older than your mother." Maeve's low, slightly husky voice seemed to draw information out of him.

"There was a twenty-two-year gap between them. She married him right out of high school. Never got an education or any kind of training."

"They must have been very much in love."

Will snorted. "She married him for security. Her father was verbally abusive and she wanted to escape. Mum and Dad liked each other, though. They made a good partnership. That was enough."

"Do you really think so?" she asked mildly.

"It was for them." Even as he said it, anger rose in him, born of lifelong resentment toward a man who'd left marriage too late to be a father to his young family. "He saddled her with four kids and no means of support."

"What did she do?"

He shrugged and kicked at a stone lying in the grass. "We moved into Mornington, and she took a job waiting tables."

"That's when you started to miss the space and freedom of the farm."

A sigh escaped his lungs. "I don't know why it

should matter after all these years—now I'd rather live by the sea than out in the country—but somehow it does."

"'The child is the father of the man,'" she quoted. "No matter what changes we go through in our lives, deep inside a part of us longs to return to the world of our childhood. It may not have been perfect, but it was where we awakened to ourselves." She stopped and turned to look at him directly. "In your garden I want to recreate the essence of the childhood memories you carry in your heart."

Her words touched him someplace deep inside that he hadn't even known existed. Unable to speak, he could only stare into her warm dark eyes, absorbing the fact that she understood him at some level that seemed impossible for a near stranger. She was half Amazon, half witch.

She smiled suddenly, as if to reassure him she was perfectly normal. "Your brother and sisters—where do they live?" she asked, walking on. "Are you close?"

"My brother and one sister live in Sydney. My other sister, Julie, lives in Melbourne. We're pretty close, although we're all so busy with our own lives, we don't see one another often enough. Julie and Mike just had a new baby—a girl." His voice became gruff as he recalled the special moments he'd shared with little Caelyn.

He would have told Maeve more about his nieces and nephews, but she suddenly became interested in the instructions on the back of a seed packet she'd pulled from one of her pockets.

At any rate, they'd arrived back at the workshop. "Come in," Will said. "I want to show you something."

She hesitated, then followed him into the dim coolness of the bungalow. Will flicked on the lights, illuminating the flat rectangle of metal and glass that took up half the workbench.

"Is that *my* solar panel?" She was indignant, but curious, too.

"I've got an idea about how to increase the efficiency and store more energy," Will said. "I went by your house to talk to Art about it, and he let me take the panel to work on it."

"He shouldn't have done that, but since he did…what's your idea?"

Will gestured to the black box attached to the solar panel. "I plan to increase the voltaic output with a multiplier that will change the basic structure of the panel to allow a more rapid flow of electrons."

He glanced at her face for signs of boredom. Usually when he got technical, women tuned out; or, if they wanted to impress, took on that glazed "how very interesting" look. Ida would have grinned and told him to can it. Maeve's expression as she bent over the solar panel was serious and absorbed.

Then her expression turned to awe as she grasped the full implications of his proposed invention. "That would revolutionize the solar panel industry!"

"Quite possibly," he admitted modestly.

"Won't you also need to use a bigger battery?" she asked, turning back to the panel. "If the panel's not self-regulating, you risk overcharging and damaging the battery, right?"

"Exactly," he said, enthused by her interest. She not only understood what he was getting at but wanted to know more. "I thought your field was botany."

"I took basic physics as part of my science degree. Then, for a while I was interested in the structure of plant tissue and its influence on physiology so I took a course in biophysics. That was before I decided I'd rather spend my time outdoors than in a lab."

An Amazon, a witch and a scientist.

"It's nice to talk to someone with a science background—" she said, adding with a warm chuckle, "someone who doesn't regard you as a nerd."

"I know what you mean." He met her eyes and smile. Suddenly it seemed to Will that the electrons lying dormant in the solar panel had jumped free and were spinning in orbit around Maeve and him. The magnetic electric current thus created locked his gaze to hers.

Footsteps crunched on the gravel between the driveway and the bungalow. A cheery voice called, "Hi, there! What's going on?"

Ida. Will started guiltily.

Maeve drew back abruptly, her cheeks dusky rose. "Will was just explaining his plans to modify the solar panel."

Ida's alert eyes moved between Maeve and Will. "You mustn't let him bore you with that stuff. He'll go on for hours about electronics if you allow him to."

"It's not boring," Maeve replied. "If his idea works, it'll be a boon for my experiment in hydroponic herb production."

"Oh, he's doing it for you. That's different." Ida's tone suggested different was not better. Worse, in fact.

"He's doing it for my father, really," Maeve said. "Guilty conscience."

"I'll bet," Ida said dryly.

Will winced and moved away from the solar panel, not daring to look at Maeve. "How are you feeling, Ida?"

"Fine." She glanced at her watch. "Have you forgotten?"

The ultrasound! "No, of course not. I, uh, Maeve, you'll have to excuse me. Ida and I have to…" He floundered.

"We have an appointment at the doctor's for an ultrasound." Ida pressed a hand against her abdomen and smiled beatifically. "We're having a baby."

A cold chill spread through Maeve's limbs. *Will was going to be a father.* The expression on his face told her how much that meant to him.

He was unavailable—if the notion hadn't sunk in before, it did now, with the battering force of a pile driver. Even if Ida didn't exist, Maeve could never give him what he wanted. What he needed.

Although she told herself she'd had no expectations, she felt as though something had been stolen from her. Love. The possibility of healing.

"Congratulations!" she said to Ida. "That's wonderful."

She turned to Will and forced herself to meet his eyes, sending a silent message: whatever happened just now must never happen again.

He nodded as if he understood. Then he put his arm around Ida. "We'll see you later, Maeve."

DR. NOVITSKY, a petit, gray-haired woman with a faint Polish accent, moved the pointer around on the ultrasound screen. "Here is the back…and this is the stomach…toes…heart."

"The heart is beating so fast," Ida commented.

Fascinated, Will tried to count the beats. This was a real live baby. A tiny person depending on him and Ida. The thought was humbling. And exhilarating. He looked from the screen to Ida. Her expression was rapt, a reflection of his own mixture of awe and excitement.

"A fetus's heart beats faster than an adult's. Nothing's wrong," the doctor assured them.

"Can you tell the sex?" Will asked.

Dr. Novitsky pushed the gel around Ida's flat belly with the ultrasound probe. With her other hand she set the dials on the instrument and clicked to record a photo. "Are you sure you want to know?" she enquired with a smile.

Will glanced at Ida with a shrug. "I don't care what it is," he said. "But if you want to know…"

She reached for his hand. "I'm happy to be surprised." She asked the doctor, "Does it have all its fingers and toes?"

"There's no evidence of spinal abnormalities," the doctor replied, interpreting her question as concern over more than the number of digits.

Will hadn't even considered that possibility, but the news was a relief nonetheless. Enthralled by the underwater movements of the fetus, he could have watched all day, but once the doctor had taken the necessary measurements, she ended the session.

He and Ida emerged from the air-conditioned consulting room into the blazing afternoon sun, Ida carrying the blurry gray-and-white image of their unborn baby as reverently as she might a masterpiece. Will had been excited at the thought of a baby before, but nothing had prepared him for how pumped he felt now. The pregnancy was suddenly real to him. His role as a father had begun.

"This weekend I'll start fixing up one of the spare bedrooms for a nursery," he said, as they walked back to the parking lot.

"We'll have to go shopping for baby things," Ida told him enthusiastically. "We'll need a crib and a car seat—"

"And a globe of the world," Will interjected. "She could grow up to be a scientist."

"A high chair and a pram—"

"I'll start an education fund for her right away."

"A bassinet and a playpen…"

"A bank account in her name, with savings bonds."

"Bath toys…"

"We'll subscribe to *Australian Geographic.*"

"Will, be serious," Ida laughed.

"I am," he replied, indignant. "I'm thinking ahead."

Arm in arm, they continued, Ida with a skip in her step. "What shall we call him?" Ida said.

"You mean *her,* don't you?" he answered with a grin.

"I like Miranda for a girl and Jason for a boy. Or would you like to name him William?"

"Maybe you should call him Richard."

Ida stopped dead, the joy draining from her expression. "Are you going to throw Rick in my face for the rest of our lives? Because if you are—"

"No." Will clutched her shoulders, aghast to see tears spring to her eyes. "I just thought you might want to remember him."

"He's not dead, and I'm not raising a monument to our so-called love affair," she said fiercely. "I don't care if I never hear his name again. And I definitely don't want my baby named after him."

Will pulled her into his arms, hating to see his friend hurting. Ida's chest rose and fell on a deep sigh. "She's really beautiful, isn't she?"

"Who?" he asked, bewildered by the abrupt change of subject.

"Maeve. You're attracted to her, aren't you?"

"No! Okay, maybe a little."

"A lot. I could tell." Ida sighed again and pulled away. "And she's attracted to you."

"No." He was firmer on that. Had to be.

"She planted Sweet William in your urns, for crying out loud. It's not too late to back out, Will. I don't want to hold you to anything you don't want to do."

"Don't talk like that, Ida. I'm not backing out. I want this baby. I want us to be a family. I'm sorry if I made you feel bad earlier this afternoon."

"You couldn't help it. There's no romance between us—there never has been. It's just that sometimes I wish…"

"What?"

"Nothing. It's not important."

"Let's just take it one day at a time, okay?" he said, squeezing her hand.

"Okay." Swinging her shoulder bag over to her other arm, she said, "I guess I'll pick up some files from the office and head home. Are you going back to the factory?"

"I think I'll catch a few waves."

MAEVE PARKED her utility truck on Birdwood Avenue in Melbourne and walked through the main gate of the Royal Botanical Gardens. Tall, broadlimbed trees from around the world shaded vast lawns, and a web of footpaths wound through the park and around the ornamental lake. Maeve took the path to the far side of the park, where the Plant Craft Cottage nestled into the verdant slope.

"Rose?" Maeve called, stepping through the open door. Receiving no answer, she moved farther into the cottage, past the small library and the gift shop to the workrooms at the back.

As well as volunteering at the cottage and growing hydroponic herbs, Rose was an avid amateur collector of tropical cacti. So when Maeve had wanted a special plant for Will's moonlight garden, she had come to Rose.

Rose was bent over a drafting table, working on a botanical watercolor of flowering chives. At the sound of Maeve's footsteps, she glanced up and pushed back wisps of silver-blond hair from her finely lined face. "Hello, darl'."

"Hi, Rose," Maeve said, entering the room. "How is your new series coming along?"

Rose shook out her cramped fingers. "The cottage curator wants to make framed prints for sale in the shop, as well as the usual greeting cards."

Maeve inspected her friend's delicately beautiful and scientifically accurate composition. "It's lovely. Will you save me one?"

"Of course. Take your pick when they're done." Rose rinsed her brush in clean water and set it aside. Her loose cotton floral dress swirled around her bare ankles as she swiveled to face Maeve. "What brings you out on a working day?"

Maeve hitched herself onto one of the stools that lined the workbench. "I'm making a moonlight garden for a client. I've got a good collection of scented white and blue flowers. Now I'm looking for a mature *Selenicereus grandiflorus*. Do you know where I can get one?''

''Ah, the Queen of the Night. A rare plant and a favorite of yours.'' She arched her eyebrows shrewdly. ''I take it this isn't a common or garden-variety client but a special one?''

Maeve was appalled to find herself blushing. ''Yes, although I'm not sure why I'm going to so much bother. He's my father's boss and he's closing the factory where Dad works.''

''But he's special,'' Rose persisted.

Maeve got off her stool to move around the room, her gaze roving over tools and bits of plant material on the benches. ''He's…complicated. Charming. Clever. He's figured out a way to boost the energy output of the solar panel so I can continue with my experiment on your herb production.''

''I like him already.'' Rose tilted her head. ''Are you interested in this man?''

''No,'' Maeve said firmly. ''He's engaged to a really nice woman, and they're going to have a baby.'' She fell silent, then sighed. ''Something's missing from their relationship, though, some spark of passion. I can't figure it out. I don't know if it's wishful thinking on my part or—'' Maeve broke off. She didn't want to think these things, much less express them.

But Rose had known her too long. ''You're attracted to him.''

Maeve lifted a lid on a woven basket to inhale

the luscious scent of moist potpourri. "I suppose so, if you like that type."

"Uh-huh. What type is that?"

"Oh, you know, typical surfer," she said, struggling to sound offhand. "Tall, tanned, hair streaked with gold, warm blue eyes."

"I see what you mean," Rose said. "Pretty unappealing."

"Oh, Rose." She turned, wringing her hands. "I *am* attracted to him. A lot. More than just looks—I feel a connection. The worst part is, he's attracted to me, too."

"Oh, dear." Rose's lips pursed and her eyebrows drew together. "Has anything happened between you two?"

"No, nothing! He hasn't made a pass or anything. He's not the kind of guy who would if he was committed to someone else." Maeve flung her hands wide. "I don't even want to like him, for goodness' sake! He's the man who's putting my father out of work."

"What will you do?" Rose asked quietly.

"From now on, I'll go to his place only when he's not there. And…I'm thinking of going away for a while after I finish the garden."

"My dear, is it that serious?"

"It could be, if a relationship was allowed to develop. But I wouldn't ever come between him and his fiancée." Or force him to choose between herself, and having children.

"I'm glad to hear it. By the way, you're welcome to stay with me in Emerald. If nothing else, the Dandenong Mountains are a relief from the heat of Melbourne.''

"Thanks, Rose, that sounds marvelous.'' She picked up a skein of soft, moss-dyed wool and turned it over in her hands. "Graham's been in touch. He wants me to come sailing with him at the end of March. He says he's changed his mind about kids and wants us to try again.''

Rose's clear gray eyes regarded her. "Do you want to try again?''

Maeve shrugged. "We had some good times.''

"But whether to have more children wasn't the only problem you two had, was it?'' Rose asked, probing gently.

"No,'' Maeve said slowly, recalling how often she'd poured her aching heart out to Rose. "That was five years ago, though. Perhaps he's changed.''

"And perhaps you're simply running from an untenable situation with this other man,'' Rose said. "You've got to search your heart for what you truly want.''

Maeve lifted unhappy eyes. "What if I can't have what I want?''

"Then you must learn to do without. Sometimes love hurts.'' Rose got up to give Maeve a hug. "Now, dry those tears, child. I know where you can find the perfect specimen of *Selenicereus*.''

CHAPTER SEVEN

MAEVE WAS GLAD to leave Melbourne's peak-hour traffic behind, and as the crowded city streets gradually gave way to solid but flowing highways, the turmoil in her mind settled. She would turn off her feelings for Will, do her job, and then get out.

By the time she reached Mount Eliza, she was humming softly and looking forward to a relaxing evening pottering in her garden. As she drove along her shaded lane, the scent of eucalyptus resin wafted through the open car windows and the magpie's warble filled the air. She waved to old Mrs. Griffiths, who was tending her beloved standard roses, then turned the last gentle bend, which led to Wandin Cottage.

A police car was standing in the driveway.

Dad!

Maeve brought the ute skidding to a halt behind the police cruiser. She jumped out and raced into the house, the screen door banging behind her. "Dad? Where are you? Are you all right?"

A police officer stepped out of her father's bedroom, blocking her path. His grim expression almost stopped her heart.

"Where's my father?" she demanded, trying to push past him into Art's room.

"Your father's fine, Ms. Arden," said the sergeant, whose gray brush cut belied his unlined face. "Mr. Hodgins is in the kitchen, giving the details to the constable."

"Details of what?" she demanded. "What's wrong?"

"Your house was broken into. When your father came home from work he found the front door pushed in."

Maeve reacted deep inside. *Someone had broken into her home.* Her own private place. With a gasp, she flung her arms around her waist as though someone had struck her in the solar plexus.

Dimly, she heard footsteps at the door and a voice say, "What's going on?"

Will. What was he doing here?

His hand gripped her elbow and an arm went around her shoulders, supporting her. She struggled to free herself, close to weeping with fury over the violation of her home. Will only made her feel more vulnerable. She didn't want to need him. And she certainly didn't want him seeing her in this state.

Ignoring her protests, he led her down the hall. "When did the break-in occur?" he asked the sergeant.

"And your relation to Ms. Arden is what, sir?"

"I'm...a friend of the family."

"My father works for him. And at the moment, so do I," Maeve said, pulling herself together. She glared at Will and tugged her arm out of his grip. "I'll ask the questions."

But at that moment they entered the lounge room, and Maeve stopped dead, her mouth falling open in renewed horror. The TV was gone. The CD player and tape deck were missing, as well. "Oh, no!" she wailed.

A horrible thought struck her. Kristy's baby bracelet.

She ran back to her bedroom at the front of the house. Skirting the high brass bed piled with lacy pillows, she went to the mahogany dresser, French-polished to a high gloss, and pulled open one of the small top drawers. She tossed aside the lacy bras and panties she wore on special occasions and removed a black velvet jewelry case, which she cracked open. She scrabbled through the gold necklaces and opal earrings. Not until she found Kristy's baby bracelet nestled safely at the bottom did she breathe a sigh of relief. Eyes closed, she pressed it to her lips.

"Good thing you don't hide your valuables in an obvious place," Will said from the doorway.

Maeve's gaze snapped to his.

He glanced at the small bracelet of coral beads in her hand. "Sweet. Was it yours?"

She dropped the bracelet back in the case so he couldn't see the letters engraved in gold on the center beads. "Yes."

Then she shoved the case back in her drawer. If she ignored him, maybe he would go away. Quickly she checked the back of the drawer, where she kept a small amount of cash. Still there, thank God. She rested her head against the top of the dresser, weak with delayed shock and relief. Clearly the thieves had carried off only what they could grab.

Then she remembered her lacy underthings, strewn over the bed and Persian carpet. For a split second, her imagination put her in them and herself in Will's arms. Her cheeks burning, she retrieved the spilled lingerie, as Will regarded her with amusement, sympathy and— *No.* She refused to think about what else burned in that warm gaze.

Straightening, she found Will glancing around her room, from the lace curtains at the windows, to the fresh flowers by her bed, to the framed prints of lush pre-Raphaelite paintings on her wall. Then he turned his bemused eyes on her, as if trying to reconcile her romantic and sensual side with the brawny woman who wielded a chainsaw and turned the soil in his garden.

"Excuse me. I have to check my computer," she said, pushing past him. Damn it, they'd tacitly agreed not to acknowledge any feelings between them, much less intensify their heat. Somehow, Will's intrusion into her bedroom seemed to complete the invasion begun by the burglars and left her scared and vulnerable.

But by the time she reached the kitchen she'd cooled enough to wonder if the heat had all been in her mind. After all, he'd done nothing amiss. Said nothing. Maybe she'd misinterpreted the look in his eyes.

Then she saw the corner of the kitchen where she'd set up a mini-office after Art had moved into the second bedroom, and forgot all about trying to sort out the vagaries of mind and heart. Her computer, printer and scanner—all were gone.

Her father, who'd been sitting at the table, was on his feet and at her side in a trice. "There now, Maevie, the insurance will cover the loss," he said, wrapping her in his arms.

"All my gardens were in that computer," she wailed, and sank into a chair. With a glance at Will, who'd followed her into the room, she added, "Your garden, too." She'd drawn his house and garden on a grid and marked each existing and future plant and shrub in its exact location.

"Don't you have backup floppy disks?" he asked.

"Yes, but reprogramming a new computer and reentering all my data will be a hassle. I didn't budget time for this kind of delay." She clenched her fist on the tabletop. "When I get my hands on those thieves, I'll bloody murder them."

The constable across from her filling in the incident report looked up. "You don't want to be making a statement like that in front of the police."

"Oh!" She threw her hands in the air.

"Of course, she didn't mean it literally." Will bent over and briefly squeezed her shoulders, saying close to her ear, "Everything will be okay."

Amid the turmoil and chaos, she found comfort and strength in his grip. She didn't dare turn her head for fear she'd do something silly like lift her mouth to be kissed. Then his hands slid from her shoulders, and without another word, he filled the kettle and put tea bags from the canister on the bench top into the teapot.

"Any cash or other valuables missing? Jewelry? Camera?" the constable asked Maeve.

She shook her head. "No, thank goodness, although I don't understand why not."

"Probably they were surprised in the act and scarpered. What make was the TV?"

"Some obscure brand. Wilson, I think. Terrible reception."

"Approximate age?" the constable added, jotting down the information.

"Twenty years. Maybe thirty."

The constable raised an eyebrow. "You were lucky they got away with as little as they did."

"You're lucky you weren't home when they broke in," Will amended. "You might have been injured." Arms crossed, he regarded her. His hard gaze contradicted the compassion he'd shown a moment ago. "What kind of security system do you have?"

She pushed a hand wearily through the hair escaping from her braid. "We don't."

He swore and straightened away from the bench top. "I'm not saying this to tout my own product, but I have an excellent tamperproof alarm on the market. People who care about their safety or the contents of their home shouldn't be without it.'' He glanced at Art, who frowned down at his folded hands.

"It's a good alarm, all right. The best,'' Art said quietly. "But too expensive for us.''

Maeve felt a twinge of conscience. Art had recommended she buy one, even offered to pay half, but she'd declined, thinking no one would break into a modest cottage on a no-through road. Plus, the alarm was pricey, and she couldn't justify the expense at a time when more money seemed to be going out than coming in.

"I made the decision. I guess it was the wrong one.'' She propped her head in her hand, elbow on the table. "No sense locking the barn door after the horse has bolted.''

"Nonsense,'' Will said. "Thieves often return once they think you've replaced the stolen items. I'll give you one of my alarms and install it personally.''

"That's extremely generous—'' Art began.

Maeve snapped up her head. "But we can't accept it.''

"Exactly what I was about to say,'' her father added gently.

"Don't be foolish,'' Will said, pacing the kitchen. "I...I was planning to give all of my employees one as a parting bonus. Yes, that's it. You can have yours now.''

Maeve exchanged a glance with her father. Nei-

ther believed for a moment that Will had had any
such intention until thirty seconds ago.

"Sounds an excellent plan," the sergeant said
firmly, as though his approval sealed the accord. The
doorbell rang. "That'll be my men, come to take
fingerprints."

The constable went to let them in. Maeve slipped
out the back way before the police officers could
reach the kitchen. She lifted the garage door and
flipped the light switch to scan the interior. Nothing
seemed to have been disturbed. Her tools and her
bags of potting mix and fertilizer were all as she'd
left them. Even the stacks of empty terra-cotta pots,
ripe for smashing by vandals, were intact.

She retreated to her garden and, suddenly exhausted, sank into the wooden swing. Her eyes fell
shut and she tuned her senses to the floral scents and
birdsong, trying to distance herself from what was
happening inside her house.

"Are you all right?"

Will's voice brought her back to reality. "You
still here?"

"Don't be rude," he admonished mildly. He sat
beside her and pushed off with his feet, making the
bench swing gently. As lightly as a breath of air, the
back of his hand touched her forehead. "Maybe you
should lie down."

His voice held nothing but concern for her health.
So why did the slight pressure of his fingers on her
skin send her heart rate soaring? Why did she long

to nestle into the crook of his shoulder, to wind her arm about his neck—

She jumped to her feet. "You shouldn't be here. Why are you, anyway?"

He stood and pulled a key from his pocket. "To give you a key to my house. I'll be working long hours from now on and won't be at home when you come."

"I don't go into my clients' houses when they're not home," she said, resisting the urge to accept the key in his outstretched hand. The urge to enter his life as someone more significant than a gardener.

"You might want to use the bathroom, or make a cup of coffee…" He pressed the key into her palm and folded her fingers over it, then wrapped his hand around hers. "Take it."

"I don't want it," she said almost desperately, aware that the jagged strip of metal was still warm from his touch. Either Will had moved or she had, but somehow they stood only inches apart. His eyes were so blue, so warm, so…close. "You've got to leave. I don't want your security system, or your concern, or—"

The back door creaked open, bringing her abruptly to her senses. Wrenching her hand from Will's, she turned to see her father glowering from the doorway.

"The sergeant wants to speak with you," Art said to Maeve, before his outraged gaze fixed on Will.

"I'll be right there." She glanced back to Will, searching his frozen expression for a clue to what she should do. She wanted to return his key, but she was afraid her father would leap to further erroneous conclusions.

Art came down the steps toward them. "Go inside, Maeve."

As she walked toward the house, she heard Art growl at Will, "Be off with you. I don't care if you are my boss. You keep your cheating hands off my daughter."

Maeve slipped the key in her pocket and went inside.

MAEVE STAYED AWAY from Will's house for five days. She filed a claim with her insurance company, bought a new computer and re-input all her records, both financial and botanical. Then she worked with her assistant, Tony, on the landscaping jobs he'd taken over while she'd been preoccupied with Will's place.

On the sixth day she decided her continued absence was not only ridiculous but simply not an option. She had plants to get into the ground and landscaping to do. The fencing subcontractor had to be instructed on the finer points of the kissing gate, and the bricklayer was coming on Thursday to build a cubby house behind the lilacs.

She timed her arrival for nine o'clock, when she knew Will would be at work. Even so, she drove cautiously down the driveway and only relaxed when she saw that his Mercedes wasn't sitting in its usual spot outside the garage.

The fencing subcontractor arrived shortly after, and she showed him where she wanted the cream-colored wrought-iron fence. The kissing gate she had commissioned separately, from an ironwork specialist. When it was ready, she would call the fencer back to install it.

The bricklayer was two hours late, but he turned up eventually. Maeve showed him a sketch of what she wanted—a small enclosure with walls four feet high and a door facing the lilacs. Around the outside, completely enclosing the brick structure, she erected a sturdy trellis, then planted jasmine vines. The flowering vines would grow up and over the top to completely enclose the cubby. Near the door, she left a gap just big enough for a child to slip through.

By the time Will and Ida's baby was old enough to play outside alone or with a friend, he or she would have a private space with a roof of green leaves and light. Will would have to prune the fast-growing jasmine, but she didn't think he'd mind.

The bricklayer worked quickly and competently, and before the afternoon was over the structure was complete. Dark red-and-black mottled bricks with ragged edges gave the cubby an aged appearance, and all that would be required in addition was a wooden bench and perhaps a table of rustic design.

After the bricklayer left, she stood back and viewed their handiwork through half-closed eyes. An image formed in her mind of the cubby in three years' time, overgrown with flowering greenery, cool and inviting on a sweltering day like today. In her fantasy, she glimpsed small brown limbs and the back of a tousled dark head duck through a gap in the foliage to disappear into his or her own world.

Without warning, she thought of Kristy, who hadn't lived to run and play in the sun. Maeve strode away from the cubby, her jaw clenched, fiercely trying to quell her grief for her lost child. Sorrow flowed from some inexhaustible well deep inside and poured through her, weakening her limbs. Halfway across the lawn she dropped to her knees as if to pray, except she'd learned long ago that her prayers went unanswered. *Oh, Kristy. Oh, my baby.*

She wanted to weep huge gulping sobs, but she held them in check. She hadn't given in to her grief in years, and never in a place that wasn't her own. Her tears dried unshed, leaving her with a throbbing head and an ache in her chest that felt as though her heart would never heal.

For a long time she sat on the grass at the edge of the cliff and stared vacantly at the shimmering water, waiting for the numbness that always followed a grief attack to block the pain. The angle of the sun made her check her watch at last. Will could arrive home at any time.

Wearily, she gathered her tools and loaded her empty pots and equipment into the ute. It wasn't until she'd backed around and started down the driveway that she remembered Will's house key was in her pocket, unused. She'd planned to put it under a pot by the back door and later leave a message on his answering machine telling him where he could find it, but she'd forgotten in her hurry to get away. She glanced at the house through the rearview mirror, wondering if she had time to go back.

Beep. Her gaze snapped forward at the sound of a car horn. She stepped on the brakes just in time to avoid a front-end collision with Will's Mercedes. Maeve reversed up the driveway, her sweaty palms slipping on the wheel. Damn, this was a stupid situation.

She waited for Will to drive past. Her heart stopped when he slowed to a halt beside her. Oh God, he was going to get out and talk to her. Thoughts flashed through her mind: all the things she wanted to say to him, all the things she couldn't say. His garden, the cubby…Ida.

But he didn't get out of the car. Nor did he roll down his window. He simply looked at her, then nodded gravely. Stiffly, she inclined her head. He released the brake and motored slowly toward the garage.

Maeve threw her vehicle into gear and continued on her way, her heart beating hard and fast.

MAEVE EMERGED from her bedroom early one Saturday morning in mid-February to find her father sitting on the hall chair, pulling on his boots. "Why are you dressed for work, Dad? It's the weekend."

Art finished tying his laces and stood. "We're pushed for time getting the orders out before the factory closes. Will asked everyone to come in today."

"I can't believe you're doing this." Maeve drew her dressing gown around her. "He's putting you all out of work, and you're jumping through hoops for the guy!"

"I've got to admit, my respect for him has dropped," Art said, frowning. "I don't think much of your behavior, either—"

"Nothing happened!"

"Well, he's still my employer, and I've never had cause to fault him on that score. As long as I work for Aussie Electronics I'll stick to the terms of my contract." Art picked up his workbag. "That includes reasonable overtime."

"You are so blind, you know that?" she called after him as he went out.

"See you tonight, Maevie." And he shut the door.

Maeve had planned to take the morning off, thinking Will would be at home on a Saturday. Now that she learned he was at work, she briefly contemplated driving down to Sorrento. But only briefly. One fool in their family was enough.

She made herself coffee and booted up the computer to catch up on some accounting. The phone rang. Absently, she reached for it. "Hello?"

"Maeve."

Her heart sank. *Graham.* "Hi. Where are you?"

"I just sailed into town. I'm moored in Mornington Marina. Can you meet me for lunch?"

"Not today," she lied, to put him off.

"Okay. You say when."

"Uh…" If he'd sailed all the way from Sydney just to see her, she would have to have lunch, at least. "Tuesday?"

"Fine. Noon at the Grand Hyatt. See you then."

Grand Hyatt. He was obviously trying to impress her.

She gave up attempting to work. After her shower, she clipped her hair back in a silver barrette and put on a flowery sleeveless dress that hung loosely to mid-calf. Taking her coffee to the back garden, she sank into the wooden swing. But the gentle rocking motion conjured memories of Will's touch. She rose to wander restlessly, pinching off dead heads here, pulling weeds there.

She really ought to get some sort of security alarm. Briefly she contemplated buying the cheaper Japanese version of Will's alarm, then guiltily dismissed the notion. That sort of thinking on a large scale had brought down Aussie Electronics and cost her father and all the other workers their jobs.

Inside the house, the phone rang again.

With a groan, Maeve returned to the kitchen.

"Hello? Sorry, he's at work. May I take a message?" She listened at first with disbelief, then growing excitement. Another electronics firm wanted Art to come in for a job interview. "I'll let him know right away," she said, scribbling down the details.

Maeve slipped on a pair of sandals and headed out to the ute. She'd never interrupted Art at work before, but the personnel officer had suggested Art get back to him right away, as they'd already completed interviews with the other candidates.

Ten minutes later she pulled off the highway into the industrial park in Mornington. So this was the famous, and soon-to-be-defunct, Aussie Electronics, she thought as she turned into a visitors' parking spot in front of the building.

"Hi. Renée, isn't it?" she said, approaching the immaculate blond woman behind the reception desk. "I'm Maeve, Art Hodgins's daughter. We've talked on the phone once or twice."

Renée set aside the bills she was stuffing into envelopes. "Nice to meet you, Maeve. How can I help?"

"I'd like to speak with my father, if that's possible. It's rather urgent."

"Not a problem." Renée rose and led the way toward a door in the far wall. "No one's sick or injured, I hope?"

"Nothing like that. My coming here won't get Art into trouble, will it?"

"Goodness, no," Renée replied with a laugh. "Mr. Beaumont is very easygoing. Anyway, it's nearly morning tea break."

Renée led her down a long corridor, past a glass-windowed meeting room and a series of offices. Maeve had a bad moment when she saw Will's name on one of the open doors. She strode past, but was unable to stop herself from casting a sideways glance into the room. *Empty.* She breathed a sigh of relief.

"I guess the workers aren't too happy about the factory closing down," she ventured.

"Mr. Beaumont is doing his best to find us other employment," Renée said loyally. "There are one or two agitators in the group, but most understand the situation." She opened a door and stood back to let Maeve go first. "Right through here."

Maeve entered a vast high-ceilinged room filled with rows of wide workbenches. Skylights flooded the room with natural illumination, supplementing banks of incandescent lights and high-intensity lamps at individual work stations. She followed Renée down the long side of the room, gazing around curiously as she went. The technicians in their coveralls and white paper hairnets were perched on stools, assembling various electronic devices. A conveyor belt ran along the outside of the bench, carrying the partially assembled components to the next station. Between the rows of benches, a woman pushing a trolley delivered parts to the appropriate workstations. Maeve slowed as she went past a young technician soldering capacitors onto a circuit board under a magnifying lamp. He winked at her behind his safety glasses.

She smiled and moved on. Seeing Will's factory and all he'd created with his vision, energy and sheer hard work, she realized he, too, must feel the loss on a personal level.

"Good—Art is at his desk," Renée informed her, as they approached a cubicle in the middle of the room.

A small crowd of technicians stood around the desk. Maeve could just see the top of Art's head. Then a gap appeared in the group and her pace slowed abruptly. Will was there, too.

"It's okay," Renée assured her. "He won't mind."

Maybe not, but *she* did. She forced herself to continue.

Will was handing out cardboard boxes from a stack beside the desk, while Art ticked off names on a list. From the smiles on most of the workers' faces, whatever was in the boxes was good.

"What's going on?" Maeve asked Renée.

"Mr. Beaumont is giving one of his security alarms to everyone at the factory as a parting bonus," Renée said almost reverently. "Even the janitorial staff will get one."

Two of the technicians, however, exchanged their smiles for scowls as soon as they turned away from Will and Art. They brushed past Maeve, and one of them knocked her arm without noticing or apologizing.

"Thinks he can palm us off with a bloody alarm," the taller one with a bushy mustache grumbled.

"We're working overtime so he can give away the product and look like a good guy," the short round one growled.

Maeve glanced at Renée who confided in a low voice, "McLeod and Kitrick. They've only been here three months, but they've been rabble-rousers from the start. I think Will would have let them go when their probationary period was up, but now he needs all the help he can get. Trouble is, they know it.''

''What can he do about them?''

''Nothing. But don't worry. They're in the minority.''

Maeve had the evidence before her eyes. When the whistle blew for tea break, the workers surrounding Will seemed content to stay and finish their chat rather than rush off. He may or may not have planned all along to give his employees an alarm each, but at least he'd kept his promise.

Which meant he would also keep his promise to personally install Art's alarm. She was trying to be good—why did temptation have to leap into her path?

''Go ahead if you want, Renée,'' she said, after thanking the other woman for bringing her this far. ''I'll be all right now.''

Renée departed, and Maeve hung back, waiting until the group around Art's desk drifted away, leaving only Art and Will.

''Hello,'' she said to Will, attempting a polite smile.

He nodded coolly. ''What brings you to the factory?''

''I've an important message for Art. About a job interview.''

Oh, did she enjoy seeing Will's eyebrows rise! Then she frowned; after the initial surprise, she could swear his expression had changed to one of satisfaction. Okay, so he was a nice guy. Big deal. Art didn't need him. She didn't need him. So long, buster.

''Are you sure?'' Art said, puzzled. ''I never applied for any jobs.''

''What?'' Maeve said, equally bewildered. ''Then how did they get your name?''

Art turned to Will, a questioning look on his face.

Will shrugged. ''I called in a favor.'' He clapped a hand on Art's shoulder. ''Best of luck, mate.'' With a conspiratorial wink for Maeve, he walked away.

Maeve stared after him. She could cheerfully have put a bullet through his twenty-four-karat heart.

CHAPTER EIGHT

ON MONDAY NIGHT Ida sipped a glass of club soda at her desk. She glanced at the stack of files she still had to get through, and sighed. Maybe she should just work at home. Sally had left an hour ago, and outside on Mornington High Street, the street lamps were winking on.

As she was shoving files into her briefcase, the phone rang. Who would be calling here at this time of night? She shrugged and let the answering machine pick up. While the message played, she crammed her swollen feet into her high heels, wincing at the pain in her small toes. She paused at the door. She might as well listen while the caller identified himself or herself, so she would know what she'd be dealing with in the morning.

"Ida?" a familiar voice said. "It's me, Rick."

Ida froze. Her heart did a somersault, and her briefcase fell from her hand and thudded on the floor.

"Ida, are you there? I tried your house, but no one answered."

A long crackling pause followed. Ida lunged for

the phone, terrified he was going to hang up. She stopped abruptly when he spoke again.

"I'll be leaving L.A. in a few minutes on a flight for Melbourne," Rick went on.

Oh my God! Her heart leaped. He was coming back!

"I get into town on Tuesday. Will you have lunch with me? If you can swing it, meet me on the Swanston Street Bridge at noon."

Ida bit her lip. The bridge was their spot, where he'd first kissed her. Her hand hovered indecisively over the receiver.

She heard Rick sigh. "I guess I'll see you when I do," he said.

The phone went dead.

Ida collapsed into the chair behind her desk, tears of joy and terror spilling down her cheeks.

Her engagement party was coming up, then the wedding. How was she going to explain to Rick that she was getting married? How was she going to explain the baby?

"I'VE PUT THE CONTROL PANEL for the security alarm here in the hall closet," Will said, brusque and matter-of-fact. "Should anyone attempt to break in, the infrared motion sensors attached to the windows and points of ingress-egress will relay a signal back to the control panel and set off the alarm."

Maeve tried to focus not on Will but on his instructions, as he pointed out the various control buttons. Perversely, his aloof, businesslike manner only increased her awareness. That his short-sleeved shirt and surfer-style shorts exposed enough of his tanned muscular body to be thoroughly distracting didn't help. She'd retreated to the backyard to repot some plants while he installed the alarm, but now she was forced into proximity while he taught her how to operate the device. She only hoped she would remember enough to be able to pass on the information to Art when he came home.

"Sorry, what was that again? That button there?" she said.

His gaze swiveled to hers, and the bottom seemed to drop out of her stomach. She realized this was the first time he'd looked directly at her since he'd arrived. If he was the honorable man she believed him to be, being around a woman he felt attracted to couldn't be easy for him, either. Which made it all the more generous of him to personally install the alarm. Which made her like him all the more. Which made the fact that he wasn't available even worse....

"Did you get it that time?" he asked. His gaze was a disconcerting combination of regret and camaraderie, rendered more confusing by his small smile.

Feeling her cheeks burn, she turned away. "Sorry, I'm not really with it today."

"I don't want to leave you unprotected. I mean, I want to know the alarm's working before I leave," he quickly amended. "You need to program it to accept your password."

"I'll read the instruction manual."

"Maeve." His low voice melted her bones. "We can do this."

Slowly, she turned back to him, unable to resist.

"Your password should be something Art will recall easily, too," he said in a more normal voice, not quite reverting to his former businesslike tone. "Can you think of a four-letter word common to you and your father?" He paused, then added with a grin, "And it better not be a word for what you'd both like me to do."

"That would be easy to remember, you must admit," she said with a laugh. "Let me see... Oh, I know." She pressed out the letters K-A-T-H. "It's short for Kathleen, my mother's name."

Will flipped down the cover on the control panel. "You can always call me if you can't figure something out."

He would have moved away, except that she touched his arm. "I...I wasn't very gracious when you offered me the alarm, but I want you to know I appreciate it."

"No worries." He gathered his tools and moved toward the door.

"Would you like a cup of coffee, or a beer?" she asked.

"I'd better not." On the doorstep, he leaned against the jamb and studied his sandals. "I saw the cubby you made," he said at last, his voice husky. For one moment their eyes met. He laid a fist on his chest above his heart. "It touched me—here."

Her heart filled with joy. A joy she was careful not to reveal. "Just doing my job."

She stood on her veranda twined with climbing roses, and waved him goodbye. They'd been good. With neither touch nor word had they betrayed Ida. And while the glances they had exchanged might be construed as revealing desire, they had not acted.

Maeve went about her day feeling a special glow within. It was only later, as she lay in bed and recalled the time they had spent together, minute by minute, that she realized the glow stemmed not from any virtue of hers, but from the deepening bond she felt with Will.

MAEVE HAD ANOTHER rush job on her books, so she didn't get back to Will's until the following week. She arrived about noon, bearing armloads of cut flowers from her garden. A simple "Thank you" for the security alarm hadn't seemed sufficient, and, anyway, his house could use brightening up.

She punched in the code he'd given her to deactivate the alarm, and put the key in the slot. She would only be in the house a few minutes, just long enough to fill vases with water and arrange the flowers.

Once inside the light and colorful kitchen, she felt immediately at home. The walls were a warm yellow. The terra-cotta pots lining the window and the Mediterranean-blue tiles behind the sink and stove provided soothing accents.

Laying her flowers on the bench top, she stood in

front of the cupboards. Now, if she were Will, where would she store the vases? Then she realized that if she were Will she wouldn't own vases. But she would save empty glass jars, and the most likely spot for those would be…

She opened the cupboard under the sink. *Bingo.* There was even an old glass jug big enough to hold the spray of purple irises and yellow dahlias. These she placed on the round glass table in the breakfast nook, then stood back to admire the effect. Subconsciously, she'd chosen the perfect colors to complement his kitchen.

She moved through the ground floor, depositing white and apricot roses on the polished mahogany dining room table, a multicolored bouquet of anemones and oriental poppies in the living room and a cluster of sweetly scented white and yellow freesias in the bathroom.

Perfect. She smiled as she strolled back to the kitchen, imagining Will's face when he saw her gift—

Silhouetted against the brightly lit glass doors stood a slender figure in a skirt.

Ida.

Ida stepped into the room, staring first at the flowers, then at Maeve.

"Hi," Maeve said. "I was just…" She pulled at her braid. "Will gave me a key…so I could use the bathroom. I had all these extra flowers…" Her voice trailed off. No matter what she said, this could not look good from Ida's viewpoint.

To Maeve's surprise, a glowing smile spread across Ida's face. "They're beautiful! How thoughtful of you." She peeked into the dining room. "Roses, too! Fresh flowers are exactly what this place needs. Will is going to love them. Thank you so much."

Maeve's breath went out with a whoosh of relief. Of course, Ida wouldn't be suspicious or feel insecure. She was sure of Will's love; she was having his baby. The knowledge burned inside Maeve like a drop of acid. The pain was all the greater because she really liked Ida.

"Will's not here," she said.

"That's okay. I was going to call you later, but since you're here, I'll ask you now." Ida hesitated, then said, all in a burst, as though forcing difficult words. "Would you do the flowers for the wedding?"

She sounded unsure about what she was asking. Because it was Maeve she was asking? "Uh, well, I'm not too good at bouquets."

"Sorry. I didn't explain myself. Since we're having the wedding in the garden, I thought an aisle lined with big pots of flowers would be nice." She took the kettle from the bench top and filled it at the sink. "Coffee?"

"Uh, sure," Maeve said bleakly, thinking, *In another month I could sail away from here.*

Ida moved around Will's kitchen easily and naturally, retrieving cups from one cupboard and coffee from another. Maeve forced herself to picture Ida

performing the same task in a year's time, but with
a baby on her hip. The exercise backfired, catapult-
ing Maeve into painful memories. Memories of
Kristy, her chubby legs straddling Maeve's waist
while her tiny hand clutched a sleeve, bright eyes
taking in every detail of her surroundings. *Oh, my
sweet baby.*

"I also want to ask you to our engagement
party," Ida added a little stiffly. "It's a week Saturday. Just an informal barbecue here at Will's
place. I hope you can come."

"Uh…" Ida had sprung the invitation on her; she
couldn't think of an excuse fast enough. "Thanks,"
she said weakly. "I'd love to. That is, if Will doesn't
mind."

"Gosh, no. But for some reason he thought I
should ask you." She shrugged. "Men. Go figure."

Maeve quelled the sudden leaping of her heart.
The occasion was Will's engagement party, not a
date. "What are you wearing for your wedding?"
Maeve asked.

"Something loose," Ida said with a grin. "My
clothes are already getting tight."

"I can't tell," Maeve said truthfully. "How do
you feel?"

"Like a million bucks," Ida said, but her smile
flickered and her focus suddenly seemed far away.
Quickly, she turned to the fridge. "Do you take milk
and sugar?"

"Just milk, thanks." Was something wrong with

the baby? With Will? Dared she ask? "Is everything okay?"

"Yes," Ida assured her. She smiled, though to Maeve the smile looked forced. "In fact, I've just had some pleasant news. A friend of mine from San Diego called to say he'd be in town next week." She hesitated, looking as though she wanted to say more, then didn't.

"That's great." So why did Ida's expression suggest otherwise? Maeve watched the woman pour boiling water over the instant coffee and stir. "Are you nervous about having the baby?"

Ida handed over a cup of coffee. "You mean the birth? Not especially. Will and I are attending prenatal classes."

"But what about—" Afterward. Maeve bit her tongue. Just because her child had died at eleven months didn't mean Ida's would perish young. She couldn't spoil Ida's joy and anticipation with her grief. "Is Will excited about the wedding?"

Ida rolled her eyes. "Hardly. Will's crazy about the baby, but he's not exactly the romantic type."

"I guess he's preoccupied with his business at the moment."

"Hmmm, maybe," Ida said skeptically. "I mean, yes, he is, but that's not the reason. Anyway, all that hearts-and-flowers stuff doesn't matter. Will is such a great guy, I can live without romance." Although she smiled, her wistful tone suggested regret.

"Maybe he just needs a gentle reminder of how

much you would appreciate thoughtful gestures, like bringing you flowers or taking you someplace special.''

Ida's hazel eyes filled with a sorrow Maeve didn't understand. ''He's taking me to the footy game for my birthday in a couple of weeks.''

''Are you one of those rabid fans who wear team colors to the games and hang team scarves from the windows of your house during the Grand Final?''

''No.'' Ida laughed. ''I'm not even sure who's playing.''

''Well, all I know is, this Saturday it's the Bombers versus the Magpies. My father talks about practically nothing else.''

''Maybe on my birthday we should send Will to the footy with your dad, while you and I go out for a night on the town,'' Ida proposed.

''Sounds good to me, but you and Will really ought to make it a romantic occasion,'' Maeve insisted.

Ida's tight smile didn't reach her eyes. She drained her cup and rinsed it under the tap.

''I'd better get going,'' she said.

Maeve went out with her and locked the door. A bride-to-be deserved a little romance, she thought, as Ida drove off. Maeve couldn't prevent her attraction to Will, but maybe she could atone for it by doing her damnedest to see Ida got what she deserved. No matter how much Maeve herself would feel hurt.

"I HAVE GOOD NEWS and bad news," Art announced, when she arrived home that night. Clad in the frilly pink apron, he had a glass of beer in one hand and a chef's knife in the other. "Which do you want first?"

She took in his broad grin and the pair of sirloin steaks resting on the open butcher's paper on the bench top. "Looks like we're celebrating. Give me the good news."

"You know that job interview I had at A. B. Electronics last week?"

Maeve went to the fridge for a mineral water. "Yes?"

"They called today and offered me the job of foreman."

"Dad, that's fantastic! Congratulations." She put down her bottle of water and threw her arms around his neck. "Your worries are over."

His grin faded. "Don't forget the bad news."

"How bad can it be?" she asked, picking at the sliced carrots on the chopping board. "Will could close down ten factories without affecting you now." Will would still be affected, though, she thought unhappily. Then Maeve reminded herself she had no right to care about Will. That was Ida's job.

"They want me to start right away. One week from now at the latest."

"So?" she said, wanting to sound tougher than she felt.

Art sat at the table and cradled the tall glass between his hands. "I can't leave Will in the lurch.

He's got orders to fill. For the foreman to quit right now would be bad for morale.''

Maeve sat opposite him. "I understand how you feel, but you've got to look out for yourself. Will wouldn't operate the factory at a loss just to provide jobs for his employees, no matter how badly he feels about letting them go. Don't you be blinded by loyalty and work yourself into a state of unemployment.''

Art rubbed his thumbs over his glass. "I don't know…''

Maeve let out an exasperated sigh. "Will wouldn't have recommended you for the interview if he hadn't taken into account that you might get the job and leave.''

"True, but—''

"He wants you to have something to go to when Aussie Electronics shuts its doors. He wants you to do well.'' By God, she truly believed that.

"Maybe you're right,'' Art said doubtfully. "I'll have to think on it.''

"Don't think,'' she ordered. "Call up right now and say you'll accept. Will is a fair man. He'll understand.''

"Can't,'' Art said flatly. "It's after 6:00 p.m. They're shut.''

Maeve shook her head at her father. "In that case, fire up the barbie. Let's grill those steaks.''

ON SATURDAY MORNING the surf was flat, so Will set to work on Maeve's solar panel. He wondered if she would show up to garden, and found himself listening for the sound of her ute. Mid-morning, he heard the drone of the utility truck as it came up the drive.

He'd planned to wait until she unloaded her tools and plants before greeting her but found himself hovering eagerly in the doorway of the bungalow. When she appeared around the side of the house, wheeling a barrow full of gardening tools, he blinked. Instead of her usual cargo pants, she wore khaki cargo shorts, revealing long legs, shapely with muscle. Today her crop top was dark purple, and the smooth full curves of her breasts accentuated the taut midriff below.

"Come and see your solar panel," Will called.

Her face lit instantly. Then, just as quickly, her expression turned guarded. By the time she'd walked over, her mouth had curled down at the corners and her finely shaped brows had settled into a small but definite frown. Will was immediately determined to make the frown disappear.

"I heard your TV was found in the Salvation Army drop-off bin," he said. In fact, Art had told him the police had located the TV and sound system in a pawn shop in Frankston, up the highway toward Melbourne.

"Ha-ha, very funny." Her lips lifted ever so slightly.

Will leaned on the doorjamb. "They say the reception is so bad even the needy don't want it."

"Who says?" she challenged him. But the line

disappeared from between her eyebrows, and the corners of her mouth curved up to their normal resting position.

He wouldn't be satisfied with anything less than a full-blown smile. "Apparently, the next time burglars come to your house they're going to bring you a brand-new television set."

"Stop it." Her lips curled merrily and a sparkle gleamed in her dark eyes as she pretended to hit him.

"That's the face I want to see," he said, dodging her blow.

He led the way to the workbench. "This new regulator—" he pointed out the black box attached to the solar panel "—combined with a bigger battery—" he indicated the one he'd taken from Stores at the factory "—should result in a threefold increase in both the charge rate and the storage capacity. It's not finished yet, but at least I've figured out what has to be done."

"Will, you're a genius." Her face shone. "How can I ever thank you?"

"No need. I enjoyed working on it." Her excitement and delight were sufficient recompense. "But that's not all."

"What else could there possibly be?"

"The extra energy from the boosted solar panel can easily run more than one experimental system. You can heat the water to the lowest test temperature, then run feeder lines from the main water heater equipped with P.I.D.'s—potential integrated derivatives—and heat sensors to raise the temperature of the outflowing water. You can run three different test temperatures at a time.''

Maeve didn't speak.

''If that's not enough, I can increase the number of sensors,'' he added. She hadn't asked for this embellishment, but when she'd described her project design, a thermoregulater had seemed an obvious requirement.

''It's perfect. Exactly what I needed.'' Her gaze remained fixed on the solar regulator.

''What's wrong?'' Cautiously, he guided her chin toward him. Her dark eyes were luminous with unspoken gratitude. And something else? He dropped his hand, curling his fingers into his palm. He should not be touching her.

''Nothing's wrong. Thank you.'' Abruptly, she turned to go.

Will followed, hands thrust in his shorts pockets. He'd never experienced this degree of infatuation. Perhaps this growing desire, this craving, to see her, to touch her, to make her laugh, came purely from not being able to have her. Yes, that was it: forbidden fruit tasted sweetest.

Maeve paused in the doorway. ''I hear Ida's birthday is coming up.''

''That's right,'' he said. ''We're going to the footy game. The Magpies are playing Essendon.''

''Footy? Is that your idea of a romantic night out?'' Her voice held an accusing edge. ''You've gone to so much trouble over a solar panel. Surely you can dream up a more elaborate celebration for your fiancée's birthday.''

''I reckon I know what she likes better than you,'' he said shortly, frustrated by the tension between Maeve and him.

''I reckon you don't.'' Maeve stalked to her wheelbarrow. ''She's a woman, for goodness' sake. Even if she does like footy, it's not what she wants to do on her birthday.''

''Well, what would you suggest?'' he demanded.

''Candlelight, flowers, dinner out. Or better yet, make her dinner yourself. You can cook, can't you?''

''I haven't starved in fifteen years of living on my own,'' he snapped. ''Sure, I could do all that, but Ida and I… Well, we…'' His voice seemed to lose power under Maeve's scrutiny. There was nothing he could say that she would want to hear.

She shook her head. Then she bent her knees and gripped the handles of her loaded wheelbarrow. ''Thanks for what you did on the solar panel,'' she said. ''I'd better get to work.''

Maeve trudged across the lawn to the terrace, dumped her load of tools, then went back to the ute for the flats of seedlings. She spent the morning filling the hollows of the rock wall with frothy white alyssum and trailing blue lobelia—white surf and cascading blue water. The alyssum and lobelia would form part of the perimeter of the moonlight garden. She would have liked to work even farther from the bungalow—and Will—but she had dozens of plants to put in the ground.

Kneeling on a foam pad, she dug the trowel into the loamy soil. He was fighting his attraction to her, just as she was fighting hers. She didn't know what to think about that. If his feelings for her were real, that meant he'd made the wrong choice regarding Ida. But he would never leave Ida, not when they were going to have a baby. Nor would Maeve forgive herself if she took him away from Ida.

And yet, what if she never met another man who made her feel the way Will did? As though every morning were the first day of spring. As though laughter waited behind every flowering bush. As though a love like she'd never experienced before was only a kiss away.

The sound of a woman's voice made her glance up.

Ida waved at Maeve from the deck. "Join us for a cold drink?"

Maeve lifted a hand in greeting and forced a smile. "Thanks, but I've got to plant these before the sun gets too hot."

"Later, then."

Maeve nodded noncommittally and went back to her work. How could she look Ida in the face after what she'd been thinking about Will? And not just today. Lately, fantasizing about Will had become her method of coping with her feelings. The trouble with fantasies was, afterward she felt emptier than ever.

Ida's and Will's voices carried across the short distance from the deck. Maeve tried not to listen, but she couldn't help overhearing their conversation. They were talking about the baby—trying out names; engaging in laughing disputes over schools; speculating about the ways in which their lives would change, how they would conduct themselves as a family. Maeve fought not to hear the quiet joy in Will's voice when he spoke of his son or daughter, but his tone rang out more clearly than words. He loved children. He couldn't wait for this baby.

A teardrop fell on her wrist. With numb detachment she observed particles of dirt floating in the tiny pool. Whatever she and Will might feel for each other, it would never be enough for him.

CHAPTER NINE

ON TUESDAY, Maeve parked on St. Kilda Boulevard and set out for the fifteen-minute walk into the center of Melbourne to meet Graham for lunch. Huge old plane trees shaded the street and the sidewalks with their broad, leafy limbs. A green-and-gold tram rumbled by. She could have hopped aboard, but walking relaxed her. Part of her looked forward to seeing Graham; their marriage hadn't been all bad. Part of her dreaded the encounter; one way or another, he was bound to try to pressure her into what he wanted.

Just past the art gallery she left the shade behind. Street vendors plied their crafts, but she ignored them and pushed on, past the tall spire of the Arts Centre toward the Swanston Street Bridge, which would take her across the Yarra River and into the heart of the city. On the bridge, tourists jostled for camera space.

Ouch. Her high heels were pinching her toes. How on earth did some women wear shoes like this every day? She stopped in one of the alcoves along the bridge and leaned against the stone wall to slip off her shoe and wriggle her cramped toes.

She was just cramming her foot back into the shoe, when she glanced across the bridge—and blinked in surprise. Through the stream of traffic, she could see Ida striding briskly toward the city center.

"Ida!" she called. Ida didn't hear. Maeve was about to call again, then stopped when she saw Ida smile and lift a hand in greeting to someone coming toward her.

The man was shorter than Will, with reddish-blond hair, a square jaw and an even white smile. Ida hesitated a few feet away. Then the man opened his arms and Ida fell into his embrace. Maybe he was her brother, Maeve told herself unconvincingly. Or a long-lost cousin. No, she thought a second later. No one kissed a relative like that.

Maeve dropped back into the stone alcove, stunned. Was this the secret she'd sensed Ida was hiding? A lover? Ida was the mother of Will's child. How dared she have an affair with another man? In broad daylight! Maeve looked again, but Ida and the man had disappeared into the throng heading into the city.

Maeve glanced at her watch. Gosh, she was late. She slung her purse over her shoulder and hurried across the bridge, her mind whirling with what she'd just witnessed. Maybe Ida had a perfectly innocent explanation for her behavior, although Maeve's gut feeling was that the situation was exactly what it seemed.

When she got to the Grand Hyatt, Graham was

lounging in a deep leather chair in the lobby, watching a crew of Singapore Airline flight attendants check in. He looked the same, or almost. His waist had thickened slightly, and his blond hair was a little thinner on top and longer on the sides, but his tan was as deep and his clothes as casually elegant as ever. In his polo shirt, chinos and sockless Topsiders, he appeared ready to cast off, not to dine at one of the best hotels in Melbourne.

Yet as usual, he didn't look underdressed—but she felt overdressed. Like a secretary sprucing up for a date with the boss.

"Well, Graham, I see you've come arrayed in your usual sartorial splendor." Her silk blouse was stuck to her skin and her toes were still hurting.

"And you're your usual sarcastic self. Nice to see you, Maeve." He rose slowly, taking his time about unbending, and gave her a kiss on the cheek. Then he glanced at his watch.

"Sorry I'm late," she said tightly. Resentment slipped over her shoulders, as familiar as an old sweater. When she was with Graham she seemed to be forever apologizing. "Look, maybe this isn't such a good idea."

Graham lost the languid attitude instantly and reached for her hand. With his most charming smile, he implored, "Stay, please. It's great to see you."

"Oh, all right. I'm starving, anyway." She managed a genuine smile. "If we're busy putting food in our mouths, we can surely refrain from biting each other's heads off."

Graham slid his arm around her waist. "I'm betting we can be nice longer than that."

"So when are you sailing to Fiji?" Maeve asked a short time later as they circled the appetizer table. She added a slice of smoked salmon to her selection of fresh herbed goat's cheese and roasted mushrooms.

"When can you get away?" Graham countered, loading up his plate indiscriminately.

"I haven't said I'd come," she demurred. "I've got a big job on."

"Which is why I'm asking when is convenient for you," he replied evenly.

Back at their table, Maeve sipped her chardonnay. "Are you still working locum?" She'd never understood why a talented doctor would content himself with temporary work, but that had been Graham's way for as long as she'd known him.

He nodded. "Got a cushy gig over on Chapel Street at the moment. You should see the parade of gorgeous women who go through my consulting rooms with their Gucci shoes and three-hundred-dollar haircuts."

"How nice for you," she said with a cool smile. "Maybe you'll find yourself a rich wife to finance your trips."

"Hey, don't even think I would hook up with one of those society babes. If I ever divorced, the alimony payments would force me to work twelve months out of the year." His gaze softened. "Did I tell you how great you look?"

Maeve put down her fork. "Why did you really ask me here today, Graham?"

He rubbed his smooth-shaven jaw, setting free the scent of his aftershave, and his mouth below his handlebar mustache settled into what she thought of as his "serious" expression. "I want us to try again."

She found herself thinking not of his suggestion but of how cool his eyes were compared with Will's, even though both men's irises were blue.

"Well?" he said.

"We've done a good job parting amicably," she said. "Let's quit while we're ahead."

"I mean it, Maeve. I'm willing to settle down now. I want to do that with you."

"Settle down? A minute ago you were talking about taking off to Fiji." She pushed away her empty plate. A waiter in white shirt and black pants glided forward and removed it.

"For a brief trip. Kind of like a second honeymoon. Then when we get back, we do the playing-house thing." He smiled, boyishly eager and charming. "Neither of us is getting any younger, Maeve. What do you say? Give it another go?"

"Graham! I haven't seen you in years. You can't just lob in here and ask me to marry you. Again." She leveled her eyes at him. "At least, I presume you're asking me to marry you."

"Absolutely. Yes, I am. Without a doubt."

He dropped his eyes under her skeptical gaze. When he looked up again, his face seemed older, and vulnerable in a way she'd never seen it before.

"I miss you, babe."

Maeve knew every phony countenance in his repertoire, but she'd never seen anything quite like the expression now on his face. This was sincerity, she realized with a shock. "Oh, Graham."

"We could have another baby," he said softly. "You were such a great mother—"

"Stop!" She absolutely did not want to break down in the middle of the restaurant.

"Sorry." His hand closed over hers.

She dragged in a deep breath. "You say you want to settle down, but where? You can't raise babies on a sailboat, and you'd hate my cottage in Mount Eliza."

"I bought a place in Brighton. I've joined the ranks of rate payers and home owners."

"You bought a house?" she asked dubiously.

"Well, more like a condo. But it's right on the beach. You'll love it."

"There's room for my greenhouse on the balcony, is there? Are you sure your fancy neighbors wouldn't mind my mulcher parked out front?"

"There you go with the sarcasm again," Graham complained. "Look, Maeve, fighting me isn't going to bring Kristy back." He held her hand firmly when she would have tugged it away. "I've dated lots of women since we broke up, but no one special. At least, we had fun together. Didn't we?"

For one fatalistic moment she contemplated saying "Yes," right then and there. They'd both grown up some. He had been a good father, if a little erratic. And she was never going to have the man she really wanted. But... "Kristy's death was only the catalyst for our breakup. I have a different life now."

"Have you got a boyfriend?"

"No," she said slowly. "But I've got roots and they're growing deeper all the time. You're still floating around, literally as well as figuratively. Sure, you've bought a place to live, but it's a condo, not a family home. Something you can easily rent out when you get the urge to take off on your sailboat again."

Graham put his hand over his heart. "If you want a house, I'll buy you one. I've changed, Maeve. I really have."

"I don't know..." Reuniting would be so easy in some ways. Especially if he was willing to work at their marriage now, instead of hoisting sail every time they had a fight.

A hopeful smile curved his lips. "You don't have to say yes or no today. Just promise me you'll think about it."

She gave him back a half smile. "Okay."

MAEVE PLACED the last of the gardenia bushes in the garden bed bordering the pool and shoveled earth around the root ball. Tight greeny-white buds interspersed the shiny leaves. With luck and continuing warm weather, they should still be blooming for Will and Ida's wedding.

Thinking of Ida, Maeve tamped the dirt around

the base of the plant with her boot a little harder than necessary. She'd really liked Ida, difficult as that was considering her feelings toward Will. When she thought of how bad Will would feel if he knew about Ida's lover, Maeve's heart ached for him.

She tossed the shovel aside and slit open a bag of fertilizer, then sprinkled granules around the base of the gardenia bushes. Should she tell him? If *she* was engaged and someone saw *her* fiancé passionately kissing another woman on the Swanston Street Bridge, she would want to know. Or should female loyalty make her hold her tongue? After all, Will might not thank her for enlightening him. Might hate her, in fact, not only as the bearer of bad news but for witnessing his humiliation. Yet if telling meant saving him from worse hurt farther down the track, wasn't that worth the risk? Once his garden was finished, she wouldn't see Will or Ida again, anyway.

"So this is going to be the moonlight garden." Will's mellow voice sounded behind her. "It looks good by day."

Maeve straightened with a start. "I didn't notice you walk up."

"You did seem awfully absorbed. What do you think about when you're gardening?" he asked, hands in the pockets of his shorts.

"Oh, this and that." He looked...happy. "Having a good day?"

"Getting that way." His gaze lingered on her face a moment before moving around the pool to the freshly weeded rockery on the other side. "What are you going to put in there?"

"One of the most beautiful and amazing plants in the world," she told him enthusiastically, her troubled thoughts forgotten for the moment. "*Selenicereus grandiflorus,* the Queen of the Night, named for the moon goddess. It flowers one night a year during a full moon, when it gives off intense bursts of vanilla-like perfume. The flowers are a foot across, with petals of purest white surrounded by spikes of bright gold."

"Sounds like a rare plant." He grinned teasingly. "What aspect of my personality are you expressing with it?"

Maeve realized with a jolt that the *Selenicereus* wasn't so much an expression of Will's inner self as it was of hers. Avoiding his question, she said, "My friend Rose knows someone who grows them. The full moon is toward the end of the month. With luck, the one I plant could flower around the time of your wedding."

Mentioning his wedding made Maeve's throat close up. Will, too, became oddly quiet.

At last he glanced at his watch. "I'd better get going. I'm off to mow my mother's lawn."

"I'm finished here for the day. I'll leave, as well." She began to pile her tools into her wheelbarrow, reluctant, suddenly, to part from him.

"Let me help," Will said, reaching for the bag of fertilizer just as she did.

Their hands touched. Separated. And met again. Their eyes held, inches apart.

"Thanks," Maeve muttered, and snatched her fingers away. She bent for her trowel, cheeks burning.

Without a word, Will picked up the wheelbarrow and trundled it across the lawn toward her ute. Maeve followed more slowly, feeling the heat gradually fade from her cheeks.

By the time she reached the vehicles, Will was loading her barrow into the back of the ute. "You don't have to do that—" she began, then broke off as she noticed the ancient, rusted lawn mower in the back of his open trunk. "Does that piece of scrap metal even work?"

He gave her a wry grin. "Now you see why I hired a gardener for my place. I've tried to convince my mother to do the same but..." He shrugged. "It makes her feel good that I do it."

Maeve stripped off her gloves and tossed them into the wheelbarrow. "Where does your mother live?"

"Mornington."

"I'd like to meet her." His eyebrows raised. "Research," she explained, smiling. "I can't pass up an opportunity to pump your mother for information about your childhood." She pulled her car keys out of her pants pocket. "I'll mow her lawn for you," she added when he eyed her dubiously.

"I haven't been there for a while," he said. "The grass will be a mile high."

"All the more reason to use my superior equipment.'' She climbed into her truck and started the motor. ''Come on, Beaumont. What are you waiting for?''

''SHE'S VERY STRONG,'' Phyllis, coffee in one hand, cigarette in the other, observed from her front steps.

Will, about to restart Maeve's electric trimmer, pushed up his safety glasses and followed Phyllis's gaze to the far side of the yard, where Maeve was mowing through ankle-high grass as though she were vacuuming a carpet. ''She's an Amazon.''

Phyllis cast him a shrewd glance. ''Ida seen her yet?''

Will wasn't sure he liked his mother's tone. ''Ida's met her, yes. She and Maeve get on quite well. What's your point?''

''Nothing. Just...'' Phyllis gestured to Maeve with her cigarette. ''If I were Ida, I wouldn't want my fiancé gazing at the gardener as if he didn't know whether he wanted to worship her or jump her bones.''

''I do not want to jump her bones.'' He jammed the safety glasses down on his face. ''Or worship her.''

Phyllis squinted over a plume of smoke. ''You might be able to fool yourself, but you can't fool your mother.''

He stalked away to the sound of her wheezy laugh.

''Will,'' she said sharply. He stopped and turned.

Her face was dead serious. "Remember your promise."

"I remember." How could he forget?

He should never have let Maeve come here. He felt that even more keenly when he'd finished edging the lawn and returned to the house to find her and his mother side by side on the sofa, poring over an old photo album. With Maeve bent close to Phyllis, they looked for all the world like mother and daughter-in-law. Engrossed, they didn't notice him standing in the doorway.

"There's young Will and his father coming back from surfing," Phyllis said. "Well, Will surfed. His father just drove him to the beach and waited. Lord knows what would have happened if Will Sr. had had to swim out to rescue him. Never could keep that kid out of the water. When he wasn't up a tree, that is." She turned a page. "There's Will with his youngest brother and second sister. And there's the whole boiling of 'em."

"Four small children," Maeve said. "How did you manage on your own?"

"Wasn't easy. 'Course, half the time I felt like I had five kids. Ida was always around. She and Will were inseparable."

"And now they're getting married."

Did Will only imagine the strain in Maeve's voice? Or Phyllis's penetrating look? Phyllis opened her mouth to speak.

Will felt a rush of adrenaline. Part of him wanted Maeve to know the truth; part of him was terrified.

He started forward. "Mother," he said, a warning in his voice.

Maeve glanced over at him. He got the oddest feeling that she'd known he was there all along. For one fleeting moment her gaze held an ineffable sadness. Then she put on her teasing smile. "You were a scruffy little chap."

"I was adorable," he replied, grinning immodestly.

"You were a scamp," Phyllis said. "I'll get you a cup of tea." She shuffled off to the kitchen.

"Sorry yet that you asked?" he said to Maeve. He perched on the opposite arm of the couch from her.

"Not at all." She smiled warmly. "Your mother's nice. We've been having a very interesting conversation."

"Is that so." He slid off the arm and onto the sofa, keeping a good three feet between Maeve and him.

"You told me of the age gap between your parents, but looking at the photos made me realize your father was—" She broke off, embarrassed.

"Old?" The hollow ache his father's memory always engendered expanded inside Will's chest. "In many ways he was more like a grandfather than a father. Except that he didn't have the time to spend with us kids that a grandfather might." Will flipped through the pages of the album. "We had good times, though, my brothers and sister and I, as kids. We had one another."

"I suppose coming from a big family, you want a lot of children yourself." Her voice was enquiring, yet neutral.

"That's the plan." He paused. "What about you? Do you want children?"

"Me? Nah." She spoke flippantly, but the flash of pain in her eyes made him wonder if she really felt was as casual as she sounded.

"You'll regret not having them if you don't," Phyllis said, coming into the room with a third cup and a fresh pot of tea.

She settled the tea tray on the low table and poured a cup for Will, oblivious to Maeve's silence. "My favorite stage was babyhood," she rambled on. "Before they learn to answer back."

Will frowned at her and gave a tiny shake of his head, though he didn't know why Maeve was so bothered by talk of babies.

Phyllis, absorbed in pouring tea, paid no attention to his sign language. "Or maybe they're cutest when they first learn to walk. Tottering around like little drunken soldiers." She handed Maeve a cup of tea. "Maeve, darl', you're as white as a ghost!"

Will rose. "I think we've kept Maeve long enough."

"I'm fine." Maeve smiled tightly.

"Ida—now, she's the type who blooms with pregnancy." Phyllis hurried on, clearly trying to cover the awkwardness with more words. "Did you say you've met Ida?"

Maeve nodded and sipped her tea. "She's lovely."

Phyllis turned to Will. "How is Ida doing? Did the ultrasound check out all right?"

"Fine," Will said. "Ida's fine, too. Although she seems a little distracted lately—" He stopped when Maeve choked on her tea. "Are you okay?" He went to thump her on the back, but the blow turned into more of a caress. He glanced up to see his mother watching him over her glasses, and snatched his hand away.

"Ida will find motherhood quite a change from a busy law practice," Maeve said when she'd recovered.

"At least, Will's young enough to take an active role," Phyllis said. "And he'll be around to see them grow up." She shook her head sadly. "It's hard on a boy when his dad dies. It's a shock, like. Makes it difficult for them to put their trust in someone again, to love someone again."

Will put his cup down and got to his feet, uncomfortably aware of Maeve's sympathetic gaze. Ida as a topic was bad enough, without Phyllis's delving into his psyche with nothing to guide her but a mother's intuition. "I need to get going, even if Maeve doesn't."

"I'd better go, too," Maeve said, eyeing her watch. "Thank you so much for the tea, Mrs. Beaumont."

"Call me Phyllis. Thank you for mowing my lawn. Come by for a cuppa anytime."

"'Bye, Mother,'' Will said, kissing her on the cheek. ''I'll call you soon.''

He walked Maeve to her vehicle. ''You seemed upset when my mother started talking about your having kids.''

Her face closed, like a flower folding in its petals at sundown. ''It's…personal.''

''I see,'' he said, even though he saw only that she was in pain. He wished he could hold her, protect her. But all he could do was watch her slide into the driver's seat of the ute.

She pulled the door shut and fastened her seat belt. ''I have to work on another job for a couple of days,'' she said through the open window. ''I'll see you later in the week. At the engagement party, if not before. Your gate is done and the fencer will come by to install it.''

His hand rested on the window ledge. ''I should have your hydroponics regulator finished by then.'' Not much, but it was something.

Her eyes turned very bright. Impulsively, she reached up and squeezed his fingers. ''Thanks.''

Then, before he could say another word, she threw the ute in reverse and backed out of the driveway. As she drove away, Will lifted the hand she'd touched. And without thinking, brought it to his lips.

CHAPTER TEN

MAEVE ARRIVED LATE to Will and Ida's engagement party. She would rather not have arrived at all. She was finding it harder and harder to be around Will and not reveal her feelings for him. But she wanted to talk to Ida.

The driveway was jammed with vehicles, and people had started to park on the front lawn. Maeve parked her ute on the grass, tucked her engagement present under her arm and walked up to the house. She was pleased to note that the flowers she'd planted in the stone urns were a riot of pink, yellow, purple and white.

At the steps to the house she paused to check her apricot-colored dress for bits of grass and to smooth back her hair, which she'd tied loosely at her nape. All of a sudden, her pulse was racing and her palms felt damp—the unaccustomed nervousness due, no doubt, to the prospect of seeing Will in a social setting. Today she couldn't hide behind her plants, figuratively or literally.

The front door was open, but at the last moment Maeve walked around to the side of the house, through the kissing gate. She hoped Will liked the gate. Given his impending matrimony, it had seemed a good idea. Now she was so self-conscious about explaining its purpose that she had yet to mention it to him.

She scanned the gathering, seeking his blue eyes and sun-streaked hair. But he was nowhere to be seen. Nor was Ida. The gift Maeve had brought weighed her down, and she edged through the crowd on the patio to carry it inside.

"Maeve, is that you?" called a balding man with a muscular build, dressed in a skintight black T-shirt. "Ginger, look who's here."

"Hi, Alex. Ginger," Maeve said, relieved to see some familiar faces. "How's your garden faring in this heat?"

"Fabulously, thanks to your watering system." Ginger pushed her elaborately messy strawberry-blond hair out of her eyes. "I love what you're doing to Will's place."

"I'm not finished yet, but thanks. Do you know where Will and Ida are? I want to give them this—"

"In the house, I think, getting the food out," Alex said. "Try the crab dip. Ginger made it."

"Thanks, I will. Talk to you later."

She turned back toward the house—and suddenly found herself nose to chest with Will. The music and the laughter faded into background noise.

"Glad you could come," he said. "Can I take that for you?"

"It's for you and Ida." She was aware only of his eyes, warm and blue, smiling down at her.

"Thanks." He hefted it in his hands. "Heavy."

"It's a vase," she blurted out before she could stop herself. "Sorry, I shouldn't have told you."

"You have something against flowers in pickle jars?" He took her hand and led her through the crowd. "I'll put this on the dining room table and then introduce you around."

"Where's Ida?" Maeve was aware of the gently possessive pressure of his fingers wrapped around hers. This was a party, she told herself. Attitudes and behavior were naturally more relaxed. She shouldn't be so tense.

"Outside somewhere, I think." Will set the gift-wrapped vase on the table and whisked two glasses of champagne off a passing waitress's tray. "Thanks, Elysse," he said, with a wink for the pretty young girl carrying the tray.

"Good idea, having the party catered," Maeve remarked, more to make conversation than because she had an opinion on the subject.

"Ida and my mother prepared most of the food. The girl who brought us the champagne is my niece. She and her friends from technical college are serving. They not only get paid, but also get credits for their hospitality course."

Maeve sipped her champagne. "Good deal."

"Come on, let's go back outside. I should check the barbie."

They retraced their steps to the deck, their progress impeded by the milling guests, who all wanted a word with Will.

"...Congratulations, you old bastard."

"...Good to see you're finally tying the knot, Will."

"...Look forward to the wedding."

"Thanks. Thanks a lot." Will shook hands, hugged women, chatted and smiled and nodded.

Maeve followed silently in his wake. All these people were gathered for the express purpose of celebrating Will and Ida's engagement. They really were getting married. Maeve glanced around for the red-haired man she'd seen Ida kissing on the Swanston Street Bridge. Was he a mutual friend of theirs? Maybe even one of Will's mates? The thought made her stomach hurt.

She didn't see the man, but she did spot Ida, holding court in a circle of lawn chairs beside the pool. Her cheeks were flushed and she was laughing uproariously, as though she were on top of the world. A spasm of jealous anger arrowed through Maeve with a ferocity that left her breathless. How dared Ida treat Will so casually? Didn't she know how many women would love to have what she seemed to take for granted?

"Hello, Maeve."

She turned, and there was Phyllis, cigarette in one hand and champagne glass in the other. She wore a flowing turquoise muslin dress and heeled sandals.

Her blond hair was nicely waved. "Phyllis. Lovely to see you again."

"This is my daughter Julie, Will's little sister," she said, indicating a pretty dark-haired woman with a baby in her arms. "And her husband, Mike, and their children. Will's other sister is here, too, somewhere. His brother in Sydney couldn't get away from work—"

"Maeve isn't that interested in my family," Will cut in. Over both Maeve's and Phyllis's protests, he eased Maeve away.

"Just what don't you want me to find out about you?" she teased.

"What I saw behind the woodshed when I was three years old. Seriously," he added, "I just wanted to rescue you."

"I didn't need rescuing," she replied indignantly. "I like your mother."

"Hey, Will." A man with short black hair came up and slapped Will on the back, but his appreciative gray eyes rested on Maeve. "Who is this lovely lady? You've been holding out on me, mate."

"This is Maeve—"

"Ah, the Amazon who's landscaping your garden—"

"Maeve, this is Paul, my accountant," Will finished.

"Ah, the evil money man who's shutting down the factory," she said with a wry smile. Although she knew the sentiment was unworthy of her, a tiny part of her was pleased that Will should witness another man being attracted to her.

"Maeve's father is Art Hodgins, our foreman," Will explained.

Paul laid a hand over his heart with a disarming smile. "Forces beyond my control. Honest."

"Don't believe a word he says," Will said.

"Listen, Will," Paul said. "The agent in Jakarta has located a suitable factory. I've laid the groundwork for meetings with the Indonesian government, so whenever you're ready to fly over and check it out, just give me a shout. We can set it up quickly."

"Sure," Will replied, but without enthusiasm.

Someone called Will to the telephone and he was drawn away, leaving Maeve with Paul. Paul smiled and tucked her arm into the crook of his. "Come and show me your handiwork. I'm desperately in need of a landscape gardener myself."

Maeve didn't believe Paul, but he lied in such a blatant and charming manner that she couldn't take offense. She happily showed him around the grounds, and for once got to enjoy one of her gardens without a shovel in her hand.

They paused at the cliff edge to admire the view of the bay.

"What did you mean, calling me an Amazon?" she asked.

"That's Will's term for you," Paul said, watching her. "He's quite taken with you."

"He can't be," she hastened to correct him. "Unless you mean as a gardener. He and Ida—"

"In case you hadn't noticed, he and Ida aren't exactly a blaze of passion."

Maeve's breath caught. How many times had she thought the same thing? "But they're in love, right?"

"Presumably, or they wouldn't be getting married," he said with a shrug. He cast her an appraising glance. "Maybe you're a little taken with him yourself."

She laughed. "Gosh, no. Half the time I'm on his case for putting my father out of work. He's a nice guy, but—"

"He's the best." Paul's tone admitted no argument.

Maeve dropped the defensive mode. "He is, isn't he." Then, to change the subject, she added quickly, "Have you seen the cubby I'm making for him? I mean, for the baby." She strode on, her heart palpitating. How obvious were her feelings if a virtual stranger picked up on them so easily? What *were* her feelings? Nothing more than infatuation, surely. Yet where did infatuation end and love begin?

She stopped in front of the brick cubby. Already the jasmine vines had grown several inches since she'd planted them and new shoots trailed over the tilled earth. She picked up the stragglers and twined them through the latticework.

"Frankly, I'm a bit worried about him," Paul said, coming up beside her.

She brushed the dirt off her hands. "What do you mean?"

"You'd think he was having his right arm amputated, the way he's agonizing over his business. He's trying to play fair, and not everyone at the factory cares about what's fair. A couple of men he should have fired long ago are causing trouble. As for Ida, they've been friends for years and there was never any talk of marriage before this. I don't know, it all seems a bit odd. I'm one of his best mates, but he's not telling me a thing."

"He's thrilled about the baby," Maeve said. "You can see it in his face."

"Yeah," Paul admitted. "No question he wants a family. And I'm probably wrong about his relationship with Ida being fishy. Will's never been the type to act head over heels in love. I suppose that's just his style."

Phyllis had said much the same thing. As they walked slowly back toward the house, Maeve tried to think of a tactful way to phrase her question. In the end her words were blunt. "Is Ida the type to be faithful?"

"Like a cocker spaniel." Paul barely got the words out before he faked a smack to his cheek. "Sorry. I didn't mean that to sound nasty. It's just that the scars on her face don't allow her many options."

"She's smart, she's got style and she's a really nice person. Why wouldn't men find her attractive?"

"Hey, don't get me wrong. I like Ida a lot. She just hasn't had much luck with men."

Maeve plucked a leaf from a gum tree and twirled it in her fingers. From what she'd seen, Ida had been pretty lucky with *two* men. "Until now," she corrected with a lift of her eyebrows.

"Until now," Paul agreed. They approached the pool area, crowded with noisy party guests. Paul stopped and turned to Maeve. "Will you have dinner with me sometime?"

"Thanks, Paul. But I don't think so..."

"Are your affections otherwise engaged?"

"No." She glanced away from his knowing smile. "I'm just...very busy with work."

"You garden at night?" he enquired with amusement.

"Please, just accept that I can't."

He reached for her hand. "You mean, won't."

She let her hand lie in his, idly noting how Paul's touch had no effect on her. "Can't. Won't. It comes to the same thing. I'm flattered, Paul, but you and I wouldn't work."

With an exaggerated sigh he released her hand. "At least, give me your business card so I can call you about my garden."

"Okay." She pulled a card from the small beaded purse strung over her shoulder and handed it to him.

He pocketed it with a smile. "Let's go get a drink. I'm parched." As they approached the increasingly raucous crowd, he leaned closer and observed, "Ever notice how the noise level rises in direct proportion to the amount of alcohol consumed?"

From the deck, Will watched Maeve and Paul's progress around his property with growing concern. Will had witnessed Paul on the prowl enough times to be sure his friend was hitting on Maeve. His antennae went up when he saw Paul take Maeve's hand, and when she didn't tug away immediately, Will ground his teeth. Although not precisely a womanizer, Paul had inordinate success in bedding women.

The thought of Paul and Maeve together made Will choke on his drink. Telling himself that Maeve could take care of herself did no good. As her employer and host, Will felt compelled to walk down to meet them, insert himself between them and escort Maeve back to the safety of the group.

Behind Maeve's back, Paul's eyes twinkled. *I got her number,* he mouthed at Will.

"She has an ex-husband who wants her back," Will cautioned, even though he knew Paul would be unfazed by a rival.

Will turned to Maeve. "I should have warned you. My friend here is a right larrikin. Under no circumstances should you give him your phone number."

Maeve smiled demurely. "He only wants advice on his garden."

"He lives in an apartment!" Will turned back to Paul, but the accountant was already retreating with a wide grin and a parting wave.

Maeve burst into laughter. "Will, you look like an outraged father. Are you getting in practice early?"

A father to Maeve was the last thing Will saw himself as. However, the thought raised the question of what relationship he did want, so he thrust it aside. "Did I tell you I finished the solar panel? I'll drop it off early next week."

"Fantastic," she said. "Can I have a look at it?"

Just seeing her eyes light up was worth the long hours he had been ill able to afford to spend away from his factory. "Come on. It's still in the bungalow."

They strolled in that direction. But before Will could unlock the bungalow door, Alex and Ginger called him over to the odd little gate in the new fence.

"What is this?" Ginger asked, waving the hand holding her wineglass. Wine sloshed onto the grass. She, like Alex, had had a trifle too much to drink. "It's just too darling for words."

"It's a kissing gate," Maeve explained. "I thought it would be appropriate, since the wedding ceremony will take place in the garden."

"Kissing gate?" Ginger repeated. "I don't get it."

"Demonstration!" Alex commanded. "We need a demonstration."

Will thrust his hands in his pockets.

"C'mon, Maeve, darl', show us how this works," Ginger urged.

"You enter, then swing the gate to the opposite side of the semicircle." A rosy flush climbed Maeve's cheeks. "In the old days in England, a man courting his sweetheart would capture her in the circle of the gate and steal a kiss."

"Show us." Alex lifted the latch and ushered her through the gate, into the circle, with a flourish. "You be the girl. I'll be the boy."

"Oh, no, you don't!" Ginger protested, laughing. "You're a married man, Alex White. Will, get over here."

Will froze, even as a rush of adrenaline set his heart racing. While he hesitated, more people came to see what the commotion was about and started egging them on. Maeve waited, looking troubled and uncertain.

"Come on, Will," Alex said. "You've never been backward about coming forward." He took Will's arm and half dragged him to the gate. "Pucker up, Maeve."

"Let's get Ida to help Will demonstrate," Maeve suggested.

"Aw, Ida's busy showing off her ring," Ginger said. "She won't mind. Jus' a little kiss."

The assembled guests began to chant. "Kiss… kiss…kiss…"

Will suddenly found it hard to breathe. Even though kissing Maeve would mean absolutely nothing. Her lips would taste of summer nights, but they would not spark a fire in his blood. Her skin might feel as satiny as a gardenia petal, but touching her would not set his soul ablaze.

One kiss would not lead to another.

"Kiss…kiss…kiss…"

Maeve now looked profoundly uncomfortable.

"Quiet, you pack of mongrels," Will said. "The steaks are nearly ready. Why don't you head over to the barbie."

His friends tried to protest, but seeing that Will was adamant a kiss wasn't going to happen, they drifted off, grumbling good-naturedly.

Will walked over to Maeve. "Sorry about that."

He opened the gate, intending to let her come back through. Instead, he found himself stepping inside the semicircle with her.

"Thank you," she said. Her lips parted slightly. Her eyes grew dark.

Afterward, Will wasn't certain whether he bent to her or she lifted her face to him. All he knew was that a hush fell around them, and he grazed her mouth with his. Suddenly, he was in a garden paradise; soft, lush, warm, scented. Longing overwhelmed him. He needed all his strength not to gather her into his arms. His eyes opened, and met Maeve's luminous gaze. The unspoken vibrated between them.

In a daze, Maeve released her breath. The sun seemed brighter, the sky a sharper blue, the flowers more vivid. Will seemed larger than life, yet the longing and despair in his eyes, the curve of his lip, his bent head and strong jaw, moved her almost to tears. She loved him.

Without speaking, Will lifted the latch and opened the gate, releasing her. She moved past, yearning, but not daring, to brush against his body.

Movement in a group of guests near the house drew her gaze. She turned, and stared into a pair of stark hazel eyes.

Ida had witnessed the kiss.

For one awful moment Maeve thought Ida would burst into tears or angrily demand to know why her fiancé was kissing another woman. A frozen heartbeat later, Ida looked away. She must have made some joking comment, because the woman beside her laughed.

Without glancing at Will again, Maeve hurried off—and lost herself in the crowd. The kiss had meant something to Will; she'd seen it in his eyes. She hugged to herself the knowledge that he returned her feelings, even if he could never tell her.

But as she moved toward the patio, her elation slowly deflated like a balloon the day after a party.

In a little over a month he would marry Ida in this very garden.

She scooped a tumbler of scotch from the tray of a passing waiter and wandered through the sliding glass doors into the empty kitchen. "Cheers," she muttered, raising a bittersweet toast to the vase of flowers she'd culled from her own garden.

"What are we drinking to?"

Maeve spun around, to see Ida standing in the doorway.

"What shall we drink to?" Ida repeated, coming into the room. Her eyes glittered and her cheeks were flushed. "Love?"

Maeve's gaze never left Ida's face. "Okay," she said cautiously, raising her glass again. "To love."

"Are you in love, Maeve?" Ida said, circling behind her to finger a deep-blue iris petal.

"I, uh…" She gulped her scotch. The hard liquor burned her throat and stomach. "Are you?"

Ida's gaze shot to Maeve. "What do you mean?"

Maeve had imagined confronting Ida in a fury of righteous indignation. Yet now that they were face-to-face, she felt nothing but a sick despair that a woman she could have liked as a friend would hurt someone Maeve loved. Will deserved better than a fiancée who ran around on him.

"I saw you the other day on the Swanston Street Bridge. I called to you, but you didn't hear. You were too busy kissing another man."

The flush in Ida's face faded, leaving her scars

vivid against her white cheek. "You don't under-stand..."

"No, I don't." Maeve set her glass on a table and crossed her arms over her chest. "Perhaps you'd better explain."

Ida's cheeks turned crimson. "It's none of your business."

"I don't care. What you're doing isn't fair to Will."

"You're in love with him," Ida shot back, grip-ping her glass so hard her knuckles were white.

"I don't want to see him hurt. That's all."

Ida's narrow-eyed gaze said she didn't believe the lie any more than Maeve did. "Do you think I want to hurt him? Will's been my friend for over twenty years."

"Then tell him about this other man. Or I will." He might not thank her for the news, but, at least, he'd be spared future heartache.

Ida paled. "You want him for yourself."

"Get rid of your boyfriend."

"Don't you dare issue me an ultimatum."

"You're carrying Will's child, for God's sake!" Ida's eyes filled with tears. "Stop it."

"Get rid of the boyfriend."

Ida sank onto a chair and buried her face in her hands. "I can't do that."

She looked so miserable, Maeve had to resist the urge to comfort her. At least, the baby meant something to her. "Then, please, break off your engagement to Will."

"I can't do that, either." Ida wiped at her eyes.

Exasperated, Maeve stood over her. "You've got to do something. You can't hide this guy from Will indefinitely. How do you think Will would feel if he found out? He's looking forward to being a father so much."

"It's not his baby," Ida mumbled.

A cold chill swept the back of Maeve's neck. "What did you say?"

Ida raised a tear-stained face. "My baby's father is Rick, the man you saw me kissing on the bridge."

"I don't understand."

"My relationship with Will is platonic," Ida said dully. "He knows the baby is Rick's. It's okay with him."

Platonic? Then all this time... Maeve stumbled to a chair and dropped into it. "I still don't understand. Where does Rick come in?"

"He's my friend from San Diego. I met him while he was working here for six months. When his time was up, he left."

"And you were pregnant, so Will did the noble thing and offered to marry you?"

"No. When Will and I decided to marry, I didn't know I was pregnant. We'd both reached a point in life where we wanted to settle down and start a family, but neither of us believed we were going to fall in love. So we agreed to join forces."

Ida reached for a cocktail napkin from the stack beside the tray of clean glasses and dabbed at her nose. "The baby was unexpected, but Will says he doesn't mind that the first one isn't his." She gave Maeve a wan smile. "In a way, I think he was relieved the need for procreation was delayed."

Will and Ida didn't sleep together. Suddenly, everything made sense—the fact that they rarely touched, the awkwardness when they did. He didn't love Ida, not in a romantic, sexual way. In spite of everything, Maeve's heart sang.

"What about Rick?" she demanded. "Does he know about the baby?"

Ida blew her nose. "No."

"He looked awfully glad to see you. I think you should tell Rick he's going to be a father."

"It's not that simple—" Ida broke off, as a man and a woman entered the kitchen. She waited until they'd found the corkscrew they were looking for and left, before she continued. "Rick doesn't want kids," she explained. "He told me right from the start that he wasn't ready to settle down. He's younger than me, too. He's only thirty."

"Why did he come back to Melbourne if it wasn't to see you?"

Ida shrugged wearily. "His job. He'll be here a few weeks this time. Maybe a month."

"Still," Maeve persisted, "you shouldn't force Will into marriage when he's not even the father of your child."

"No one's forcing him."

A few moments passed before the information sank in. Will had chosen to marry a woman he didn't love and to act as father to another man's child, all because he wanted a family. A family Maeve, couldn't—wouldn't—give him.

Ida gazed at her sympathetically. "When Will and I decided to marry, we tentatively agreed that if…the need arose…we could have intimate relationships with other people."

"What are you saying?" Maeve fought a rising tide of nausea.

Ida glanced around the kitchen to make sure it was still empty. Her voice dropped, and she held Maeve's gaze. "I…I wouldn't mind if you and he have an affair."

Furious, Maeve pushed to her feet, and her chair toppled over. "Oh, so you'll let him screw around as long as he'll stay with you in a phony marriage?"

"That's an awful way of putting it."

"It's the truth."

Ida linked her fingers protectively over her abdomen and the unborn baby she was carrying. "Rick won't marry me. I have to think of the baby's future. He or she needs a father. So, no, I'm not letting Will go. Nor does he want to break our engagement. I've known Will most of his life. We won't have love, but we'll have something better—a lasting relationship."

Maeve stared at her in horror. "You're mad, the

pair of you. You deserve each other. I feel sorry for Rick. And for the baby.''

She stumbled through the house and out the front door, praying she wouldn't meet anyone, least of all Will. The effort he'd put into her solar panel, the sidelong glances, the inadvertent touching of their hands—had those been, not the tortured resistance of a forbidden love, but a deliberate prelude to an affair?

She wove through the parked cars blocking the front of the house. He didn't believe in love. That was what it boiled down to. Her skin crawled with shame at the fantasies she'd created of kisses from a man honor bound never to touch her lips. What a fool she was. A silly romantic fool who ought to have known better.

"Maeve, where are you going?" His voice sounded behind her.

Damn, damn and triple damn.

Reluctantly she turned, but kept walking, backward. He was standing at that stupid kissing gate. God, when she thought about how her heart had been in her eyes…

"Got to go," she said, giving a casual wave. "Thanks for the party."

"Wait," he called, bewilderment in his voice. He pushed open the gate and hurried through the maze of cars toward her.

Maeve pulled her sunglasses from her purse and

put them on, but she was too late: he'd already seen the evidence of tears.

"What's wrong? Did Paul behave like a jerk?" Will's scowl suggested Paul would regret it if he had.

"No, of course not." She glanced at the blockade of cars surrounding her ute, which was wedged between a white Ford and a silver BMW. Retreat was impossible; she'd have to stand and fight. Better, perhaps, to get all the pain over with at once. "I talked with Ida. She told me about your platonic relationship. And…and Rick's baby." Her heart pulsed with pain when she saw Will wince. Not being the father *did* bother him. "I'm sorry about that."

He brushed away her concern. "Is that what upset you?"

"Yes. No." She ran a hand through her loose hair. "I just think the whole setup is wrong. It's bad for you, bad for Ida, bad for her baby…"

"It's…what we wanted. What else did Ida say?"

"She…she said you two had an arrangement. That you were allowed to see other people." Maeve swallowed. "She hinted that you and I—" She broke off. The intensity of his gaze robbed her of speech.

His expression changed to one of incredulity. "She actually said it would be okay for us to sleep together?"

Maeve eyed him narrowly. "Wasn't she telling the truth?"

"She suggested that in the beginning. But later I got the impression she wouldn't be happy with such an arrangement." Will rubbed his jaw. "I wonder what changed her mind."

Maeve burned with the desire to enlighten him. A remnant of female loyalty caused her to hold her tongue. "You'd better ask Ida that. I've got to go."

He grasped her wrist, his grip strong enough to detain her but quickly turning gentle. "Now that you know…Maeve, I feel something for you."

"No. No." Tears threatened, tears of anger and a biting sense of loss. "There's no future for us. Love isn't meant to be a clandestine coupling in some sordid hotel room."

"Making love with you couldn't be anything but pure and beautiful." His voice was low and compelling.

"No." She backed up between the cars, spitting out her words. "Maybe you can divide your allegiances, but I can't. Nor will I play second string. You must have zero respect for me even to suggest it. Not to mention what that says about your so-called friendship with Ida." She was shouting at him now, any threat of tears drying in the hot wind of her anger. "There are a few things you should know about Ida, too."

"I know Ida inside out."

"You don't know everything."

"Maeve!" Will started after her.

"Stay where you are," she warned. She reached her ute and fumbled for her keys. To her relief, a narrow path between the cars would allow her egress.

She climbed in and started the engine. In the rear-view mirror, she saw Will staring after her, his jaw clenched so tightly he must be grinding his teeth. Laboriously, she executed a five-point turn into a position from which she could back out through the gap between vehicles. Her body flooded with adrenaline, she revved the accelerator in fits and starts until at last she burst onto the driveway, and, tires squealing on the bitumen, escaped down the road.

CHAPTER ELEVEN

IDA CHECKED HER HAIR in the ladies' room mirror, then combed her flippy curls forward over her cheek in an attempt to hide as much of the scar as possible. Quelling a pang of guilt, she slipped off the engagement ring she and Will had bought together and put it in her makeup bag, before going to the hotel lobby to meet Rick.

His coppery-blond head turned at the tap of her high heels on the marble floor, and his smile spread at the sight of her. In his light-brown suit that fit his solid physique perfectly, he was so gorgeous that she still didn't know why he bothered with her.

Why, oh, why couldn't he be the one? He wasn't staying in Melbourne; she shouldn't torture herself by seeing him. But she hadn't been able to stop herself from saying yes when he'd asked for a second date.

"There you are." His lips were deliciously cool and lingered on hers. "I missed you on the weekend," he said, taking her arm as they went into the restaurant. "Too bad you couldn't have gotten out of your cousin's engagement party."

"Yes, too bad." Ida's stomach churned. Did she

have the courage to tell him? Maeve was right: sooner or later, Will would find out. Or Rick would find out about Will. She could end up with no one.

When they'd been seated at a window table, Ida took a deep breath, straightened her spine and reached for his hand. "Rick—"

He glanced up from the menu and gazed at her with clear blue eyes. "Yes?"

"I...I was wondering if you wanted to go to the art gallery later. The new exhibit is a collection of paintings by Turner."

"I'm sorry, Ida. I was going to tell you first thing. I have to wrap up affairs at the bookstore sooner that expected. My boss in San Diego called and wants me to cut my trip short. There's some crisis back home."

Smile, Ida. Don't let him see your disappointment. This was an excuse if ever she'd heard one. "When are you leaving?"

"Next Monday evening." He reached for her hand. "I'll be working overtime all week, but we'll have the weekend together."

"Friday's my birthday."

"Great," Rick said. "We'll celebrate."

Yeah, great. They'd have just enough time for one more romp in bed. Look where that had landed her.

A waiter appeared. "Make I take your order?"

Ida glanced at the menu board, but the words blurred, and, anyway, she couldn't be bothered reading it. "I'll have the special."

Rick took his time choosing. When he'd finally placed his order, he asked Ida, "Would you like red or white wine?"

"I've got a slight headache. I'll just have mineral water."

The waiter left, but before Ida could screw up her nerve again, Rick said, "Did I tell you about the ranch house I'm building outside San Diego?"

"No." As he enthusiastically described the community he was moving to, the countryside and the amenities and the friends he'd made there already, her heart sank. His life was happening on the other side of the Pacific Ocean. Far away from her. And their baby.

Yet how could she not tell him? "Your new home sounds very nice."

"Have you ever been to California?" When she shook her head, he added, "You'd love it." He hesitated. "I have holidays in late July. You could come for a visit."

Ida did a quick calculation. She would be nine months' pregnant, and no airline would allow her on board. "I...I'm going to be pretty busy in July."

She saw his mouth tighten, and knew she'd blown it. Although he was probably just being polite when he asked her to visit. Rick was like that. "Rick? I—"

"Look, don't worry about it. Some other time." He glanced at his watch, even though they'd barely been there twenty minutes.

Tell him, you coward. Do it. Just do it.

"Rick, I'm pregnant and the baby is yours."

To her horror, the color drained from his face. His jaw dropped, his mouth worked, but he couldn't seem to speak. She waited, while he gazed at her in shock. Worse than shock, she'd seen the flash of fear in his eyes.

"Don't worry," she added, smiling. She was an expert at smiling. "I'm not asking you for anything. You see, the truth is, the engagement party the other night was for me. I'm getting married."

WILL PACED THE CLIFF TOP at Sorrento Ocean Beach, moodily watching the flat water lap the shore. After his disastrous confrontation with Maeve, he was in the mood for crashing white water. The surf was not cooperating.

Over and over, Will tortured himself with the memory of the passion and longing in her eyes after their kiss. Followed by the hate and disgust she'd displayed when she'd thought he'd asked her for an affair. Had he really done that? Their exchange had happened so fast, been so fraught with emotion, that he hardly knew what he'd said. For one brief moment he'd glimpsed paradise—then the gates had clanged shut. He despised himself for making her feel second best. Maeve deserved so much more than he could give her.

Will kicked at the dirt, and pebbles sprayed down the cliff. His life was out of control. He was committed to one woman and falling for another, who seemed to move farther out of reach with each encounter. She'd spoken of love, but he didn't know what that word meant to him.

Farther along the cliff, Mouse sat smoking a rollie and staring out to sea. He wore his wet suit peeled to the waist, revealing tattoos etched across sinewy biceps. Will and Mouse had been surfing the same beaches for years and had never exchanged more than a few words.

Mouse finished his cigarette and stubbed it out in the sand. He picked up his board, and as he padded past Will on the way to his panel van said, "Nothing good coming this way today, mate."

Will acknowledged the truth of this with a grunt. He should have checked out the surf conditions on the Web site, but he'd come out here to forget his troubles for an hour or so before going to the factory. The plan hadn't worked. He'd merely brought his worries along for the ride.

At least, the situation at the Mornington plant, potentially explosive, had settled down. He'd moved the troublemakers, McLeod and Kitrick, to a section by themselves to reduce their opportunities to foment discontent. The bonuses and extra incentives he'd introduced to show his gratitude for loyalty and cooperation seemed to have lessened the grumbling.

Will wiped the perspiration off his forehead with his T-shirt. The sultry weather didn't help matters. He couldn't remember a summer as hot as this one, not even from his childhood, when summer seemed to last forever.

He bent to pick up his board. For the sake of his employees' morale, he ought not to be late for work. He was pushing them too hard, and he'd better not give them one more thing to complain about.

An hour later, he turned in to the service road of the industrial estate. Seeing a crowd in front of the factory and cars blocking the road, he frowned. Had there been an accident? A fire?

He pulled to the side of the road and jumped out. Hand-lettered signs waved above the heads of his employees. A small group, including Renée, stood to one side, looking upset. As Will approached, McLeod climbed onto the flatbed of a ute and raised a megaphone to his mouth, shouting for solidarity.

Good Lord, they were on strike.

MAEVE WALKED into her kitchen that afternoon, just as Art was putting down the phone. "Hi, Dad—" she began, then stopped, noticing his expression. "What's wrong?"

"That was Renée. The workers at Aussie Electronics are on strike." Art paced to the fridge and yanked out a bottle of beer. "I warned Will that McLeod and his mate were up to no good," Art raved as he carelessly poured out a glass. "Bloody bastards!"

"Look out, Dad. Your beer is foaming all over the floor." Maeve wrung out a dishcloth and crouched to mop up. "You said yourself, Will's been working everyone too hard."

"He works harder than any man Jack of 'em. Don't those morons realize that if he doesn't fill his contracts, they won't be getting the bonuses he's promised 'em?" Art took a long swig of beer. "I'll have to go back and see what I can do to help out."

Maeve rose with the dripping dishcloth in her hand. "Are you mad! You just started a new job. They won't give you leave this soon."

"I'll quit if I have to," Art replied grimly.

"No, you won't!" Maeve tossed the cloth into the sink. "This job is way too important for you to pass up. Where are you going to get another position at your age?"

"How can I leave Will Beaumont in the lurch, when I wouldn't have had any job at all for the past five years if not for him?"

"You don't know that you can do any good. Why sacrifice your future for something so tenuous? Sheesh!" she added, pushing her hair back from her forehead. "I thought we already had this conversation."

"The situation has changed. It's no coincidence they struck the moment I was off-site. McLeod wouldn't have had a hope of getting the others to go against Will if I'd been there."

"Dad, you're not Will's guardian! Let him handle his own problems. He's more than capable."

Art wasn't listening anymore. "I knew I was

wrong to desert him in his time of difficulty," he said to himself. "I'll get over there first thing in the morning. Losing one day's production won't be too serious if I can stop the strike quickly."

Maeve threw up her hands in despair. "All right. Do what you want. You're not worried about rent or food or anything as ignoble as the mundane necessities of life. You can just stay on here forever—"

Art snapped out of his monologue and tossed a sharp glance her way. "Are you worried about my staying here forever?"

Oh, hell. Why had she blurted that out? "No, of course not," she said, backpedaling. "This is your home for as long as you want. You know that."

"You can set your mind at ease," Art said, drawing himself up with dignity. "I'll be finding my own place just as soon as the strike is settled. I'll not be a burden on my daughter."

"Don't be silly, Dad." She put her arms around his shoulders, truly sorry she'd spoken in haste. "I was just mouthing off. I'm worried about you. Your work is a big part of your identity. I don't want you to go. Honest." And somewhat to her surprise, she realized that what she'd said was true. "Who would cook me a decent meal, if you weren't around?"

"We'll talk about it when things are settled," he replied, seemingly mollified. "But I'm going back to Aussie Electronics tomorrow, and I don't want to hear another word against it."

Maeve went into the back garden and got out a bag of wild-bird seed to fill the feeder. The sound of grain being poured brought a small flock of rainbow lorikeets fluttering down from the top branches of the gum trees. She pottered among her flower beds, seeking but not finding respite from her concerns over her father, and the aching emptiness in her heart whenever she thought of Will.

She was no longer angry with him. He was caught in a difficult situation and had spoken on impulse during an emotionally charged encounter. And although she would never agree to having an affair, she was beginning to think she'd overreacted. Maybe he hadn't even meant that.

Regardless of what happened with Will, the kiss they'd exchanged had convinced her of one thing. She couldn't go away with Graham. Better to tell him sooner than later.

She went inside to call, but his cell phone was turned off. He was sleeping or showering, probably. In which case he'd be done by the time she got there.

The setting sun spilled gold and red across the water as Maeve walked down the clanking wharf to Graham's thirty-five-foot fiberglass ketch. The boat deck was deserted when she came alongside.

"Ahoy," she called, and rapped on the hull. "Anybody home?"

No response. A horrible thought struck. What if

his cell phone was turned off because he was entertaining some other woman?

Graham poked his head through the gangway. His face lit at the sight of her. "Maeve. Hop aboard."

"I'm not disturbing you, am I?" she asked, taking in his wrinkled shirt, his tousled hair. "I tried to call."

He stretched his arms over his head and yawned. "Just having a power nap. I've been practicing and I'm rather good at it now."

"I'll bet." She grabbed onto a stanchion and swung her foot over the gunwale.

Graham took her free hand, pulled her up and captured her into a light embrace. He smiled and kissed her on the lips. "Nice to see you."

"You, too." Gently she extricated herself from his arms. "The boat is looking good."

"Have a seat," he said, indicating the cushions lining the cockpit. "Like a glass of chardonnay?" Pausing in the gangway leading down to the galley, he added hopefully, "Or is this an occasion for champers?"

"I've had enough champagne this week to last me a good while, thanks. Chardonnay will do nicely."

He disappeared below, and a few minutes later returned with a slender green bottle in an ice bucket and crystal glasses between his fingers. "So where have you been supping bubbly lately?"

Maeve took the glasses from him and held them

out to be filled. "Just an engagement party for one of my clients."

"I didn't think you usually attended your clients' social functions. Not wise to mix business with pleasure, or so you used to say."

"This was different." Maeve sipped her wine and watched the setting sun. "I suppose it's too late to go for a sail?"

"Yes, although I'm glad you're interested." Graham settled onto the cushion next to Maeve.

He'd changed his shirt and combed his hair. The faint whiff of toothpaste when he leaned toward her brought back memories of mornings sharing a bathroom and evenings when the laughs outnumbered the fights. The days before tragedy had torn their marriage apart.

"I went to see Kristy this afternoon," Graham said.

Maeve toyed with the halyard dangling from the mast. He meant he'd gone to the Frankston Memorial Park, where their daughter was buried. Years ago, Maeve had visited Kristy's grave on what would have been her first birthday and had spent the rest of the week crying. She'd never gone back.

"I took her some flowers," he went on. "Pink carnations."

Still Maeve couldn't speak. Part of her wished she could act as casual as Graham sounded. Part of her thought him unfeeling.

"Maeve, it's time to let her go," Graham added softly.

"Yellow pansies were her favorite," she whispered. Blinking, she raised her untasted wine to her lips. "Tell me about your last trip," she said. "Where did you go?"

Graham regaled her with stories of the Marquesas Islands. They talked and joked and finished the rest of the bottle, then drank coffee until Maeve was fit to drive home.

"Thanks, Graham," she said, when at last she rose and stretched. "I'd better leave."

"The moon's almost full," he pointed out as he walked her up the wharf to her ute. Casually he slid an arm around her waist. "If you stayed overnight, we could go sailing first thing in the morning."

"Or perhaps we could sail some Sunday afternoon."

Graham cupped his hands around her cheeks and gave her a searching gaze. "Have you thought about coming with me?"

"You mean to Fiji?"

"Fiji and beyond." When she didn't answer, he added, "You don't have to make up your mind about 'beyond' right away. I meant what I said about not wanting kids, Maeve. I'm nearly forty. I'm over the urge to change nappies in the middle of the night. We'll do it your way. No kids."

Before she could answer, he lowered his mouth to kiss her. She turned her face away so his lips met her cheek. "I'm sorry, Graham," she said. "I can't. I...I'm in love with someone else."

He was silent a moment. "Will you be marrying him, then?"

"No. The situation's...complicated."

"Well, if you change your mind, you know where to find me."

"For a week or two," she said.

"Uh-uh-uh." Graham wagged his finger. "I've enjoyed the break from your sarcasm tonight. But actually, you're right. Once my locum's up next week, I might as well take off." He smiled wistfully at her. "Got no reason to stay, do I."

"It was good to see you again, Graham. I'm sorry things didn't work out."

"That's life, as they say." He turned serious. "Take care of yourself, Maeve. You seem... fragile."

"I'll be all right." She hoped. If nothing else, she finally felt a sense of closure on her relationship with Graham.

That night, the moonlight shone through the lace curtains as she sat cross-legged amid the pillows on her high brass bed and brushed out her hair, dark against the voluminous white cotton. She thought of Graham's attempted kiss, and realized that as well as not wanting to encourage him, she hadn't wanted to erase the memory of Will's kiss. If she closed her eyes, she could still feel with extraordinarily accurate recall the smooth warm imprint of his lips on hers. With a sigh, she turned out the light, and in the solitude of her bedroom, in her fantasies, she carried their sensual brush with desire to its logical conclusion.

A dog barked in the wee hours, waking her. She pulled back the curtains to find the moon had set, leaving the sky inky black. She lay awake for hours, her mind churning with memories of Kristy and worry over Art. This time she wouldn't let herself even think about Will. Problems always looked darker in the night, and already her thoughts regarding him were as black as pitch.

At last she got back to sleep, only to be awakened, seemingly minutes later, by the clock radio. She dragged herself out of bed, slowly ate, then dressed. Art had already left, presumably for the factory. She hoped his sacrifice would avert further strike action, but she wasn't going to hold her breath.

She went out to the garage to pack her gear into the ute, and blinked sleepily at finding her solar panel and thermoregulator lying on her workbench. Will must have come by early, while Art was still here to open the garage door for him. Maeve searched for a note. Sure enough, a smaller scrap of paper fell out of the folded sheet of typewritten instructions.

With trembling fingers, she smoothed out the handwritten message. It contained only two words: *Forgive me.*

A tear rolled off her cheek and onto the paper. *Yes, Will.*

She spent the morning at a house in Rosebud, working with Tony to install a watering system and put in a herb garden. Creating the herb garden was pure fun. Tony turned the soil, while she laid paving blocks in the pattern of a star within a circle. In the center, Maeve planted a mix of lavender and valerium. Then she arranged the perennials—sage, thyme, rosemary, marjoram and oregano—in the arms of the star, and filled in the segments of the circle with annuals such as parsley, basil and coriander. Under the warm sun, the herbs gave off their pungent aromas as she placed them in the ground.

"Thanks, Tony," she said, when they were done and the worksite was cleaned up. "I'm going to the Beaumont place now. Are you okay to finish installing the watering system on your own?"

Tony waved a hand. "Piece of cake."

Maeve loaded the leftover herb plants into the back of her ute. She'd overbought, as usual, on the basis that it was better to have too many plants than too few. These she could repot, or, better yet, she could plant them in Will's terrace rockery. Neither he nor Ida was into cooking, but herbs were decorative as well as useful. Ida might feel more domestic once she had the baby. Although, the thought of Ida sprinkling Maeve's herbs in Will's dinner made Maeve's chest hurt.

Tonight was Ida's birthday, she realized an hour

later as she tucked perennial herb seedlings into pockets of soil between the stones of Will's rockery. The annuals she arranged in a terra-cotta pot on the patio by the sliding doors into the kitchen.

Then she strolled down to the pool to check on the *Selenicereus*. The buds were full and ripe. The Queen of the Night was not going to wait for the wedding; she was going to bloom tonight. Maeve thought back to the calendar. Of course. Tonight was the full moon.

Flowers that bloomed only once a year sounded to her like a darn good excuse to miss the footy game. She glanced at her watch. Will should be home soon; she could tell him about the *Selenicereus,* plus thank him in person for the solar panel. And just maybe they could reestablish some sort of friendly relationship. If he didn't show up, she would stay and watch the *Selenicereus* bloom—an event so rare it ought to be witnessed.

She stowed her gardening tools in the ute, moved the sun-baked vehicle farther into the concealing shade of a camellia, and went back to sit on the edge of the rockery. But the stones hurt her bottom and the late-afternoon sun had lost none of its heat.

The lounge chair in the dappled shade by the pool looked too inviting to pass up. She hesitated only a moment before she removed her boots and socks. Sitting on the lounge, she dipped her feet in the pool. Air-cooled water circulated between her toes. Slowly she stretched out full length, feeling her weary muscles relax. She was so tired. The moment she heard Will's car pull up the driveway, she would be on her feet. Surely shutting her eyes for just one minute couldn't hurt....

IN THE LOBBY of Aussie Electronics, Will peered through the vertical blinds. One by one the picketers drifted away, leaving McLeod and Kitrick behind in their portable trailer to keep watch overnight and make sure no new supplies entered the building. Will pressed his fingertips against his temples in an effort to relieve the shafts of pain piercing his brain.

"How long can they keep this up?" Art asked, coming up behind him, his workbag in hand.

"Longer than we can," Will replied. "McLeod still refuses to negotiate. He's cutting his own throat, but if neither you nor I can make him see that his strategy is getting them nowhere, I don't know where we go from here."

A handful of supporters had crossed the picket lines to keep the assembly line running, although at a fraction of full capacity. Even Renée had donned a white coverall to wheel the delivery trolley around the factory floor. But the supply of components would run out within days if the stalemate wasn't breached.

"I've been thinking," Art said. "I've got an idea."

"Go on." Will found that if he took shallow breaths the pain was marginally less intense.

"Well, you've got the shareholders demanding a bigger profit and that's why you have to move overseas, is that right?"

"More or less." The pain spread from his forehead around to the back of his neck. "What's your idea?"

"Why not buy the shares back? I mean, those shareholders are strangers. They don't care about us as long as they make money off the company."

"I can't afford to buy the shares back. I don't have the cash, and the bank refused a loan." He gripped Art's shoulder. "I can't tell you how much I appreciate your coming back to help out, Art. I've been trying all day to get hold of Ron at A. B. Electronics to buy you some more time." He felt sure that if he explained the situation, Ron would see that the loyalty Art displayed to Will would one day be Ron's, if only he could be patient.

"Never mind that right now," Art said. "I meant, the employees could buy back the shares. I read about a factory in America where the workers bought out the company. For a while they struggled on low wages, but the factory stayed open and in the end became even more productive. If there was even half a chance of their keeping their jobs, I reckon the blokes on strike would come back to work and ride out the rough times with you."

"The thought had occurred to me." But a glance at the arithmetic had made him dismiss the possibility. He owned fifty-five percent of the company.

Even if his employees owned the other forty-five percent, Aussie Electronics wouldn't have enough capital to stay afloat. Will would have to sell some of his shares, and in doing so he would lose control of his company. He hadn't striven all these years to become an employee in his own factory. "I'm not prepared to accept the consequences of that course of action."

Disillusionment that was painful for Will to witness crept into the older man's gaze. "I'll be on my way, then."

Will eased the Merc out by the rear entrance to avoid another confrontation with McLeod and his henchmen. All he wanted to do was go home and put an icepack on his head, but he had a date with Ida. At last he would find out why she'd changed her mind again about a nonexclusive relationship. There'd been no opportunity to get her alone at the party, or even afterward, with their families around helping to clean up. And she'd been unavailable every time he'd called in the days since. If he didn't know better, he'd think she was avoiding him. Her birthday, however, was noted in his pocket organizer, and he presumed he was still penciled in on her calendar, too.

But when he got to her office to pick her up as arranged, he found a note pinned to her door. She wasn't able to see him tonight, after all. No explanation, no elaboration other than that she would call him tomorrow. A new locus of pain began to throb in his temple.

She'd stood him up. And he'd gone to so much trouble, taking Maeve's comments to heart and organizing a special dinner instead of the footy game. He couldn't say he'd planned a romantic evening, because that wasn't what he and Ida were about—but he'd bought seafood for the barbecue, a really good wine and a selection of the finest chocolates available in Melbourne. What more could a friend ask for?

The bouquet of flowers in his hand sagged at his side. A noise behind him made him turn to see Ida's secretary, Sally, carrying a stack of file folders. "What happened to Ida?" he demanded. "Is she sick? Did she go home?"

Sally hugged the folders to her chest. "I don't know."

An appalling thought struck him. "Nothing's wrong with the baby, is there?"

"No," Sally quickly reassured him. "As far as I know, the baby's fine."

Will moved the bouquet to his other hand. "So, what happened?"

"She left with Rick—" Sally clapped a hand to her mouth. "Maybe I wasn't supposed to say that."

Rick. Suddenly he recalled Maeve's saying there were things he didn't know about Ida. "If you see her, tell her—" His mouth set in a grim line. "Never mind. I'll tell her myself."

He drove over to her house, but her car wasn't in the carport and no one answered the door. He went around the back, found a plastic bucket by the outside water tap and filled it half-full. He stuck the flowers in the bucket and parked them in the shade next to the front door. Then he got back in the Merc and cruised down the sunlit street, his fingers pressed to his aching forehead.

When had Rick gotten back into town? And why hadn't Ida mentioned it? What was happening to their friendship? A month ago she would never have betrayed him like this.

At home, Will popped a couple of headache tablets and trudged upstairs to change into his swimsuit. Maybe a cooling swim would clear his head. What the hell was going on with Ida and Rick? A crazy notion ran through his head—they'd eloped to San Diego.... Unguarded, his heart leaped at the thought of freedom. And Maeve.

But according to Ida, Rick didn't want to marry, wasn't ready for children. One thing he'd learned about Ida in the past month—she wanted security. She might not balk at a little fun on the side, but— That was it: she was picking up where she'd left off with Rick, just while he was in town.

Upstairs was unbearably hot and stuffy. He stripped off his shirt and pants, and opened the window. On the far side of the bay, the sun had begun its descent into the heat haze that stretched upward from the horizon. Port Phillip Bay shone like molten pewter.

Below in the garden, Maeve lay sleeping by the pool.

CHAPTER TWELVE

THE FAINT ONSHORE BREEZE caressed his bare shoulders through the open window. Despite the acrimony of their last meeting, he felt a shiver of anticipation.

Why hadn't he seen her ute? What was she doing here?

Answers were not to be found in his bedroom. He grabbed a towel from the linen closet, hesitated, then took out another. He'd prepared a romantic dinner for two. Ida was off somewhere with Rick. Why not share with Maeve? If she would stay.

His head still throbbed with pain, but now he didn't mind quite as much. He pulled shorts on over his bathing suit, threw on a T-shirt and went out through the sliding doors and across the patio. On silent feet he padded down to the pool. Maeve slept as one enchanted.

Dropping to a crouch beside the lounge chair, he took the opportunity to gaze at her without fear of censure or inhibition. Tendrils of damp hair clung to her temples where they'd escaped from her braid. Her chest rose and fell with each breath, her tanned skin glowing with perspiration. He ached to slide his hand down her bare midriff to her taut abdomen.

"Maeve," he whispered, not sure how long he could restrain himself from touching her. But not for anything would he frighten her.

She shifted in her sleep, stretching one arm over her head. The movement lifted her breasts in the black crop top with a soft jiggle that made his groin tighten.

"Maeve, wake up."

Wake her with a kiss, a small voice murmured in his mind.

Her bare feet were tender, vulnerable; her toenails painted a deep pearlized pink.

She was soundly asleep, her eyelids moving rapidly. What did she dream of? He scarcely dared hope she dreamed of him. If she woke up and saw him so close she would probably hit him.

Wake her with a kiss. The thought pounded in his right temple with the insistence of a jackhammer. Slowly he lowered his face to hers. Felt the soft warmth of her breath on his lips—

Her eyes snapped open.

"Will!" She struggled to a sitting position, glancing at the sky. "What time is it? Have you been watching me?"

"I was trying to wake you up," he said. "What are you doing here?"

"The *Selenicereus* is going to bloom tonight."

She rose from the lounge chair and moved around

the pool to the rockery. Holding one massive, near-to-bursting bud in her palm, she said, "Come dark, the blossoms will begin to open. I didn't want you to miss it. Forget the footy game." She added, her voice strained, "Ida would enjoy this so much more."

"We're not going to the footy game." A shooting pain tunneled through his frontal lobe. He winced and pressed the heel of his hand against his skull.

"What's wrong?" she asked, gently letting the *Selenicereus* bud fall back.

"Just a headache. Maeve, about what happened at the party—"

"It's okay," she said.

"No, really. I'm sorry. I hope you know I have the greatest respect for you—" He broke off as another shaft of pain struck.

"I can make you a herbal pack that will help."

"I've taken a painkiller with codeine. It should kick in any minute."

"Okay," she said dubiously, and stepped back. "I'd better go and let you rest before you meet Ida." She gave him a tight smile. "I'm glad you decided against the footy match for her birthday. What did you plan, instead?"

"A barbecue seafood dinner here in front of the sunset."

"Very nice," Maeve said. "The *Selenicereus* will be a bonus."

"That's what I had *planned*," he added. "Ida

can't make it— *Ow*." He grabbed his head with both hands.

"Come, sit down." She took his arm and pulled him toward the lounge chair.

"I'm fine. Honest," he protested, but he let her push him gently into the chair and swing his feet up.

She moved behind him and began gently to massage his temples. "How does this feel?"

Like heaven. "Good." He tried to twist around to see her. "Did you get my note?"

"Yes," she said softly. "Of course I forgive you. We were all a little overwrought that day."

Thank God. Will's tension eased a fraction.

"What happened to Ida tonight?" Maeve asked. "Is she okay?"

"Apparently so," he said dryly. "She went out with Rick."

Her hands stilled on his head. "So she finally told you he was in town. Are they getting back together?"

"She didn't say," he said with bitter bluntness. "In fact, I didn't even know he was in Melbourne until her secretary let it slip. I gather you've been kept informed."

Maeve came around and sat on the edge of the lounge chair, facing him. "She told me about him the day of your engagement party. I didn't think it was my place to tell you. Look, I know you have your heart set on being a father to her baby, but shouldn't you encourage her to tell Rick the baby is his?''

"I have. She swears he's not interested.'' Will lay back on the lounge chair, shutting his eyes with a sigh.

"I'm going to pick some of the lavender and valerian I planted today and make an infusion for your head,'' she said, rising. "Then I'll go and let you rest.''

"Don't leave, Maeve.'' He reached for her hand. "Stay and see the Queen of the Night in all her glory.''

Her smile reached her eyes. "I'd love that.''

"Have dinner with me, too.'' When she frowned, he added, "It would be a pity to waste those tiger prawns.''

"Mmm. Tiger prawns.'' She glanced down at herself. "I'm still in my work clothes.''

"You look beautiful in anything.'' The coming of the full moon must be making him a little crazy. Nothing in his life had ever seemed as urgent as having Maeve spend this evening with him.

"You must be feeling down about Ida.'' Her voice was low and rich with sympathy. "Maybe you love her more than you realize.''

"I don't love her, not in the way you mean. But I am worried about her. I'm afraid Rick will break her heart again. First thing tomorrow I'm going to track him down and demand to know his intentions.''

Maeve's warm chuckle fell softly on his ears. "That would sound pretty strange coming from the fiancé."

His smile was brief. "It would, wouldn't it."

"I'm going to make you that infusion now," she said. "While you recover from your headache, I'll run home and change."

Will shut his eyes and must have dozed. A short time later Maeve was pressing a cool, musky-smelling cloth to his forehead and a cup of warm liquid into his hand.

"Drink up."

"What is it?" He started to take a sip.

"Lavender tea."

He choked it down only because she'd made it. "Hurry back."

She smiled into his eyes, and then her long cool fingers stroked his eyelids shut. "Sleep if you can."

As MAEVE SPED through the evening, she prayed there were no speed cameras on the Nepean Highway tonight, because she'd get a ticket for sure. She didn't know what the night would bring, and for once she wasn't stopping to analyze the possibilities. *Don't think, just act.*

Art wasn't home when she arrived. He was probably at the pub with his mates from work, she decided as she stepped under the shower. Good. She didn't want to have to explain why she was spending that evening with Will.

When she opened her wardrobe, her long white muslin dress fell off its hanger and landed in a soft puddle at her feet. Must be a sign, she decided, and drew it over her head.

This was not a special occasion, she told herself, slipping gold hoops through her ears. He'd asked her to dinner as a friend, nothing else. He was still engaged to Ida, although Maeve no longer believed he would go through with the wedding.

She drove back down the peninsula to Sorrento, feeling as if all her Christmases had come at once. When she got back to Will's house he was firing up the barbecue on the patio. His welcoming smile made her feel this night was special to him, too.

"How's your headache?" she asked, a little shy, now that she was here.

He poured a glass of wine from the bottle in the cooler. "I don't know what you put in that potion, but my headache has completely disappeared," he said, handing her the glass.

"I've had a lot of practice with headaches," she explained. "Graham used to get migraines."

"Speaking of your ex," Will said, his voice too casual, "when are you sailing to Fiji?"

She lifted the glass to her nose, assessing the wine's complex bouquet. A special wine for a special occasion. *Ida's birthday,* she reminded herself. Even knowing that didn't take away from the magic of now. "I'm not going."

Will poured himself a glass. "I thought you said he'd changed."

She met his gaze. "Somehow, it's not enough."

Will touched his glass to hers. "To...?"

Fantasies? Futures? Feelings she could barely contain? Any of those, or all, seemed appropriate on this whimsical night. "To the Queen of the Night," she suggested.

Will smiled into her eyes. "Queen of the Night."

She savored the richly fragrant wine. "Thanks for the solar panel and thermoregulator," she said. "Couldn't you produce those in your factory to boost sales?"

"The solar panel is a possibility, but would require a lot more development. As for the thermoregulator, there isn't a big market for such specialized equipment." He paused. "Understandably, you're not happy about your father coming back to work for me, but I want you to know I really appreciate what he's doing. When all this is over, I'm going to try to make it up to him."

Maeve nodded. She didn't want to talk about this now.

"Art proposed that the employees buy out the company to save it from going overseas," Will added.

My idea, Maeve thought. "Is the scheme viable?"

"Possibly," he admitted. "But if the employees bought me out, I could lose control of research and development. I would certainly lose the power to make decisions.''

''Wouldn't that be better than seeing the factory go overseas? To me, having control over my life means having the power to choose as opposed to being acted upon by external forces.'' She gave him a half smile. ''Is Ida aware you're such a control freak?''

''Yes, unfortunately for her.''

Mention of Ida brought an awkward silence. Guilt washed over Maeve. ''Would she mind my being here tonight?'' she said at last.

''Judging by her absence, I'd say not.'' Will gazed speculatively at Maeve for a moment. Then, abruptly, he rose to his feet. ''Let's throw those prawns on the barbie.''

Maeve lit the half-dozen citronella candles set around the patio, while Will cooked. They dined al fresco, washing down succulent prawns and salad with more of Will's delicious wine, followed by fresh strawberries and chocolate.

''You understand the way to a woman's heart,'' Maeve said, relishing a melting shard of Belgian chocolate. ''Ida doesn't know what she's missing.''

Will leaned across the table and placed his hand over hers. ''Could we not talk about Ida, just for tonight?''

At this moment, with his blue eyes gazing into hers, Maeve didn't care if she never heard of Ida again. ''Agreed.''

She turned her hand over so their palms met, then slid her hand away before his fingers could lace through hers. After so long avoiding all contact, things were happening too fast. "Let's see if the flowers are blooming."

They walked down to the rockery, where the setting sun burnished the rocks with a red-gold glow. Despite the late hour, the heat had not left the day. All along the slanting waist-high wall of rock and earth, the *Selenicereus* cactus spread its trailing vine, dotted at irregular intervals with ripe buds the size of a man's fist.

"Look," Maeve said, excited. The bud she'd examined earlier had unfurled, its glowing white petals surrounded by golden spikes.

Will bent to smell the flower. "There's no perfume."

"Be patient. It comes in bursts. Another half hour and the whole rockery will be a mass of flowers."

His hand slid around hers. "Let's go watch the last of the sunset while we wait."

She followed him across the springy turf. The balmy breeze sifted through her light dress, and the scents of the myriad flowers she'd planted perfumed the air. Will's hand held hers. From the cliff edge, they gazed over the bay at the indigo sky, slashed with crimson on the horizon. Boat lights winked on the darkening water. The full moon, a massive golden orb, was rising from the sea.

Will inclined his head till his nose touched her scalp. "You're not wearing your usual fragrance…"

She grimaced. "Sweat and dirt."

"Sweat and dirt can be sexy."

His low voice next to her ear was hypnotic.

"Tonight you simply smell like…clean hair." He sounded surprised, and smelled again. "Not shampoo or hair goo or perfume. Just hair." Bending lower, he nuzzled the curve of her neck. "And your skin smells like skin."

"You're tickling me." Laughing, she put a hand on his chest, but not to stop him. "I don't wear scented products."

He played with a strand of her hair. "Do you believe people do things during a full moon that they wouldn't normally do?"

In the magical golden light, he looked like some eager wild child. Her heart beat with the rhythm of a tom-tom. "What kind of things?"

"I don't know—howling at the moon. Flinging yourself off high cliffs."

"You'd break your neck."

"I thought you were a romantic." Facing her, he slid his arms around her waist and drew her to him. "Everywhere I look in this garden, I see you."

"Silly, it's meant to be about *you*." She slipped out of his embrace and started to walk back to the pool.

"We're two of a kind," he said, following.

"God, I hope not." Her laughter floated on the sultry air.

"Maeve, I'm being serious."

And he was, for once. She stopped and, hesitantly, trailed her hand up his arm. "I know what you mean. I feel it, too."

He pulled her back to him. "Show me how that kissing gate works again," he murmured close to her lips.

"We're a long way from the kissing gate," she demurred.

"You're not wrong." He touched his lips to hers. Tenderly. Tantalizingly. "Who goes through the gate first?"

She inhaled his warm breath, mingled wine and chocolate. Wanting a taste, she ran her tongue along his lips. "I go first. You follow."

His arms enclosed her, pressing her body against his from thighs to chest. "Enter."

A light push of her tongue gained her access to his mouth. He captured her with a gentle sucking, drawing her deeper in an intimate caress. Maeve felt heat spill through her, felt her breasts swell like buds ready to burst. An intense wave of vanilla fragrance wafted their way.

Will broke the kiss to whisper against her lips, "I thought one was supposed to hear bells."

Abruptly, she took a step backward, removing herself from his embrace, from his warmth. "Will, is there going to be a wedding?"

His chin sank to his chest. "I don't know."

"We have to talk about Ida." She touched his arm, then quickly withdrew.

"You know what I think bothers me the most?" he said. "Ida always used to come to me when she had a problem. But ever since we got engaged, our friendship has become more and more strained. Like this thing with Rick. She couldn't even tell me she was seeing him. It's as if she's afraid of how I'll react. She never used to worry about that."

"Will, if losing her friendship is what bothers you the most about her seeing Rick, then you should not be marrying her."

He sighed. "She could be making love to Rick right now and it wouldn't bother me. In fact, I'd be happy for her."

"Is that the kind of marriage you want?"

"No, but I made a promise to my mother not to hurt Ida."

"It seems to me Ida's hurting you."

"I don't understand why she didn't at least call," he said. "I'm not gaining a wife—I'm losing a friend."

"She's avoiding a decision, afraid of losing everything."

"Maybe," Will conceded. "On a solicitor's income she could easily provide for her baby, but being pregnant has changed her. Made her fiercely protective of the child."

"Of course it has. The worst thing in the world

for a mother is to lose her child—'' Maeve broke off, not wanting to pursue that topic.

Ignoring Will's sharply inquisitive look, Maeve thought carefully about what to say next. She didn't want to sound as though she were speaking from self-interest. ''Marriage is about more than pragmatic choices. Certainly, you and Ida might be reasonably happy as platonic partners, but you'd be cheating yourselves out of the ultimate experience of life.''

Will stared at her blankly.

''Love,'' she said, exasperated. ''I'm talking about love.''

''I don't know what love is,'' he said sadly.

Maeve smiled at his innocence. ''Yes, you do. You just don't recognize it.'' She was certain he loved her, and she was going to show him what that meant. Elated at the chance to give him something truly meaningful, she stroked his jaw. ''Come,'' she whispered. ''I'll show you.''

The risen moon had lost its golden tone and now shed a brilliant silver light over the garden. Shadows from the giant fig tree spread inky fingers across the pale grass.

Will let her lead him to the thick grass beside the pool. Rich vanilla fragrance drifted from the snowy banks of *Selenicereus* along the rockery. More flowers had blossomed. Under the moonlight they and the frothy clumps of white alyssum took on an almost fluorescent quality, while the cascading blue lobelia and banks of forget-me-knots glowed dazzling white. If magic existed in the universe, it was here, tonight, in this garden.

And Maeve had created it.

His heart leaped to his throat as Maeve slowly unbuttoned his shirt and smoothed her hands over his chest. She took his mouth in a kiss deeper than any they'd exchanged.

"I've wanted you," he murmured, sliding his hands down her dress to touch her breasts. "I've dreamed of you." His body trembled. "Do you want me, too?" He needed to hear her say it.

"Every minute of every day." Pushing his shirtfront aside, she planted kisses across his chest.

He pulled free long enough to bring two thick beach towels from a lounge chair and lay them on the grass. Then he turned to see Maeve releasing the tiny pearl buttons at her neck. He watched reverently as they slipped free of their loops, one by one, revealing tantalizing glimpses of pale rounded breasts beneath the fabric. Slowly she slipped the gown off her shoulders and let it slide to a pool of glimmering whiteness at her feet.

Naked, Maeve's long smooth limbs glowed in the moonlight. Her thick hair flowed over her full breasts to hang like a curtain around her slender waist. Maeve belonged in his garden. She was a part of all she'd created, a wood nymph whose spirit had entered the very plants and soil she'd shaped for his use.

She knew him better than anyone, and in ways not his mother, or Ida, or Paul could fathom. Even with Maree, he'd never felt this all-consuming passion. He threw off his clothes and took Maeve into his arms. Under the all-knowing, beneficent face of the moon, he made love for what seemed the first time in his life.

When at last they lay cradled together, the moon had moved a few degrees closer to the crown of the Monterey Bay fig. The air was still as warm as if it were day.

"That was magic," he breathed.

"That was love," she said, smiling.

He held her more tightly. "Whatever it is, I can't give this up for friendship. Maeve—"

"Let's go swimming."

"Okay." He'd rather talk about their future, but they would have plenty of time for that later.

Maeve dove straight in at the deep end and came up grinning. "It's wonderful!" she exclaimed. "As warm as a bath."

Will walked across to the pool controls. He ignored the switch for the underwater light—the moon was illumination enough—but he opened the valves to the jets, and suddenly water arced across the pool from a dozen miniature waterfalls.

Maeve was doing the breast stroke away from him, her long legs churning bubbles, when he dropped over the side. The water slipped over him like warm silk. Like Maeve.

He swam after her. Just as he reached a hand out to grasp her ankle, she folded into a duck dive and shot to the bottom. He dove, only to see her glide across the pool underwater.

They circled each other around the pool, laughter bouncing off the surface, tension simmering below. He faked her out on her next pass, and they surfaced, panting, face-to-face in the moonstruck water. Her dark hair gleamed wetly, and a liquid light shone in the depths of her eyes. Water lapped at the top curve of her breasts. He could see their round shapes wavering dimly beneath the surface.

Reaching for her waist, his hands slipped on her taut skin, then he pulled her in close. "Gotcha."

Legs entwined, mouths joined, they slowly sank through the water, her breasts against his chest. When his toes touched concrete, he propelled the two of them back to the surface.

Will rolled onto his back, still holding her hand, and gazed up at the fat silver moon. The spray from the jets sounded like a symphony and the heady scent of the *Selenicereus* made his blood race through his veins. He'd never felt happier, or more alive, than at this moment.

"The man in the moon is looking at us," Maeve said.

"Hope he likes what he sees." Will sculled with his free hand until his body lay alongside hers. Her long hair floated across his arm. He felt so relaxed with her, yet stimulated by the slightest touch, the fleetest glance. An image of his future children floated into his mental view. A girl with long dark hair like her mother, and a boy who grubbed around in the dirt, examining the roots of a plant.

"Maeve?" he said dreamily. "Did you ever think about getting married again?"

Silence. Then she said, "I'm getting cool." She removed her hand from his, and stroked across the pool. Then disappeared.

Will hung in the water, disoriented. Where had she gone?

Suddenly, he was being pushed up from below, lifted right out of the water to splash down a few feet away. Maeve bobbed behind him, laughing. He lunged after her, but she was too quick for him. She pulled herself out of the pool in a sluice of water. He just glimpsed her lithe naked form, before she wrapped herself in another of the big white towels sitting on the lounge chair.

He climbed from the pool, and, still wet, scooped her up and placed her, laughing, down on the grass, where he made love to her again. The rich scent of vanilla mingled with the musky scent of their bodies. And he knew that for the rest of his life his mind would link the two, and remember the night something rare and precious bloomed beneath the full moon.

They swam once more in the moonlight, and basked in the glorious scent of the *Selenicereus* until midnight came and all the flowers closed their petals for another year.

The moon had slipped behind the fig tree by the time he led her through the house and up the stairs to his bed.

"Maeve," he murmured minutes later. "Will you marry me?"

The only reply from the pillow next to his was the gentle, even sound of her breathing.

"Never mind," he said, drawing the sheet up to cover her. "I'll ask you in the morning."

CHAPTER THIRTEEN

MOONLIGHT FILLED Maeve's dreams, but she awoke to sunlight. Will lay on his stomach at her side, his face buried in the pillow. As she looked at his tousled head, her heart turned over. Last night truly had been magical. And just for the moment, she wasn't going to think about what today would bring.

She ran a finger lightly down his spine. "Good morning."

Sleepily, he rolled over and opened his arms to gather her into their loving shelter. She snuggled close, lazily stroking the dark, curling hairs on his chest. Golden silence cocooned them, rich with memory and meaning. She could lay here forever....

Almost against her will, the scent of his skin started the blood hurrying through her veins. She stirred against him, and he turned to her, already growing hard. They made love, indolently at first, then with energy, and finally with an urgency that tossed the covers from the bed and raised a sheen on their skin.

"Awake now?" she asked, subsiding onto his chest.

"Maeve, you're a revelation." He still pulsed inside her.

She tightened around him, suddenly unable to speak. The moment was coming closer. She didn't want to give him up. Not when she'd wanted him for so long, and had him for such a short time.

"I've been thinking," he said. "We could build you a greenhouse over by the box hedge—"

"Don't, Will." Nothing, not even love, would alter his desire to have children. She knew that as surely as she knew she loved him. Ironically, that he was a family man at heart only made her love him more. He was whole, and she was not.

"I'm not a free man. But I intend to rectify that."

Maeve rolled off him and lay on her side, pulling him over so they were face-to-face. "I have to tell you something. It will change your mind about…about you and me."

"Nothing will change my mind. Not after last night." He stroked her hair off her face, tucking the long strands behind her ear. "Say you'll marry me."

"Oh, Will." Gazing at his open countenance, she could have wept for what she was about to do to him. How could she have released the love inside him, only to destroy it with a few words? A revelation, indeed.

"What is it? Are you worried about how Ida will feel?"

"No. Well, yes, of course I'm worried about her,

but I believe in the long run she'll be better off not marrying you.''

He smiled. ''Thanks a lot.''

''You know what I mean.'' Maeve gave him an affectionate push.

Push led to shove, and before she knew it, he was on top of her, pinning her hands above her head. ''Uncle!'' she cried, breathless with giggles.

He kissed her, long and tenderly, making sweet love to her mouth. Then, still gently but firmly holding her wrists, he looked into her eyes. ''Now say, 'I'll marry you, Will.'''

''I love you.'' Love was all she could give him. And it wasn't enough.

His eyes were as serious as she'd ever seen them. ''What's the problem?''

''I don't want children.''

He released her wrists and slid off her onto his side. ''I don't understand.''

She turned her face away so he wouldn't witness her grief. ''I had a child once. A little girl named Kristy.'' Her throat closed up, and she couldn't speak.

Will pulled her back against his chest and cradled her hips in the curve of his pelvis. With his arm around her and his hand resting below her heart, he was as close as he could get. If only, Maeve thought, they could stay like this forever.

''Go on,'' Will said.

''She was a beautiful child. Happy, bright.'' Her

voice trembled, but she made herself go on. "She was so full of life. And even as a baby, so sweet and affectionate. She would put her little arms around my shoulders, tuck her face into my neck and hug me." Tears slid from Maeve's eyes and down her cheek, wetting the pillowcase. "I loved her more than words can describe."

Will held Maeve in silence. Finally, with quiet dread in his voice, he asked, "What happened to her?"

"One morning, I went into her room—it was past eight o'clock, far later than she normally slept, but I wasn't worried. I certainly didn't expect anything to be wrong. When she'd gone to sleep the night before she'd been perfectly healthy, not even a sniffle." Remembering, Maeve felt her palms go damp. Her voice tightened. "I looked down at her and at first couldn't understand why she seemed so still. Then I realized—she wasn't breathing. I went to pick her up. She was…stiff. Cold. Dead."

She felt his shocked silence, then his arm clamped more firmly around her. "Maeve, Maeve." Will keened her name.

Maeve drew in a shuddering breath. "Sudden Infant Death Syndrome. She died without a sound in the night. Oh, Will," she cried, doubling over with the pain. "When I found her, she was blue."

Will turned her in to his chest and folded her in his arms, rocking her as she clung to him and sobbed.

Long minutes passed before she could calm herself. At last she lay still in his embrace, emotionally drained and still grief-stricken that her life could go on when her child's had ended.

With infinite tenderness, Will kissed her swollen eyes. "Aren't you able to have more children?"

The message hadn't sunk in. He wouldn't sound so calm if he really understood. "There's no physical reason I can't."

In the silence, she could almost hear the pieces fall into place in his mind. When at last he spoke again, his voice had a strained quality. "I thought from things you said that it was Graham who hadn't wanted children."

"He wanted to have another baby right away. I couldn't face it. I still can't."

"Maeve," he said gently, urgently. "Don't do this to yourself. I'm sorry about Kristy, but your life has to go on."

She forced herself to look Will in the eye. "I shouldn't have made love to you knowing it would come to this, but I…I wanted you so badly. It was selfish. I'm sorry."

"Sorry?" He gave a humorless laugh, then shifted away from her on the bed.

"Will," she said desperately. "More than anything in the world I would like to marry you. But you want a family. I don't want to stand in the way of your happiness."

He grasped her wrist again, and this time his grip

burned her skin. "You convinced me I shouldn't marry Ida. Made passionate, beautiful love with me. Bowled me over so utterly and completely I virtually forgot my name. And now you're just going to walk away. What do you think that's going to do for my chances to be happy?"

"I'm sorry, Will," she repeated, miserable.

"And what about you?" he said. "Can you be happy walking away from what we experienced together last night? Having another baby might heal you. God knows, staying childless hasn't ended your suffering."

"I'd better go." She slid off his bed to pluck a scrap of white lace from beneath a chair. Tears welled in her eyes as she clumsily thrust a leg into her panties. Damn it, where was her bra?

He got off the bed and reached for his bathrobe. "If you're looking for your bra, you didn't wear one."

His eyes locked with hers, and for one brief moment he and Maeve were transported back to the previous evening, when their love was newborn, full of splendor and promise. Then Will's eyes turned cold and Maeve reached for her dress.

Later, she would weep. Right now, she had to leave. Before she begged him to take her with or without children.

That was when she realized that subconsciously she'd been hoping all along he would say that. She yanked her dress over her head and heard a seam tear. What a fool she was! He was right to despise her. She'd screwed up both their lives.

She jammed her feet into her sandals. "Goodbye, Will."

He turned his back on her without a word.

Tears blurred her eyes. Maeve walked out of the room, down the stairs. And out of his life.

WILL'S NUMB SHOCK lasted only until he heard the front door shut. Then boiling anger took over.

Damn her. She'd found his heart, feasted on it, then spit it out. His fists clenched, and his eyes screwed shut to stop the tears from leaking out. He felt like breaking something. The way she'd broken him.

Instead, he stood under a scalding shower and scrubbed his skin raw. He could remove all traces of her scent, but memory was more difficult to extinguish. And feelings he tried to rebottle had grown too large to contain.

He felt like the soiled towels he gathered later from the garden—used and tossed carelessly aside. Even the *Selenicereus* flowers hung wilted and spent on the vine. Their brief, spectacular inflorescence now seemed vulgar and pointless.

As he stood in the middle of his glorious garden, everything seemed pointless. The brilliant sunshine mocked his grief and the magpies' sweet warble was a painful counterpoint to his suffering. But somewhere deeper even than his personal pain, his heart ached for Maeve and for the baby girl she'd lost.

Ruthlessly he shut that part of his emotions down. He didn't need her. If Ida still wanted to get married, fine. If not, he'd crawl into his cave and be happy all on his own, God damn it.

He considered going surfing, but for once the idea didn't appeal. When he was out on the waves he thought too much. And he wanted Maeve off his mind, not on it.

So he walked back to the house and called Ida— not that he expected her to be at home. He counted thirteen rings before he finally hung up. He'd deal with that situation later.

What he needed was action. Something to take him out of himself. Hell, why not right out of the country? Still holding the phone, he dialed Paul's home phone number.

"Listen, Paul, how soon can you be ready to check out that factory in Indonesia? Tomorrow? Fantastic. I'll pick you up on my way to the air-port."

ON MONDAY MORNING, Maeve headed south on the highway to Mornington to see Ida. Even if she couldn't be part of Will's future, she needed to know what his future was to be.

At the intersection with Mornington Road, she pulled to a halt in the right turn lane, waiting for a gap in the traffic. While she waited, she fanned herself with her hat. Temperatures had soared once again, and she was almost glad to hear the radio weather person issue a storm warning for later in the day.

Just then Will's silver Mercedes approached in the oncoming lane. Of all the horrible coincidences. The traffic light turned from green to orange, and to beat the red light, Will stepped on the accelerator. He roared through the intersection, eyes forward, looking as if he were a thousand miles away. This would be their punishment, she thought: doomed forever to cross paths but never again to meet.

A few minutes later Maeve was knocking on Ida's open office door. Ida glanced up from her paperwork, her scarred face alight with expectation. When she saw her visitor was Maeve, her features settled into a blandly neutral expression.

"What can I do for you?" Ida asked coolly.

Maeve shut the door and took a seat in the visitor's chair. "Did you have a nice birthday?"

"Very nice," Ida replied. Spots of color flushed her cheeks, but her chin rose defiantly.

"Will wondered why you didn't call."

Ida shrugged and fiddled with her pen.

"He's upset that you're not talking to him," Maeve went on.

"If you know that, I'm willing to bet you did your best to console him." Ida glanced pointedly at her watch. "I'm expecting a friend." She emphasized the word *friend* as if to exclude Maeve.

Maeve felt rather sorry for Ida. Her posturing was so obviously a defense mechanism. Keeping her own expression unreadable, she asked, "Rick?"

"Yes." Ida sighed heavily. "What exactly do you want?"

"I want to know what your intentions are with regard to Will. You hurt him, not so much because you stood him up, but because you aren't treating him like a friend. Have you talked to him since Saturday night?"

Ida doodled on a pad of yellow legal-size paper. "I stayed in Melbourne all weekend, hashing things out with Rick. I wanted to call him, but... Look, this is none of your business," she said, suddenly aggressive. "Or are you trying to find out if he's up for grabs?"

"I just...I would like him to be happy." She paused. "*Is* he up for grabs?" She wasn't asking for herself, but to find out what Ida's plans were.

Ida threw down the pen she'd been twisting between her fingers. "No. Yes. I don't know."

"Please, at least call him. Right now, he badly needs—"

"A friend?" Ida cut in. "Why? What did you do to him?"

"I, er, nothing."

"You slept with him, didn't you."

Maeve pinched the bridge of her nose. This was not going the way she'd planned. "It was a once-off. It'll never happen again."

"Why not? He loves you. Don't you love him?"

Maeve got to her feet. "I shouldn't have come. Look, just give Will a call. Talk your plans out. He needs to know where he stands."

"Because he's going nowhere with you, is that it?" Ida rose, too, and leaned over her desk. "Maybe you'd better sit back down and tell me exactly what happened between you two."

Maeve sank back into her chair. "There's not much to tell," she said dully. "When you stood him up, he invited me to stay for dinner. We had one wonderful evening—and now it's over."

"Because Will said it's over?" Ida's hazel eyes were focused squarely on Maeve, pen in hand as if she planned on taking notes.

"No," Maeve admitted slowly. Ida would cross-examine her until she got at the truth; she might as well spill her guts and get it over with. "I don't want children, so it wouldn't be fair to Will to continue with the relationship. Maybe I should have mentioned that before we made love, but it seemed kind of presumptuous." She held up her hand as if testifying under oath. "I swear, I never meant to hurt him."

"Never mind that," Ida said. "Why don't you want children?"

Did she really have to go through the agonizing explanation again? Ida's unrelenting expression said she did. "I lost a baby to SIDS five years ago," she said tersely.

"Oh. I'm sorry." Ida's hand dropped to her abdomen as if to protect her unborn child.

"It's okay." Suddenly, Maeve was so jealous of Ida she couldn't bear to look at her.

"No, it's not." Ida came around her desk to crouch beside Maeve's chair. As if they hadn't been fighting for the past ten minutes, she put her arms around Maeve. Maeve held herself stiffly, biting her cheek to keep the tears at bay.

Ida sat back on her heels and pressed Maeve's hand to her softly rounded belly. "Can you feel her moving?"

Maeve wanted to snatch her hand away. The life growing in Ida's womb was a painful contrast to the emptiness of her own. And the gift she couldn't bring herself to give Will.

Then she felt a faint flicker of movement, and memories of her pregnancy came rushing back. The hopes and dreams she'd once held so dear. Now hopes and dreams shone in Ida's face. "I envy you so much," she whispered.

"Me?" Ida hand went automatically to her scar. "But you're so beautiful."

Maeve smiled sadly. "Not all scars are on the outside."

Ida got awkwardly to her feet. "I'll call Will," she promised. "We'll sort things out. But Maeve, he wants a family, and I promised him I'd give him children."

"What about Rick? Did you ever tell him the baby is his?"

Ida's face crumpled. "I blew it. He wants rights to his child, but he's through with me. When you arrived I thought—hoped—you were him, coming to tell me you'd changed your mind." She sighed and glanced away. "He's leaving for San Diego tonight."

"Oh, Ida. I'm so sorry."

"I'll call Will right now." Ida went back to her seat and dialed a number. Holding the receiver to her ear, she took a tissue from a box on her desk, then pushed the box toward Maeve.

Maeve blew her nose and glanced around the office, while Ida waited for Will to answer. Next to Ida's framed law degree was an original watercolor of Mother's Beach here in Mornington, painted by a local artist. Children played in the sun-sparkled shallows, and a golden retriever romped eternally through the foam after seagulls. Bittersweet longings curled around Maeve's heart.

"What!" Ida exclaimed. "When did he go?"

Maeve spun around. *What is it?* she mouthed.

Ida dropped the phone back in its cradle. "Will and Paul just left for Indonesia to look at a factory."

"So he's really going to move offshore." Maeve reached in her pocket for her car keys. "I'd better leave." She forced herself to add, "Let me know what you're doing about the wedding. The garden's ready, but I need a couple of days' notice to bring in the potted flowers for lining the walkway. I'll be away for a while. My assistant will finish making the arrangements.''

"Maeve…'' Ida's gaze beseeched her for understanding and forgiveness.

Maeve squeezed her hand. "Take care of yourself, and your baby.''

"Thank you.'' Ida paused. "I'll watch out for Will, too.''

Maeve came out of Ida's office building, took one look at the lowering black clouds and hurried to her ute. The emotional storm in her heart was reflected in the atmosphere. As she pulled out of the parking lot, lightning flashed over the bay and the first heavy pattering of raindrops hit the dusty dry earth.

WILL GAZED out the window of the taxi transporting him and Paul through the colorful palm-lined streets of Jakarta. They wound around bicycles and jeepneys, drove past construction sites where the workers wore sarongs and inched along traffic-choked roads beneath the shadow of high-rise office buildings.

"So what do you think?'' Paul said enthusiastically. "Can't you just picture Aussie Electronics operating out of a tropical hub of commerce?''

"I'd hardly be able to call it Aussie Electronics, would I?'' Will replied.

Paul shrugged. "What's in a name? I think once you see the factory your mind will be put to ease.

From the specs, the facilities appear to be just about perfect.''

The factory they'd come to check out was on the fringe of the city, in a light industrial zone. On one side of the empty building was an American running shoe factory, and on the other a German manufacturer of office furniture. At the security gate they left the taxi to meet an Indonesian agent acting for the British owner.

"Good afternoon, gentlemen," the agent said, smiling and shaking hands courteously. He wore an immaculate gray business suit despite the steamy heat. "Very pleased to meet you."

Mr. Wayanamundra conducted the tour, interspersing his description of the many modern features of the factory with assurances that the Indonesian government would expedite relocation with a minimum of red tape.

"Low taxes and competitive wages are just some of the many incentives for foreign investors," Mr. Wayanamundra said, his words echoing in the huge, empty production room.

Paul shot Will a glance that said, *Didn't I tell you so?*

"This factory will meet all your technical requirements," the agent went on, indicating the fitted-out workbenches. "The previous occupier manufactured electronic toys." He added with a smile, "And if you need a computer desk or filing cabinet, why, you only have to go next door."

Will laughed politely, then sobered. "What's the current political situation? I know that not long ago the capital was unstable. Our news reports covered the riots and demonstrations."

"That is all finished now," Mr. Wayanamundra reassured him. "The rebel factions are completely under control. Foreign investors have nothing to fear. In any case, this industrial park is guarded by the very highest security systems." He paused at a door and drew a set of keys from his pocket. "Through here are the offices, modern and up-to-date."

Will could find nothing to complain about with regard to either the offices or the factory. The building fit all his requirements, plus had room for expansion should he wish to add to his line of products in future.

But as they left the building, he looked back, trying to imagine the name Aussie Electronics written across the front. No matter how hard he stretched his mind, he couldn't see it. He waited while Paul thanked Mr. Wayanamundra effusively for his time, added his own thanks, then fell silent in the taxi on their return to the hotel.

"So what do you think?" Paul asked for the third time, after they'd registered and settled into their room.

"I think I'm hungry. Let's go find something to eat."

He knew Paul was frustrated with his recalcitrant

attitude, but so far the trip had made him more un-
easy about the move, rather than less so. The problem was, he couldn't pin down what was bothering
him.

THE NEXT MORNING Will and Paul met with government officials and leaders of the local business community. While Paul and the Indonesians negotiated
terms and conditions, Will recalled what Maeve had
said about true control being the power to choose
the direction of your life. Here he was having to
choose between the lesser of two evils: selling out
or moving offshore. He'd never felt less in control—

"Right, Will?" Paul said, interrupting his mus-
ings. "Refreshments would be nice." The accountant shook his head with a meaningful lift of his
eyebrows. *Wake up!* he clearly was saying.

"Er, right," Will replied, glad to discover he was
only agreeing to the cup of coffee the pretty, solemn
secretary had just placed in front of him.

Despite Paul's silent injunction to take part in the
discussions, Will went on with his internal dialogue.
The solution to his crisis teetered on the edge of his
understanding, and his brain would not leave the
problem alone.

Selling out would mean jobs lost, trust broken,
plus all the uncertainty and effort of building a new
business. Moving offshore would entail losing control of day-to-day operations, and he hated losing

control. Which was why he couldn't contemplate selling majority ownership to his employees.

He sipped the strong bitter coffee and sighed. He'd been through this over and over again. Something was missing, some essential factor in the equation.

The secretary, or tea lady, or whoever she was, offered him a pastry from a tray. He took one, noting with mild interest that her gold necklace consisted of the letters of what must be her name. "Thank you…Made."

Her response was to beam with pleasure. Speaking softly but emphatically in Indonesian, she bowed and smiled repeatedly before moving around the table with her tray. Will smiled back, uplifted by the moment of personal contact.

That was when the root of the problem struck him. Personal contact. The Indonesians he would employ should he relocate to Jakarta would be nothing more to him than faceless workers. And he would be merely the foreign investor who was, possibly, as much a source of resentment as of employment. Yes, those workers would have lives and families, problems and aspirations, just like Renée and Art and the rest. But he wouldn't ever be here long enough to get to know them. He would never ask so-and-so about his kid's graduation, or commiserate with them over who won the Grand Final, or have a beer with the gang at a Christmas barbecue.

His problem wasn't losing control but losing personal contact.

"Will?" Paul was looking at him strangely.

He realized then that he'd gotten to his feet. "Thank you all very much for your time," he said, including the gathered bureaucrats and businessmen in one polite glance. "Gentlemen, I have made my decision. Aussie Electronics will remain in Australia."

CHAPTER FOURTEEN

RETURNING HOME from Melbourne Airport, Will peered through the streaming rain, trying to keep in sight the red taillights of the car ahead. Thick black clouds had turned day to dusk, and periodic flashes of lightning illuminated the city skyline.

Traffic crawled through the city and out to the eastern suburbs. Gutters overflowed and low sections of the road were underwater. The wind blowing the storm in from the southern ocean had taken down power lines and uprooted small trees. By the time Will pulled into his driveway he was exhausted.

The big house was cold and empty. Before he even turned on the lights or changed his damp clothes, he went to the study and listened to the messages on his answering machine. There were no messages from Maeve. But Ida had left three.

With a sigh, he picked up the phone and dialed her number. "Ida? I just got back. Are you okay?"

"Will, we need to talk."

He wanted only to sleep. And time to think before he dealt with Ida. But her voice was strained, almost desperate. He could imagine her twisting the phone cord, worry wrinkling her forehead beneath the wisps of auburn hair. "What's wrong?"

"Can I come over?"

Whatever was bothering her must be bad if she was prepared to drive through the storm. "Sure."

He turned on all the lights, took a hot shower and made himself scrambled eggs and toast. He'd just put on a pot of coffee, when the doorbell rang.

Ida's spiky hair was dripping, her clothes disheveled. She gazed at him with wide wet eyes, then flung herself at him. "Oh, Will."

He closed his arms around her. Silently, he led her into the lounge and sat her in front of the fire he'd lit to dispel the gloom. "Hang on a tick. I'll get us some coffee."

When he returned he gave her a cup and took a seat facing her on the couch. "Well?"

Ida's eyes flooded with tears. "I'm so sorry I didn't call you on my birthday. Maeve said you were upset. I feel terrible."

Mention of Maeve set off a maelstrom of complicated emotions. He ignored them to concentrate on repairing his relationship with Ida. "I was upset. I thought our friendship meant more to you than that. I was worried about what you were going through. And hurt that you couldn't confide in me."

"Oh, Will," she whispered. "Can our friendship survive our marriage?"

"That, my dear, is the sixty-four-thousand-dollar question."

She lifted her gaze to his. "Are you in love with Maeve?"

That question he didn't want to answer, least of all to himself. But what was the use of avoiding the issue? Slowly he nodded.

She took a deep breath. "Then I release you from your promise. You don't have to marry me."

The fire crackled in the silence that followed. From outside came a distant rumble of thunder and the steady drum of rain on the tile roof. Will tried to analyze the feelings her announcement evoked, but his heart was a whirl of mixed emotions, while his head spun with contradictory thoughts.

"What's happening with you and Rick?" he asked, putting off a response. To respond would require a decision.

Ida shrugged unhappily. "In a word—nothing. He wants to know his child, which was a nice surprise after what he'd told me earlier. But he's through with me."

Will sipped his coffee. "Perhaps he's just angry you took so long to tell him about the baby. Give him time to adjust to the situation. After all, he came back to Melbourne to see you—"

"He came back for his job," she replied automatically.

"He didn't have to call you." Will noticed her averted eyes. "You didn't tell him you were getting married before he had a chance to ask you himself, did you?"

She hung her head. "I might have."

"Oh, Ida!" Will exclaimed. "If you put him off every time he tries to get close, of course he's going to keep his distance. Can't you accept that he might love you and want to be with you? Possibly even marry you?"

Tears trickled down her cheeks. "I wish I could believe that, but I can't. I just can't."

Will gazed at her in sorrow. He'd thought he knew Ida, but he'd had no idea she was that low in self-esteem. He wagged a finger, putting on a comical voice. "'A fine mess you've got us into this time, Ollie.'"

Ida smiled bleakly.

Will got up to poke a crumbling log back on the fire. And thought about how you never really knew a person until tough decisions came up.

He turned back to Ida. "If you're not going to be with Rick, what are you going to do?"

"Marry you—if you'll still have me?"

He wasn't sure he could do that, even with Maeve out of the picture. "But is that what you want? A moment ago you were releasing me from my promise."

"I wanted to give you the option." Her eyes filled again. "Because I can't decide. That's why I came here tonight. To ask you as a friend to make the decision for us both." She leaned forward and took his hand. "Maeve says she doesn't want children. So if you still want to marry me, I'll do it. And I'll do my best to forget about Rick and be a good wife to you. I mean, in the long term, after the initial attraction has worn off, what's the difference between deep, lasting friendship and love?''

''For crying out loud, Ida, what a question. Of course there's a difference between friendship and love.''

But for the life of him he couldn't have said what that difference was. Marrying Ida would be an easy out. He would have a wife and child—the family he'd always wanted. They would have to make room in their child's life for Rick, but Will thought he could cope with that. He and Ida could continue with their plans as if this whole summer had never happened. The heat, the madness, Maeve—all would vanish in the calm, rational cool of autumn. No one need ever know that for a short space of time he'd been lifted to the sublime and dizzying heights of love. And if he regretted missing out on passion, how much more might he regret never having children?

He scooted closer to Ida and put his hand on her belly. ''How is he doing?''

Ida smiled. ''Really good. The morning sickness has passed.'' She touched his hand and gazed at him beseechingly. ''I know it's not fair to burden you with the decision, but I've driven myself crazy with worry over what to do.''

''Give me a little time to think things over.''

"Thank you." She rose from the couch. "I'd better go."

"Do you want to stay in the spare room?" he said. The rain was no longer torrential, but it still fell steadily.

She shook her head. "Rick might phone from San Diego in the morning."

"Ida—" He broke off. He was too tired to protest, and she was beyond lecturing. "Drive safely."

He saw her to her car, then watched until her taillights disappeared down the driveway. If he could keep Maeve out of the equation, he just might be able to make a decision regarding Ida.

McLEOD'S VAN was still parked in front of Aussie Electronics when Will pulled up the next morning. The sight of pickets striking at his factory enraged him. Until he remembered he'd come here today to make his factory *their* factory, and put everyone, including himself, back to work.

"Where were you yesterday, Beaumont? Business so good you can afford to take a day off?" McLeod, in his shorts, singlet and thongs, jeered from the steps of his van. "How about using some of your profits to keep jobs in the country, instead of selling out like everyone else?"

Will strolled over to the group, hands in his pockets. His employees parted to give him access to McLeod, some of them watching with interest for the coming confrontation, but many averting their eyes in embarrassment. Will pretended not to notice their discomfort. "G'day, Tom. Rita. Hi, Noel. How's the new grandson?"

Then he let his gaze drop slowly from McLeod's unshaven jaw to his dirty toenails. "Profits aren't as great as you obviously imagine."

"Bullshit," McLeod said with a derisive laugh, and glanced around at his group of supporters. A few laughed with him. Most did not.

"Come inside and see for yourself," Will said. "I've instructed my accountant to open the books."

"They'll be the cooked version," McLeod sneered.

Will ignored the gibe and turned to the assembled crowd. "I'm offering the employees of Aussie Electronics the opportunity to collectively purchase controlling interest in the business. An injection of funds on this scale will be sufficient to keep the Mornington plant open and Aussie Electronics right here at home, where it belongs."

"What's the catch?" someone called.

Will thrust his hands in his pockets and thought a moment. "The catch is, I'll be on contract as head of Research and Development, and Paul will continue as the firm's accountant. We want to protect all our jobs. Any of you who are interested, come inside. We'll discuss this further with Art and Paul."

"It's a trick," McLeod scoffed, as the men and women laid down their signs and turned to follow Will. "He's just trying to get you back to work."

"Good!" someone shouted. "Getting back to work is exactly what we want."

Negotiations proceeded for the rest of the day. Paul had come out from Melbourne to give the assembled employees a frank and realistic rundown on the company's finances. At the end of a long and sometimes heated discussion, Will was asked to leave the room so the matter could be put to a vote.

Before he left, Will glanced over the group. McLeod and Kitrick hadn't joined the discussions, and he was glad. The rest were good workers and, until circumstances had pushed them to the wall, loyal employees. He could do worse than put his fate in their hands. After all, they had done the same for him every day at Aussie Electronics.

Oddly enough, just knowing that after today they might all be sharing equally in the good times and the bad eased some of the pain he felt at losing his company. He wasn't losing a company, he argued to himself; he was gaining a hundred partners.

Even so, the twenty minutes he paced the corridor alone was an agonizing wait. Virtually everyone had to agree, to make the scheme work. Paul had told him the company could be kept afloat by selling shares, but regaining their competitive edge would require everyone to agree to a pay cut. Will had taken the lead by accepting a twenty-percent drop in salary.

He was gazing out the plate-glass window at the horses in the paddocks and wondering how long he would continue to have this view, when he felt Paul touch his shoulder.

"Congratulations, you old bastard," Paul said, shaking his hand. "Your employees have voted overwhelmingly in favor of buying out controlling interest in Aussie Electronics. They've got some ideas to increase productivity. And they're amenable to a ten-percent wage cut."

If anyone had told Will three months ago that he'd be overjoyed to sell his company to his employees, he would have said they were mad. But his shoulders sagged in gratitude and relief as he pumped Paul's hand. "Thanks, mate."

The cheer that greeted him from the assembled workers when he returned to the factory floor raised his spirits even higher. Tears came to his eyes as he moved among the men and women whose fortunes were now bound irrevocably to his.

He came at last to Art. The older man clasped his hand with both of his. "I'm proud of you, lad. You did the right thing."

"I hope you'll consider taking your old job back."

Art grinned. "I never really left it."

Will hesitated. "How's Maeve?"

"She's packing her things. She's going away for a while."

"To Fiji with her ex-husband?" Will asked. *Please, no.* Although he knew it was irrational, if he couldn't have her he didn't want anyone else to, either.

"Nah, she wouldn't go anywhere with that clown. She's going to the Dandenong Mountains to her friend Rose's place in Emerald. She says she needs to be alone for a few days. Or a few weeks." Art gave him a piercing glance. "You wouldn't know what that's all about, I suppose?"

Will looked him in the eye. "I'm sorry, Art. It's between Maeve and me."

"Are you going to fix whatever's wrong?"

"If I could, I most certainly would. More than that, I can't tell you."

Art studied the toes of his work boots while he thought about that. Then, glancing up, he said, "Come by for a beer sometime."

"Thanks, Art. I will."

THAT EVENING, Maeve parked her ute next to Will's Mercedes in the parking lot at Sorrento Ocean Beach and walked to the cliff edge to scan the waves below. She'd tried his house first, but when he wasn't there, she'd gone looking for him. She wanted to tell him how pleased she was about his decision to sell the factory to the workers. She wanted to say goodbye before leaving for Rose's house. And to see him one last time.

The rain had washed the air clear, and the wind had whipped the waves into towering walls of green. After a moment she spotted him, sliding down the cascading slope, pivoting and sliding again, hugging the curl, dragging a hand in the water, eking every second of energy and motion out of the wave, until, fully upright, he slowed to a wobbly halt in the rushing foam at the edge of the shore.

Longing surged through her. In spite of her intention not to try to talk to him, her feet started to move of their own accord down the path to the beach. As he bent to pick up his board, he glanced up at the cliff. She lifted a hand in greeting. He didn't return the gesture. At the sight of the stern set of his brow, she dropped her arm slowly to her side.

So. There were to be no further goodbyes. Head down against the buffeting wind, she walked back to her vehicle. Suddenly, she was glad she was getting right away from the peninsula. In the hills around Emerald she wouldn't accidentally bump into him in the shopping mall, or at a stoplight. Or torture herself by haunting the surf beaches in the vain hope of glimpsing the man she loved.

WILL HAD BEEN DOING OKAY until he'd looked up and seen Maeve. He hadn't come to any brilliant conclusions about Ida, but for the few moments he'd flown down the crest of the wave, his mind had been mercifully free of the need to make irrevocable decisions.

Maeve had thrown him off balance, literally and figuratively. Conflicting emotions and unfulfilled dreams flooded his consciousness, destroying his concentration. The next wave he caught, his timing was off and he tumbled into the trough. His board caught him a painful clip on the shoulder as he was pushed under by the crashing wall of water. The next two waves he missed entirely, drifting on the receding swell like a piece of flotsam.

Bruised in his body and battered in his mind, he picked himself out of the shallows and trudged up the hill to his car. Making love with her had inserted doubt into his future. And like the dilemma over his factory, nothing could begin to go right in his personal life until he knew what was truly important to him.

Back home, he hosed down his board and rinsed off his wet suit. Yes, he wanted children. But why exactly did he want them? Was it to carry on the family name? His brothers had already accomplished that, and, anyway, he honestly couldn't say having a Will Jr. to walk in his footsteps was critical to his happiness.

Was it to make up for what he'd lost as a child when his father had died? But no one could ever really make up for that. Or was it so he wouldn't be lonely in his old age? Maybe. Yet who was to say his children wouldn't move away or neglect him? He hoped neither would happen, but he felt instinctively that having children because of what they could do for you in future wasn't a good reason.

He hung his wet suit over the clothesline to dry and wandered back to the house, avoiding looking at the rockery or the spot on the lawn where he'd found love with Maeve.

Ida's question also niggled. What was the difference between love and friendship? Why would marrying Ida be better or worse than marrying Maeve? Aside from the children factor, that is.

Will changed and loaded his rusty lawn mower into the back of the Merc. A half hour later, he was unloading it onto his mother's footpath.

"Where's Maeve?" Phyllis asked, squinting against the smoke that curled up from the cigarette tucked between her lips. Below her cotton shirt and shorts, her thin legs ended in a pair of worn pink thongs.

"Don't know." Will checked that the tank held enough petrol by shaking the mower until he heard liquid slosh. Then he set it back on the ground to haul on the cord. It wouldn't start.

"That mower of Maeve's was high class."

"It was nice," he agreed, and gave the cord another yank. Still wouldn't start. He cursed under his breath.

Phyllis sucked in a deep drag and blew the plume of smoke out through her nose. "She did a wonderful job on your garden."

Phyllis was doing her best to sound him out on the subject, but he didn't feel like talking about her. "I thought you were going to quit smoking."

"When you become a father, I'll quit smoking."

"At the rate I'm going, that may never happen."

THE SECOND PROMISE

Bent over the mower, hauling on the cord, Will felt himself turning red from exertion.

"What about Ida? Aren't you two getting married?"

"I don't know," he snapped. There were too many things he didn't know at the moment for his peace of mind. Too many questions unanswered. And no one to answer them except him.

"Don't get testy with me because you've got yourself in a mess over two women. I just hope you haven't broken your promise to me."

"I will not hurt Ida, Mother, I swear."

"I didn't mean that promise. I know you wouldn't consciously hurt her. And maybe Ida needs to take the initiative where the father of her baby is concerned. No, I meant the second promise—to be true to yourself."

To be true to himself, he had to know what was most important to him. He'd thought it was children, but since Maeve had left, he was beginning to have doubts. Yet to give up his dream... "Long before I ever wanted a wife, I wanted children."

"*Wife* is generic. What you want is Maeve." Phyllis jabbed her cigarette at him. "What are you going to do about it?"

He straightened, ready to snap at her again. Then he saw the compassion in his mother's eyes, and his irritation evaporated, replaced by utter weariness. "Her daughter died as a baby. She absolutely doesn't want any more children. What can I do?"

"You could start by talking to her. Did you ever hear of 'Love conquers all'?"

"A cliché," he said dismissively. "Meaningless."

"Are you telling me what you feel for Maeve is meaningless?"

He refused to answer. With one last yank on the cord, he brought the mower sputtering to life.

Will returned home when the sun was low on the western horizon and his garden was alight with a reddish-gold glow. After he put away the lawn mower, he felt too restless to go inside.

His meandering footsteps took him eventually to the cubby. The jasmine had nearly grown over the "roof."

Hesitating only a moment, he crouched low and entered. The dirt floor was dry, and someone— Maeve probably—had placed inside a low wooden bench.

He sat on the bench in the center of the cubby. He felt a little as if he were in church, thanks to the ethereal radiance that filtered through the jasmine vines. Then he breathed in the sweet scent of the small white flowers, and in a flash he was back in his boyhood haven. His father came unexpectedly to mind. Not the awful days and lonely weeks after William Sr.'s death, but the pure deep love the man had always shown Will, despite, or perhaps because of, his frailty. He may not have been able to play footy with his son, but he'd always taken the time to listen to Will and let him know his thoughts and feelings were important. He'd given Will understanding and had held an absolute belief in Will's abilities.

Unconditional love. That was what Will wanted for his children. And why he wanted to have children—to pass on his father's legacy. He was pleased with that. It felt right. So far, so good.

The correct decision, then, must be to marry Ida and have children. Will waited in vain for the lightening of his heavy spirits, which would let him know this was the solution.

Damn, this was hard. His life up until now had been relatively straightforward, the path he'd chosen based on logic and rational thought. He'd never had to spend time sorting out his emotions. He and Ida shared similar values, backgrounds and beliefs. Those, he'd heard, were the basis of long-lasting love—or, in his and Ida's case, friendship. Yet Maeve already understood him on a level that Ida never would for all their years of friendship. How could he account for that with rationality?

He'd made a promise to be true to himself. Well, he was trying. But he must be really stupid not to get it.

Stilling his mind, he let his unfocused gaze rest on the soft greenery while he simply absorbed the last warmth of the sun and the mingled scents of flowers and leaves and earth.

Where had Maeve's understanding sprung from? Not experience or knowledge. Intuition? Partly, maybe, but it was more than that. Between him and Maeve flickered a spark that couldn't be quantified, captured or defined. With a certainty that defied logic he felt that spark could be fanned into a flame of pure joy that would light their way through good times and bad as long as they both lived.

Then suddenly he got it. The spark, the flame, was love.

Blessed were those who found love.

Blessed was how he felt when he was with Maeve.

That was the difference between love and friendship.

Love's energy hummed through him, expanding his consciousness, lifting his spirits. For one transcendental moment his understanding encompassed love in all its multitudinous glory, and at the apex were his feelings for Maeve.

Warm tears leaked from his shut eyes and trickled down his cheeks. Where confusion had filled his mind, now there was only calm certainty. Where conflicted emotions had battled for ascendancy in his heart, now love for Maeve reigned uncontested.

He would always be there for Ida and her child. But Maeve was the woman with whom he wanted to share his life.

Now he also understood that love meant relinquishing the tight control he had over his emotions.

He'd held them in check so long he hadn't even realized he was doing it. The small core of inner sadness left over from his boyhood crumbled and dissolved, and he gave himself up to love without fear.

Life was very simple, really, once you knew what you truly wanted.

"IDA?" WILL POKED his head around her office door the next day at lunchtime. "Come for a walk through the park with me."

Ten minutes later they sat on a bench overlooking the marina and Mother's Beach, while Will explained the nature of love.

"Converts always make the most fervent evangelists." Ida patted his hand with a tolerant, amused smile.

"But do you see why we can't marry?" he said earnestly. He was worried he was going to hurt her, after all. "Love is too important to knowingly base a marriage on friendship. It's not enough for me, and it shouldn't be enough for you, either. Maybe Rick won't be the one for you, but someday—"

"It's okay, Will." Ida cut him off. "I'm glad you came to this conclusion. I was too much of a coward to make the hard choice, but in my heart I know you're right."

"Whatever you and the baby need, I'll be there to give it to you both. You know that, don't you?"

"Will you be my son's godfather?"

Will grinned. "You bet."

Ida gazed down at her stomach, and her eyes glistened. "Do you think there's a chance Rick'll want me if I tell him the engagement is off?"

"Unless you ask, you'll never find out. Open your heart, Ida. Tell him you love him. You'll be surprised how good it feels."

"Are you going to be okay, Will? What about your dream of having a family?"

He sighed. "I'm not sure. That's something Maeve and I will have to work out. All I know is, now that I've come to see love as the solution, not the problem, anything seems possible. I'm going to find her and talk to her."

He took Ida's hand, unfolded her clenched fist and flattened his fingers against hers in the sign of their childhood secret club. "Friends forever?"

Her smile brimmed over. "Friends forever."

CHAPTER FIFTEEN

"BATHTIME, KRISTY!" Maeve announced to the round-cheeked baby sitting in her high chair, happily gurgling into her milk.

"Ba. Ba." Kristy banged her cup on the tray at the sound of the water running into the baby bath on the kitchen bench top.

In Maeve's dream, the bench top was in Will's kitchen at Sorrento, but she didn't think that odd.

She scooped Kristy out of the high chair and onto the changing mat next to the bath. Cooing and tickling, Maeve quickly divested her of sleeper and diaper. Holding the squirming, eager baby in one arm, Maeve tested the water with an elbow. "Okay, in you go." Kristy laughed and kicked her legs. Maeve trickled warm water down her neck and tummy. Kristy giggled, her chubby fist reaching for a loose strand of Maeve's long hair, pulling Maeve's face close to hers. For one priceless, endless moment, Maeve gazed, smiling, into Kristy's eyes, and Kristy gazed back at her. Maeve's love for her daughter overflowed.

In the space of a heartbeat everything changed. Suddenly, Kristy's eyes grew dull and staring. Her grip slackened and fell away from Maeve's hair. The kitchen disappeared, and Maeve was in the nursery. She was walking toward the crib with a sense of dread. She didn't want to look inside. No, please, no...

Kristy's pallid face was tinged with blue around her mouth. Maeve reached for her, but the vibrant bundle of love and energy was cold, her little body stiff and lifeless...

"No-o-o-o!" Maeve awoke in a cold sweat, heart pounding, and sat abruptly upright in the single bed in Rose's spare room. *Kristy. Oh, my baby.* Maeve dropped her face in her hands and sobbed. She wished she were dead.

The dream stayed with her all morning and colored her mood gray. To distract herself, Maeve squatted among trays of herb seedlings, laboriously transplanting the slender green shoots into pots for Rose to sell at the local Sunday market. Without warning, Kristy's smiling face appeared before her, and then the transformation to death happened all over again. The rich black potting soil spilled on the grass, and she wrapped her arms around herself while tears squeezed from her clenched eyelids.

Rose found her thus and crouched to take her in her arms. "In the tarot, Death means not literal death but a major change in one's life. Change can be difficult, especially when you cling to the old and fear the new."

Wordlessly, Maeve shook her head, too upset to

speak. Not wanting to accept Rose's interpretation. This wasn't a tarot reading, and she didn't fear anything but the loss of her beloved child.

Still numb with delayed grief three hours later, Maeve sat on the veranda of Rose's cottage with a cup of peppermint tea and looked out over the green and steeply sloping valley. Idly, she tracked the movement of a large pale car as it wound its way up the hills between market gardens and vineyards.

When the car turned into Rose's driveway, Maeve recognized the silver paintwork and the distinctive Mercedes hood ornament. *Will.* No need to ask where he'd gotten Rose's address. Art would hand Will the moon if he could.

Her first impulse was to run inside and escape from feelings too painful to confront. Too late. The car crunched to a halt and Will got out. The sight of his familiar figure gave rise to her second impulse, which was to run to him and fling herself in his arms.

Maeve gave in to neither. She stood tall and straight, and waited.

Will walked over to the house and stopped at the foot of the steps leading up to the veranda. "Hello, Maeve."

His face. His dear, dear face. "You should have called."

"You left town in a hurry. I wanted to make sure you were all right."

They sounded as though they were talking at

cross-purposes. Maeve thought he wanted to be reassured he had nothing to do with her sudden flight. Typical male, he wasn't likely to apologize.

"I'm fine." She forced a cheery note into her voice. His rebuff at Sorrento surf beach still stung, but he didn't have to know. "I'm having a miniholiday in the hills."

He planted one foot on the bottom step. "How long do you plan to stay?"

She noted the foot—and something else. Something calm and joyful about him that she didn't have the emotional energy to interpret. Or to deal with. "Two weeks, maybe three. I'm helping Rose with her herb nursery."

Will glanced toward the greenhouses to the right of the house. "What about your experiment? Are you just going to drop that?"

After all his work on the solar panel, she guessed he had a right to ask, but she hated the answer she had to give him.

"I don't want to," she said. "Art agreed to look after it for me. I wrote out the experimental protocol in terms he would understand, but, well, he forgot to add the nutrients to the hydroponic solution and that week's data were spoiled."

She couldn't blame Art; differential growth rates of chives and parsley wouldn't be on the top of everyone's list of priorities. Plus, he had a whole new work situation to contend with. "I'll set it up again once I return," she said.

"Except, didn't you once tell me ambient light was one of the constants? The season will have progressed, and light conditions changed."

"Yes, well, it can't be helped."

Silence fell. Then at last he said, "I should have talked to you that day at Sorrento beach. I've missed you."

She wavered, longing to forgive and forget. Then memories of Kristy insinuated themselves painfully into her consciousness. It was better this way. Couldn't he understand they had no future together? Ida could give him what he wanted. If not Ida, then some other woman.

Now she forced herself to be caustic. "How kind of you to acknowledge that...after the fact."

Will just shook his head and gave a small smile. "Can we talk? There are things I understand better now."

"I really don't see the point—"

"I'm not marrying Ida."

"Oh."

His warm blue eyes held hers. "I love you, Maeve."

Her sudden yearning for him was so strong she had to turn away so he wouldn't see it in her face. His circumstances may have changed, but her feelings hadn't.

"It's no good, Will." Her back to him, she spoke gently but firmly, feeling the tears prick her eyes. He would forget her someday and find someone else to bear his children. She was glad it wouldn't be Ida, though. Ida deserved to have a chance with Rick.

"No? Just like that, you say no?" He sounded quizzical, not angry.

She couldn't let him matter to her. And it would be better in the long run for him to be rid of her. Facing him again, she confirmed with a steady voice, "Just like that."

And just like that, he walked away. At his car he turned. "When you're ready to come home, I'll be waiting. We'll talk."

Of all the arrogant... As if they were already a couple, already married. As if her capitulation was foregone.

Except that he didn't sound arrogant. He just sounded...quietly confident, infinitely loving.

And then he got into his car and drove away.

He wasn't marrying Ida.

"More peppermint tea, darl'?" Rose appeared with a tray bearing a cosied teapot and a second bone china teacup. She saw that Will had left, and her face fell. "What on earth did you say to make him leave so quickly?"

"The truth." Maeve poured herself another cup of steaming straw-colored liquid and set the creaking wicker to rocking. "I'm not ill, Rose. You don't have to wait on me."

"You're sick at heart," Rose said softly, before padding away into the wooden cottage.

Truer words were never spoken. But peppermint tea and all the cosseting in the world wouldn't mend her broken heart.

A FEW DAYS LATER she'd gained a small measure of peace, enough to pick up her cellular phone from the wicker table beside the rocker and punch in her home number. Art answered on the third ring.

"Hi, Dad. How's it going?" She spoke with an upbeat lilt.

"What's wrong?" Art said. "You sound odd."

Maeve sighed. She should have known better than to try to fool her father. "I'm okay. How are you? How are things at work?" She hadn't even asked Will about his factory.

"No one's thinking all our troubles are over," Art said. "But we're all in it together, sink or swim. Will seems to have benefited from the change, too. He's different these days."

"In what way?" Was he pining over his lost family? How desperately she craved news of him was shameful. Especially after she'd literally turned him away from her door.

"Well, now, I don't know how to describe it. Just a look in his eye. Something deep, some kind of certainty."

That didn't sound like a man in mourning. "I heard he's not getting married, after all."

"Maybe he feels he had a lucky escape." Art chuckled at his own joke.

"Honestly, Dad."

"Maybe he's waiting for you."

"Did he...say anything?"

"No. But he did bring over one of the trucks from the factory and load up your experimental plants."

"He did what?"

"I tried to stop him, love. Honestly, I did. But he just muttered something about how you hadn't worked so hard just to drop the whole experiment."

Maeve tried to feel outraged that he'd assumed control, but all she could muster was gratitude that he'd taken the fate of her plants into his capable hands.

"When are you coming home?" Art asked.

She wanted to go this minute. "I don't know."

DURING THE WEEKS since Will had come to Rose's cottage, Maeve returned to the peninsula almost daily to keep up with her more pressing landscaping jobs. Each night she went back to the mountain. She'd driven past Will's house twice, half hoping, half terrified she would run into him. Getting over Will was turning out to be harder than she'd anticipated.

She dropped in to see Ida one day and coaxed her out for lunch at a café. She was concerned over the other woman's state of mind and curiously eager to hear how her pregnancy was going.

"This is for your baby," she said, handing Ida a package wrapped in paper bright with red and yellow balloons. She hadn't intended to go into the baby store, but it was just two doors down from the hardware store where she bought her hose fittings and, well...

She had drifted through the aisles, fingering baby blankets, inspecting the braking system on a pram. And then, before she knew what she was doing, she found herself standing over a bassinet, fantasizing about a rosy-cheeked, dark-haired baby. Oddly, the baby had not Kristy's dark-chocolate eyes, but eyes of cobalt blue glinting with gold.

"May I help you, dear?" a grandmotherly saleswoman enquired, discreetly checking out the curvature of Maeve's flat tummy.

Maeve snapped back to reality. "I'm not pregnant. I'm just looking for a present for a friend's baby. I don't plan to have any children," she added needlessly. "I don't want children."

The saleswoman's gaze changed from warm to wary. "Perhaps you'll find what you're looking for in the toy section," she said, indicating the far wall and shelves stocked with stuffed animals and colorful plastic toys.

Now Ida smiled and ripped open the paper to pull out a purple-and-green stuffed dragon. "It's gorgeous! Thank you!"

"The teddy bears seemed a little too cutesy." In fact, they'd looked adorable, but Maeve didn't feel comfortable with her sudden interest in baby toys. "What are you, four months along?"

"Four months, one week and three days," Ida said proudly. "I can hardly wait until he's born. I've got more clothes and baby furniture than you could imagine."

Remembering the joy and excitement of Kristy as a tiny baby, Maeve felt a stab of envy. Could she really resign herself to never experiencing that again? She tried to summon the feelings evoked by her nightmare, but the memory had faded, as dreams do.

"Will told me you two aren't getting married." Maeve searched Ida's face for signs she was unhappy with the way things had turned out.

But Ida merely grinned ruefully. "It wasn't one of our brightest ideas. I'm feeling a lot better now about the possibility that I'll be raising this baby on my own. That's what I planned in the first place, anyway, until Will insisted the baby needed a father."

"And won't he have one? What about Rick?"

Ida picked at the remains of her Caesar salad. "He asked me to come to San Diego…to live."

"Ida, that's wonderful! Congratulations."

Ida shrugged. "If I went, we would have to get married for me to stay in the country. I wouldn't feel right forcing him—"

"Stop right there," Maeve said. "Is Rick the kind of guy you could force into doing something he doesn't want to do?"

"Hardly."

"Well, then? He wouldn't ask you if he didn't mean it. You're going, I hope."

Ida smiled tremulously. "I want to. Oh, Maeve, I want to so much. He…he seems keen on the baby, in spite of what he told me when we first met."

"He loves you. Love changes the way you perceive things. It alters your priorities."

On her way back to Emerald, Maeve found herself going out of her way to drive past the Frankston Memorial Park, a route she usually avoided. She'd cut a bundle of white roses from her bushes at home to take to Rose. But she was sure Rose would understand if she gave them, instead, to Kristy.

Maeve walked through the rows of plain flat markers engraved with names and dates, scant reminders of lives so precious to family and friends. Tears came to her eyes when she stood before Kristy's grave and read the inscription she'd chosen from a Tennyson poem: "Oh, death in life, the days that are no more."

At the time of Kristy's death, the poem had expressed Maeve's overwhelming grief and sorrow. Now the words seemed too sad for such a sunny-natured child as Kristy. Maeve wished she'd chosen something a little more cheerful to comfort her baby through eternity. Something from A. A. Milne, perhaps. Kristy had loved her stuffed Tigger. Probably because she was the "bouncingest" baby.

Maeve smiled through her tears. Dropping to the grass, she sat for a while, remembering all the many ways Kristy had enriched her life during her few short months on earth. Finally Maeve laid the roses on the gently curving mound of green. "Goodbye, sweet one. Till we meet again."

THAT NIGHT, Maeve stood on Rose's veranda and watched the full moon rise over the valley. A whole month had gone by since she and Will had made love beneath its silvery glow. If she stood on tiptoe she could just see a shining sliver of the bay miles away to the west.

Was Will gazing at the moon right now, too? Was it the moon or the love she felt for him that drew her so strongly tonight? Would she spend the rest of her life wishing she were with him? Or did she have the courage to step out of the past?

Without allowing herself to think about her motives or even what she would say to him when she got to Sorrento, Maeve drew a light cardigan on over her cotton dress and slipped her feet into a pair of sandals. She wrote a note for Rose, who'd gone to bed early, and quietly closed the cottage door behind her.

Down the mountain lane she drove, the headlights of the ute leaping ahead to illuminate the curving road, picking out the flash of amber eyes in dark grass, then shining on a kangaroo bounding across the narrow ribbon of asphalt.

On the flat land between the mountains and the sea, she crossed paddocks of sleeping cows, rumbled over level railway crossings and slowed through small towns with their brightly lit pubs and take-aways.

Would he be home? Would he welcome her after the way she'd treated him? Could they find a common ground without compromising their dreams?

With the bright full moon to guide her, these questions and others flowed through her mind as the miles flowed behind her. Yet beneath the questions lay a growing certainty at her core: whatever else happened, or didn't happen, in her life, she wanted to be with Will.

And then she was turning into his driveway, and excitement began to build as she followed the last curving path to her destination. The house was dark except for a light deep within, probably in the kitchen. She stood for a moment, gazing at the moon, now at its zenith. The hour was late; traveling had taken longer than she'd expected. Should she go home to Mount Eliza and wait until morning?

"Maeve." His voice came low and sweet from somewhere close by.

"Will? Where are you?" Her pulse began to race.

"Here, by the kissing gate."

She saw him then, his shirt and shorts pale against his tanned arms and legs. "What are you doing out here?" she asked, walking over.

"Moon gazing. Waiting for you." His hands rested nonchalantly in his pockets and he leaned against the circle of the kissing gate as though he hung out there every night.

"You were so sure I'd come." She was fascinated by the enigmatic curve of his mouth, and suddenly there was nothing she wanted more than to see his dimple. "Say, mister, is there a toll on this gate?"

A tiny dark shadow, familiar and dear, appeared to the right of his grin. Holding the gate open so she could slip into the circle with him, he said, "You bet there's a toll."

Now she was close enough that her dress swished against his legs. Awareness ran through her. "What's the price of admission?" she enquired, already lifting her mouth to be kissed.

But instead of a kiss, his thumb came up to brush her lips, raising a delicious shiver. Her fingers curled into her palms as she resisted the urge to reach for him.

"Talk to me," he said.

"What do you want to know, exactly?"

He reached for her braid and rubbed its silky end over his lips, while his eyes held hers. "Why did you come here tonight?"

"I love you. I want to be with you."

He nodded thoughtfully. Still holding her braid, he asked, "Is there any possibility you would consider having children? It wouldn't have to be right away."

He deserved her complete honesty. "I...I'm not sure."

He frowned down at her until she thought the moon was going to set before he would react. Then, to her relief, he smiled. "Well, the answer's an improvement on the last time I asked you."

Putting his hands on her waist, he drew her closer, till their hips met and her breasts nudged his chest. A spark burst into fire in her loins. His lips were warm and firm, tenderly exploring her mouth in a melting kiss full of promise and barely restrained passion.

"You're making me want to make love with you," she just had time to murmur before his mouth began another onslaught.

"It's a start in the right direction," he said, breaking the kiss. His hands, warm and strong, hold her close.

He drew back to look at her. "Do you know what the full moon does to me?"

She smiled. "Makes you randy?"

"Don't be vulgar. It brings out the romantic in me. I won't stop wanting children, but I want you more. Maeve, will you please do me the very great honor of becoming my wife?"

Maeve glanced up at the brilliantly lit sky and back to Will. Despite the formal words, his hair was ruffled and the wild-child gleam was back in his eye.

"Yes," she answered, smiling. She loved him all the more for not pressing her. Deep down, she knew she already wanted children with him, and the knowledge filled her with profound contentment.

Taking her hand, Will pushed open the gate. "Come into my garden. It's a very special place."

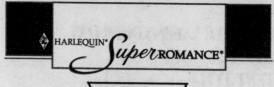

#1 *New York Times* bestselling author

NORA ROBERTS

brings you more of the loyal and loving,
tempestuous and tantalizing Stanislaski family.

Coming in February 2001

The Stanislaski Sisters
Natasha and Rachel

Though raised in the Old World traditions of their
family, fiery Natasha Stanislaski and cool, classy
Rachel Stanislaski are ready for a *new* world of love....

*And also available in February 2001 from
Silhouette Special Edition, the newest book in the
heartwarming Stanislaski saga*

CONSIDERING KATE

Natasha and Spencer Kimball's daughter Kate turns her
back on old dreams and returns to her hometown, where
she finds the *man* of her dreams.

Available at your favorite retail outlet.

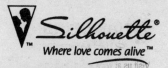

Silhouette®
Where love comes alive™

Visit Silhouette at www.eHarlequin.com   PSSTANSIS

From bestselling
Harlequin American Romance author

CATHY GILLEN THACKER

comes

TEXAS VOWS

A McCABE FAMILY SAGA

Sam McCabe had vowed to always
do right by his five boys—but after
the loss of his wife, he needed the small-town security
of his hometown, Laramie, Texas, to live up to that
commitment. Except, coming home would bring him
back to a woman he'd sworn to stay away from.
It will be one vow that Sam can't keep....

On sale March 2001

Available at your favorite retail outlet.

HARLEQUIN®
Makes any time special ™

Visit us at www.eHarlequin.com

PHTV

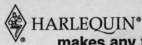